What was it about

Linda wondered, t... year after year?

Power? It radiated fr... spades. Class? It was... the rich Texas legacy ... sprang.

Linda saw all that—and more—in Clay Buchanan. From the moment she'd laid eyes on him ten years ago, when she was just sixteen, the tycoon had become the ideal against which all other men were measured—and fell flat.

But what about him? Had Clay ever felt anything for her?

Linda heaved a small sigh. No. She was simply his invaluable assistant. His right-hand man. Smart, dependable Linda.

While quietly flowering through the years, putting down deep roots, was her secret.

She loved Clay Buchanan.

And longed to be his bride...

Dear Reader

Welcome to Special Edition™. October's line-up starts with two compelling secret baby stories. In the final one of the SWITCHED AT BIRTH novels, Penny Richards' *Wildcatter's Kid*, a father is reunited with the family he never knew he had. And in book three of Cathy Gillen Thacker's HASTY WEDDINGS series, *The Maverick Marriage*, an eccentric's will prompts a divorced couple to pick up where they left off—seventeen years ago!—and finally raise their son together.

Babies continue to be a popular theme with Christine Rimmer's *The Nine-Month Marriage*, the first in three linked novels featuring the marriages of the Bravo men. Abby can't believe it when Cash proposes—just for the sake of their baby! And an unexpected arrival brings together an unlikely twosome in this month's THAT'S MY BABY story, Diana Whitney's *Baby on His Doorstep*. Watch out for the follow-up novel, coming next month.

Finally, two confirmed bachelors have their minds changed by two very determined women. *The Rancher Meets His Match* is Patricia McLinn's latest, and a marriage of convenience with her handsome tycoon boss makes Linda Douglas the *Texan's Bride* thanks to author Gail Link.

Enjoy them all and come back next month—please!

The Editors

Texan's Bride
GAIL LINK

SILHOUETTE

SPECIAL EDITION ®

Silhouette, Silhouette Special Edition and Colophon are registered trademarks of Harlequin Books S.A., used under licence.

*First published in Great Britain 1998
Silhouette Books, Eton House, 18-24 Paradise Road,
Richmond, Surrey TW9 1SR*

© Gail Link 1998

ISBN 0 373 24163 1

23-9810

*Printed and bound in Spain
by Litografia Rosés S.A., Barcelona*

This book is for my editor, Tara Gavin, who loves the classic romance stories as much as I do. Thanks for all your support.

And for all those readers who wrote and asked me if I was going to write books on the other Buchanan brothers. Thanks so much for caring about my characters—it means so much.

Plus, I can't forget to thank my inspiration, the man who gave Clay a physical form, Texas native son Matthew McConaughey—totally genuine.

GAIL LINK

A bookseller since 1977, Gail realized her dream of becoming a published author with the release of her first book, a historical novel, in 1989.

Gail is a member of the Romance Writers of America and Novelists, Inc. She has been a featured speaker at many writers' conferences, and several publications have featured her comments on the romance genre. In 1993 Gail was nominated for the *Romantic Times* Reviewer's Choice Award for Best Sensual Historical.

In addition to being a voracious reader, Gail is also an avid musical theatre and movie fan. She would love to hear from her readers, and you may write to her at P.O. Box 717, Concordville, PA 19331, USA.

Other novels by Gail Link

Silhouette Special Edition®

Marriage To Be?
Lone Star Lover

Prologue

The Encantadora ranch, Texas

Today was the day Linda Douglas had been waiting for. Excitement ran through her veins like one of the Hill Country rivers—fast and strong, the current carrying her along in its wake.

She couldn't wait to meet Clay Buchanan.

Her grandfather, never one given to fulsome compliments, showered this young man with praise. He was the golden boy, the chosen one, the heir apparent to the empire.

"Mark my words, Linda," her grandfather had said to her on numerous occasions. "Clay Buchanan is the best of the best. Smart. Tough. The finest head for business that I've seen in my seventy years. He's got vision, and he isn't afraid to take a chance. There's plenty of them that are. But not him. No, sir. He tripled the trust fund his granddaddy left him in under a year. Study him, girl. Learn from the best. If you ever want to reach the top, let him show you the way.''

To the impressionable, teenage Linda Douglas, Clay Buchanan was already a legend at the age of twenty-eight. Groomed for success, he'd proved everyone correct. Where he led, others followed. While girls her age mooned over rock singers or movie stars, Linda's heroes were found in the pages of the *Wall Street Journal* and *Financial Times*. Business was her forte and Clay its guiding light.

Now, thanks to her grandfather, she was going to meet the man himself.

Her eyes quickly scanned the crowd of people that had gathered at the ranch to celebrate the Fourth of July until she found who she was searching for.

The one thing her grandfather had neglected to mention about the oldest Buchanan son was that he was handsome as sin. Pictures she'd seen in newspapers and magazines didn't near do him justice, Linda thought as she walked arm in arm with her grandfather across the grounds toward the Independence Day barbecue.

Clay was standing beneath the wide-spread limbs of a live oak, laughing at something a tall, slender, dark-haired youth with a toddler in his arms was saying. She watched as Clay chucked the little girl under the chin. The child responded with a gurgling laugh of her own. Seconds later the younger man ambled off in the direction of a softball game that was being played across the field.

''Howdy, Clay.''

''Hello, Ethan.'' Clay extended his hand toward Linda's grandfather, shaking it firmly as he reached out his other hand to clasp him on the shoulder. With a welcoming smile on his lips, he shifted his gaze to Linda, who stood at her grandfather's side. "Who's the charming young lady on your arm?"

"This here's my grandbaby, Linda."

"Hardly a baby, Ethan," Clay drawled, his gaze quickly assessing the girl. He held out his hand and enveloped Linda's much smaller one. "Mighty pleased to make your acquaintance, Miss Linda," he said.

Warmth flushed Linda's cheeks as her eyes met her grandfather's client. In that instant, for her, the world had turned upside down.

"Linda, honey, are you okay?" her grandfather asked, concerned as he observed the sixteen-year-old staring blankly at the Buchanan scion.

She blinked and blushed even more. "Sorry."

"Nothing to apologize for," Clay assured her, his voice a balm to her sensitized nerves.

From the corner of her eye, Linda spied a tall, slender, striking blonde walking toward them.

Clay smiled and slid his arm around the woman's waist when she joined them, pulling her close to his lean body as she kissed him affectionately on the cheek.

"Ethan, Miss Linda, I'd like you to meet..."

Linda didn't need to hear the woman's name. She recognized the face. Who wouldn't? In the past year it had appeared on more magazine covers than she could count.

"Honey," the model said in a soft, kittenish voice, "you promised me a tour of the house."

"That I did," Clay acknowledged. "Will you excuse me?" he asked Linda and her grandfather.

"Certainly," Ethan replied.

Linda watched as the couple walked away, her newly awakened senses abuzz with sharp feelings and strange longings, all the result of this one encounter.

"Let's go get some of that chili they're cooking up over there, honey. The Encantadora's cook is famous for it—guaranteed to singe the wings off an angel and make the devil reach for water."

An hour later Linda, with a tall glass of fresh iced tea in her hand, wandered alone along a path that led to the nearby garden. Spying a seat, she walked over and sat down on the oak bench. She'd wanted to talk to Clay, to ask him questions, pick his brain. She'd carefully rehearsed what she'd say.

All that flew out the proverbial window however when Clay Buchanan took her hand and looked into her eyes. What had come crashing down on her at that moment was the force of his personality—the awareness of him not only as a successful businessman, but as a man. A wonderfully attractive man.

One who obviously liked the company of attractive women.

Linda drank a hearty swallow of her beverage, painfully aware of what she considered her own shortcomings in the beauty department. *Gawky* was the word that best described her. Could she ever hope to match the style the model on Clay's arm had displayed today? The business world, she well knew, wasn't just about brains and drive. Image played a large part in the equation, too.

Noises from the barbecue floated in the air all around her: a band played, alternating from rock to country, with an occasional Latin flavor thrown in for good measure; children laughed; adults cheered; dogs barked; horses whickered.

However, all Linda could really hear was the sound of Clay Buchanan's voice softly replaying in her head.

Her eyes drifted closed as she sat there, quietly thinking, remembering.

Minutes ticked by. She knew that she should rejoin the party. Her grandfather would be worried if she remained hidden away, but it was all so peaceful here among the many blooms artfully arranged and carefully nurtured.

Suddenly her eyes snapped open. In that moment, a butterfly landed on her jean-clad knee, its brightly colored wings flapping gently before it took off.

Linda watched it fly away, a smile growing on her lips as she drained the glass of its contents.

Her future fell into place. She knew where she was going and what she had to do to make her fondest wishes a reality....

Chapter One

Ten years later

It had been a hell of a long day.

Clay Buchanan loosened the dark blue tie he was wearing, then, with a jerk, pulled it off, dropping it to the arm of the low, plush couch of his living room. His lightweight gray wool jacket followed seconds after. Settling himself down upon the soft burgundy fabric, he closed his eyes for just a moment, letting the cool power of the air-conditioning wash over him. Outside, Houston was sweltering with an oh-so-hot and muggy early evening.

He was tired. Like a pup dragging its butt in the dirt, as Pike, one of the old ranch hands, was fond of saying. He'd just flown in that morning from an extended two-week-long business trip to Australia, checking on real estate and business investments in Melbourne and Sydney, and had gone straight to his office from the airport.

Delegate, his father, Noah, had often told him. He suggested he hire a few more capable assistants like Linda to help keep tabs on things so that he could kick back and enjoy life more.

Better said than done, Dad, Clay thought. Work was his life, the thing he was best at. It's what gave him satisfaction and kept him focused.

A clipped, British-accented voice interrupted his musings. "Welcome back, sir."

Clay opened his eyes and gave the man a weary smile. "Good evening, Basil. It's great to *be* back."

The older man returned his employer's smile with a broader one of his own. "Will you be home for dinner this evening?"

Originally Clay had been scheduled to attend a charity event tonight, but he asked his secretary to cancel. He just didn't feel up to the rigors of a social event with snap-happy photographers and intrusive reporters. "Yes, but tell Lettie not to go making anything just yet. I don't know what I want." Clay leaned forward, accepting a copy of the Houston paper from Basil's hands. "Probably just a sandwich."

Basil lifted a bushy gray brow. "Whatever you decide, Lettie will be more than happy to fix it."

Clay grinned, a pure light-up-the-room action. "I know." He'd hired the British couple last year after his longtime housekeeper-cook had given notice of her retirement. They'd worked out well, seeing to his every need, giving his newly acquired home the careful attention it deserved.

"Can I get you anything for now?" Basil asked, noting the signs of exhaustion on Clay's face. "A drink, perhaps?"

"Iced tea would be nice," Clay replied. "I've had a

strong desire for that all day.'' While he normally enjoyed a glass or two of wine about this time, this evening was made for iced tea, Texas style.

''I do believe Lettie fixed some earlier, just in case you'd be wanting some. I shan't be long.''

After Basil left the room, Clay picked up the paper and scanned it quickly, finding a photograph in the society column of himself and the woman he'd escorted to a party at the Opera House in Sydney two nights ago. His mother had called this morning and left a message at his office, anxious for details, her curiosity piqued when she'd seen a faxed copy of the article.

Under the picture of himself and the willowy blond divorcée, whom he'd squired as a favor to a friend, was the caption, ''The Next *Buchanan* Bride?''

Clay stared at the color photograph, examining the cool, self-possessed blonde with the gleaming, calculating smile.

Marry her—or someone like her? Not likely, he thought. If, and when, he wed, he'd prefer that his marriage bed be warm and welcoming. He'd want a woman of flesh and blood, not silicone and bones.

Marriage.

The word lingered in Clay's mind, bringing up memories that he'd carefully pushed aside and buried under layers of protective mental tarps. *Once* before, he'd given the matter of marriage serious thought. Bought the ring, asked the woman.

The woman that got away.

Basil walked back into the room a minute later and handed Clay a large glass, then put the silver tray and Waterford pitcher on a nearby butler's table. ''A very flattering picture of you, sir.''

Clay shrugged. ''Not bad.''

"Although, I must say," Basil remarked, "I rather think that the lady might have been a bit chilly in that outfit."

Clay glanced at the picture again and laughed softly. "Basil, I doubt the lady would have been bothered if she stood outside buck naked in a genuine Texas blue norther," Clay commented dryly.

A wry smile curved the older man's thin lips. "I believe I understand, sir."

Clay removed his steel-framed glasses, polishing the lenses before replacing them. "I thought you might."

"Then I shall leave you to your aqua vitae, sir. Whenever you're ready to eat, let me know. Your mail and messages are in your office."

"Anything urgent?"

"Nothing that seems to be so. Most of the personal messages are from members of your family, all of whom seem to have seen copies of this photo."

Clay sighed. In Texas, Buchanans made news, whatever they did, wherever they went. Consequently, nothing was secret, or sacred, to his family. "I'll reassure them later that I'm safe from becoming husband number five for Lisa Palopos."

"Five?"

"You heard correctly, Basil. Five." Clay shook his head, the repugnance he felt at the woman's attitude toward marriage evident in the hardened look in his blue eyes.

Basil nodded his head in agreement and exited the room.

Clay, alone again, sipped at the strong tea, its flavor enhanced with lemon and mint. Several moments passed before he reached down to the coffee table in front of him and picked up the slim remote lying there. After a series of clicks, the room was bathed in the familiar rhythms of cool jazz.

Abruptly he rose from the sofa and proceeded to the wide bank of glass in the high-ceilinged room. Clay stared out through the elegant French doors that led into the brick courtyard, finishing his drink in one hearty swallow, watching silently as the day slowly slipped away and the dark covering of night emerged fully.

He remained there for almost ten minutes, staring at the stars that began to fill the sky, before turning aside and walking over to the small butler's table, where he switched on a lamp and poured himself another large measure of iced tea. Beside the Waterford pitcher and serving tray, there were several silver-framed photographs.

Clay picked up one of the photographs and gazed intently at the people pictured there. It had been taken at his nephew Sam's christening last year. Happiness and love radiated from the photo, celebrating a family: Burke, Clay's younger brother, Burke's teenage daughter Jessie, his wife Emma and their son Sam in his antique gown, passed down through successive generations of Buchanans, held carefully in Emma's arms. Warmth and affection, love and security. That's what Clay saw there.

He closed his eyes. Sam *could* have been his son. Emma *could* have been his wife. He'd found her first. He'd wanted her first. He'd asked her to marry him first. He'd hoped. He'd planned. He'd even dreamed.

And he'd lost her when she met Burke and they'd fallen in love.

Clay opened his eyes and looked at the photo again. This was a family. No doubt about it. Love surrounded them; the photographer had captured it all so clearly.

He put the silver frame down.

Emma.

He still cared for her. Deeply. Tempered now by the fact that she was his sister-in-law. They'd maintained their friendship; it had been tough at first, even slightly awkward. But somehow they'd managed. He'd had to because nothing, he knew, was going to change. Emma loved Burke. Burke loved Emma. Just like the sun rose in the east and set in the west. That's the way things were and always would be.

Clay possessed a keen, analytical brain and was able to weigh profit and loss, assess situations at a glance, quickly. It was one of the elements that made him so successful in all his business enterprises. His personal loss was his brother's ultimate profit.

Yet, beyond that, Clay had come out a winner in many respects. He'd profited by keeping Emma's friendship, which was important to him. Their relationship now was solid and caring, as it should be between brother and sister-in-law.

He'd profited by being an uncle to Sam and Jessie. He loved those kids as if they were his own. Losing contact with them would have ripped out an irreplaceable chunk of his heart.

And, he profited the most in not losing his brother's love and good regard. Close as he and Burke had been, that loss would have devastated him and rendered a tear in his family the size of his beloved state.

It had been almost two years now, and Clay still hadn't found another woman who interested him half as much as Emma had.

Why?

It wasn't as if he'd been a monk, hiding from life. God knows he wasn't searching for forever—maybe because he wondered if it existed for him?—just for a woman who could take the edge off, to dull the embers of pain and loneliness that flared to life every so often, like now.

But it couldn't just be any woman.

Run of the mill wasn't his style. Nor was second best. He wanted...

What? What he couldn't have?

No. He'd long since realized that Emma had made the right choice in choosing his brother. She and Burke were more than right for each other.

Clay had listened to his heart once before, and he'd suffered the consequences of rejection. Now it was time to listen to his head, which urged that he be rational when it came to the future.

What he needed was an intelligent, uncomplicated, companionable companion. Someone to share the part of himself that he was willing to give. A self-sufficient partner who wouldn't cling or complain when business took precedence as it so often did. A cool, levelheaded woman who wanted what he did, which meant, eventually, a family, children of his own.

Children. His songs and daughters. The next generation.

Clay's glance fell to the only item of jewelry he wore, the large gold signet ring on the middle finger of his right hand, the *B* bold and distinctive. It had been his paternal great-grandfather's ring, given to him on the day he was born and held in trust, along with a bottle of port, until he reached his twenty-first birthday. From the day Clay had received the ring, he'd worn it proudly, imagining that someday he would pass it along to his own son, or grandson.

A *son.*

He'd be thirty-nine come his next birthday this August. And if he wanted a new direction in his life, then he had to get started pretty damned soon. He could control a lot of things—and did—but not time, which clicked off the years much faster now, it seemed. He'd given the matter of establishing a serious relationship a lot of thought recently. Analyzed his options. Weighed the pros and cons.

But where could he find the woman to fit the plan he'd outlined?

He was waiting for her.

And, as always, her eyes were drawn to him as soon as she opened the door.

Entering the bedroom of her Houston condo, Linda Douglas stared at the photo of the man that rested on her chest of drawers, as if memorizing each of his chiseled features, wondering if she could ever get enough of looking at him. Caught off guard, the man in the picture was relaxed, slightly in profile, a hint of a smile curving his mouth. Sunlight glinted, bathing his wavy light brown hair in a wash of gold.

Ridiculous! she thought. To be so fascinated by one man when in the course of her life she'd met so many. Rich, handsome, available.

Kicking off her navy high-heeled pumps, Linda wiggled her nylon-clad toes as she picked up the framed photo and then walked a few paces to her white iron daybed. She sat down upon the navy-blue-and-white-striped duvet cover, unable to pry her eyes away from the portrait.

What was it about this one man in particular, she wondered, that continued to hold her captive day after day, year after year?

Power?

Yes. It radiated from him. With some men, it was like a jacket they put on or off; with him it was intrinsic, part of who he was, like the color of his eyes.

Chemistry?

Most definitely yes. He had it in spades. This was a man women noticed, whether he wore formal black evening clothes, a three-piece, hand-tailored designer suit, or a relaxed oxford shirt and chinos. He possessed the long-waisted, lean body of a quintessential classical athlete with wide shoulders and slim hips.

Class?

Without a doubt. He had a quiet dignity that bespoke a true gentleman. A man one took at his word, because when he gave it, it meant something.

Pride?

Of course. It was stamped on his face and rooted in his genes, a heritage of the rich, well-mixed Texas legacy from which he sprang.

Linda saw all that and so much more in this one photo, shot on the sly at a recent event at his family's ranch. When the opportunity presented itself, she hadn't been able to resist taking his picture. Like a miser hoarding treasure, it was intended for her eyes alone.

And so it remained, the solitary photograph in her bedroom. Throughout the rest of her apartment, photographs of various sizes and shapes adorned every available space, whether hung on walls or displayed on furniture. Family, friends, places, special occasions, events. Anything and everything that mattered to Linda was on display for anyone to see. Except this picture. This one was intensely private, deeply personal.

Linda heaved a small sigh. She'd been instantly drawn to this man from the very first time she'd laid eyes on him ten years ago when she was just sixteen and her grandfather had introduced them at a Fourth of July barbecue.

Twelve years older, with his engaging smile and elegant manners, Clay Buchanan was the epitome of sophistication; Linda had tumbled head over heels in love. From that day on, he was the ideal against which all other men were measured.

Throughout high school, college and graduate school, all the males she'd met fell flat when compared to him. They weren't him. Would never be him. *Could* never be him.

A small smile curved her lips as she recalled the day she'd taken this photo. An hour or so before, she'd snapped one of him, along with his two brothers. While the youngest, Burke, was dark and intense, the middle brother, Drew, was charming and outgoing. But Clay was different. Light golden brown hair to their sable; blue eyes to their brown. Formal to their casual. King to their crown princes.

Her eyes had met his for an instant over a glass of champagne and she'd felt the connection all the way to her toes. Smooth and powerful, like a concentrated beam of light going through her body. Sharp without being painful; hot without being febrile. It had always been this way for her. And, she suspected, it would remain so as long as she drew breath.

But what about him? Had he ever felt anything?

Linda rose gracefully from the bed, smoothing down the skirt of her tailored business suit, which hugged her slim hips and long legs. Returning the photo to her dresser, she bent and inhaled the sweet fragrance of the fresh-cut flowers that rested in the old-fashioned glass pitcher that she'd bought at a local charity flea market in Fredericksburg several weeks ago. Bluebonnet blue, the seller had said.

Texas blue. The same shade of blue as his eyes.

When Clay had first discovered her proclivity for fresh

flowers, he'd made sure that her office had a new selection each day. Or, if she were traveling on business, arrangements were made that her hotel suite had a daily floral delivery.

That gesture both touched and tortured Linda. Touching because he instigated it; torturing because it was simply his way with all his valued employees, of which she was one, albeit one who worked closer to him than most of the others. She was his personal assistant. His right-hand man. Trusted confidante in all matters pertaining to business. Smart, dependable Linda.

She quickly removed the pearl studs from her ears, along with her slim gold watch, taking note of the time. What she needed was a long soak in a hot tub and a leisurely meal. What she'd settle for was a quick shower and a microwaved dinner. Reports that she'd brought home in her briefcase needed her attention tonight.

Linda quickly gave the picture one last glance as she unbuttoned her white silk shirt and headed for the bathroom. A glimmer of longing resurfaced every time she looked at him, either in the privacy of her bedroom or at the office. Like a seed that had been carefully watered and fed, the idea had germinated inside her mind, quietly flowering in secret throughout the years, growing and putting down deep Texas-sized roots—she loved Clay Buchanan.

Totally.

Passionately.

And ultimately, she acknowledged, hopelessly.

Stripping off her clothes, she set about washing her face. She'd been witness to the effect of the breakup of his relationship to Emma Cantrell. Silently watched as he went on with his life, taking care of business just as efficiently as ever. To almost everyone he was the same.

But not to Linda. She saw behind the mask he wore in public to the wound below.

Stepping into the tepid shower, she drew the soapy cleaning sponge across her flesh. Her arms had ached to give him comfort. Her mouth had longed to say the words she knew he didn't want to hear. Because he hurt, she did, also. And there was nothing she could do about it. Making something of it would have meant crossing the line and that she couldn't, wouldn't, do, no matter how much she'd wanted to.

Relaxing in her kitchen a half hour later, with a glass of tea and a plate of pasta, Linda decided that, before she tackled her evening's worth of work, she'd check her phone messages.

Two were from people trying to sell her something. The third was from her secretary, reminding her about an overseas phone call that she had to make. The fourth, from her sister, must have come while she was in the shower. ''Linda, it's Sandy. You still haven't told me if you're bringing a date yet. Let me know soon. Please! I want to finalize the seating arrangements for the wedding party this week. Oh, by the way, did you see the picture of your hunky boss in today's paper? I think you might want to check it out. Call me later. Love you! Bye.''

Linda hadn't had a chance to even glance at the paper yet today, which wasn't unusual. Intrigued by Sandy's words, she went and retrieved it from the hallway where she'd dropped it when she came in.

Opening it up, Linda automatically went directly to the business section. Scanning it carefully as she padded back into the kitchen, she didn't see Clay anywhere. Tossing that aside, she picked up another section, skimming through it until she found the picture.

It was him all right. With another woman. Not that that

was so out of the ordinary. Over the years, she'd seen him with other women, in and out of print. However, the caption that ran beneath this picture sent a shaft of pain that hit her squarely in the region of her heart. "The next *Buchanan* Bride?" it said.

Linda's fingers gripped the paper tighter as she stared at the image of Clay and the beautiful woman at his side.

Had he met someone in Australia that had captured his interest so much that he wanted once more to take the ultimate step in a relationship?

The newspaper slid from her fingers as tears welled in her eyes. She knew that it would happen someday. That was inevitable. Still, that didn't lessen the pain, or ease the heartache.

Somewhere, in the back of her mind, in the secret places of her heart, Linda had harbored a secret fantasy that someday she could be the woman to make him forget all the others that had gone before. That she could be the woman to restore his faith in love by giving him hers.

That she could be the only Buchanan bride that counted—Clay's.

Chapter Two

"**W**hy not ask Clay to accompany you, Linda? I'll bet he would. You've been out with him to social functions before, haven't you?" Sandy said between bites of her grilled salmon steak. "After all, this is a special occasion."

"They were business-related affairs, nothing personal," Linda reminded her sister as she lifted the forkful of honey-lemon spiced chicken salad to her lips. "Corporate affairs that required we both be there. No big deal."

"So what?"

Linda shot her sister an amused glance. "Big difference, sis."

Sandy rolled her eyes. "Why?"

Linda sighed. Thank God, her younger sister had no idea of how Linda really felt about Clay. If Sandy did, then she'd have never asked. "Because this wouldn't be about business, that's why."

Sandy raised her eyebrows. "And that would be so terrible?"

"It wouldn't be appropriate."

"Oh, give me a break, would you?" Sandy protested in a wry tone. "It's not as if you'd be asking him to marry you and father your children."

That remark brought a sweet stab of painful pleasure to Linda's heart. *If only.*

"What's the worst that the esteemed Mr. Buchanan can say?" Sandy proposed, head tilted to one side as if in consideration. "No. That's all. I mean I know it's not the type of wedding that he's used to going to. It's not going to be black-tie and caviar with the cream of Texas society in attendance." At that, Sandy chuckled. "Certainly not with our budget. It'll be down-home and fun. More like a fiesta." She ate another bite of her smoked salmon, then added, "Besides, here's his big chance to see you in that gorgeous dress that you'll be wearing."

Linda thought about the beautiful item she'd purchased for the event, recalling the effusive saleswoman's comments about how very romantic she looked in it and that her boyfriend was sure to just eat her up when he saw how lovely she looked. "Prettier than the sun breaking through a mess of clouds on a rainy day."

Linda hadn't corrected the older woman's assumption that she had a boyfriend, lover, significant other or whatever. She didn't say that for her there was only the dream, which never talked back, which never held her close, or whispered words of love in her ears.

"Or, if you don't ask him to come with you," Sandy said, "I can always get Rick to ask around the hospital and see if he can find you a date. Lots of prospects there."

"Gee," Linda murmured dryly, "thanks."

"Well, if you'd give some thought to something more

than your work, you might just have a private life,'' her sister scolded gently. ''And this conversation wouldn't be necessary.''

''I'm quite happy with my life,'' Linda stated, taking another forkful of the chicken salad.

''So am I, big sister,'' Sandy retorted, ''but I still managed to find time for a personal relationship, or two, along the way.''

Which left her several up on Linda, who silently acknowledged that fact. She'd realized a long time ago that for her to make love she had to be in love. Which she was. But, with a man who wasn't hers to have. Maybe someday she'd grow out of it. Move on with her life, find another man to care for who would reciprocate her feelings.

However, she strongly doubted that. Like her grandfather, Ethan, she was a one-love kind of person. Her parents had divorced when Linda was twelve and Sandy ten. Though her mother and father each had eventually found happiness with another person, a part of Linda had wished that they'd found it with each other, and that theirs had been a true and enduring love. It was possible; she'd met couples who had found the ideal mate for them. Clay's parents were a prime example. In the past year or so since becoming Clay's personal assistant, she'd had more occasions to spend time with them and she liked what she saw. She admired the way, after all their years as man and wife, Noah and Santina were still so much in love. And both of Clay's brothers seemed to have found this kind of forever love, as had her sister.

''Hello?'' Sandy chided, attempting to regain Linda's attention.

''Sorry, I was just thinking about something,'' Linda explained.

"Probably business, right?" Sandy laughed. "Are you sure you don't want me to fix you up with a cute doctor? We've got a few hunky fellows on staff, even a couple in the ER."

"No, thanks," Linda quickly replied. "The last doctor you introduced me to was a vain, pompous jerk who only wanted to spare enough time from talking incessantly about himself to get me into bed."

"Sorry. They're not all jerks. After all," she said, a dreamy look in her eyes, "there's Rick."

Linda gave her sister a warm smile in return. "Your fiancé might be the exception."

"I doubt that," Sandy declared. "Luckily, I do know a few others who might fit the bill. All they need is a good woman, and you, my dear sister, are the best."

Linda took another sip of her heavily lemoned iced tea. "Thanks, but no thanks."

"If you change your mind, let me know."

"I won't."

Sandy stared at Linda across the expanse of the small cherry table in one of the private dining rooms belonging to her sister's boss's company. It was a real kick to eat here, especially after the crowded cafeteria at the hospital, where, although the food was actually quite good, there was always a long wait in line and jostling for position at a table.

She was well aware that Linda was stubbornly independent. Once her sister made up her mind, there was usually no changing it. When she did something there were no halfway measures. It was all or nothing. Sandy realized that she should have known better than to expect that Linda would be other than who or what she was. It was one of the reasons she loved her older sister so much, had counted on Linda's dependability while she, Sandy, was growing up.

"God, I could really get used to eating in a place like this."

Linda said, "One of the perks of working for a man like Clay. He likes to see that his employees are well cared for. There is a larger dining room on the floor below with a buffet catering to whatever anyone could want. He has at least ten chefs on staff here." A smile crossed Linda's mouth as she paused. "Unlike some employers, Clay's a very generous man, one who treats the people who work for him like family." Her green eyes took on a deep luster of pride as she continued. "He's good to them. Bonuses. Profit sharing. Respect. It's one of the reasons I admire him so much."

"Honey," Sandy protested, "you don't have to defend him to me."

"I know," Linda said. "It's just that I get tired of hearing how greedy and heartless so much of corporate America is. Granted, I've met my fair share of nasty SOB's who wouldn't spare the time to help anyone unless there was something in it for them. But not Clay."

"Noblesse oblige, eh?" Sandy asked.

"Without a doubt," Linda confirmed. "He takes his responsibility as head of the company to heart. In another time, he would have been a wonderful clan laird. The kind of man you could always count on to protect his people and look out for their best interest. A real leader."

"Okay. Then back to my original suggestion, ask Clay to be your date for my wedding."

Linda took a sip of her iced tea. "You're not going to let it go, are you?"

Sandy was adamant. "No way."

Linda considered the idea. She'd never asked a personal

favor of Clay before. What was the worst thing that he could do? Turn her down. Still...

"I'll think about it."

"You can't afford to think too long, Linda. The wedding's in another month, and I'm sure he's got quite a busy calendar as it is." Sandy finished the remainder of her salmon, keeping to herself the secret she'd long suspected—that her sister was interested in Clay Buchanan as more than a mere business associate. That had been the main reason why she'd made her suggestion of him as a date in the first place, as a burr-under-the-saddle maneuver to get Linda to go for what she really wanted. Linda was smart—top of her class at Wharton's prestigious Business School—but when it came to men, she could be clueless. Clay Buchanan was smart, handsome, rich and straight—plus, best of all, single.

The phone on a nearby smaller table buzzed softly.

"Excuse me," Linda said, rising to answer it. "I'll be there in five minutes," she promised the person she was speaking with, checking her watch. "Yes, she likes Earl Grey with lemon. No, I'll have another glass of the iced tea. Fine." Linda hung up and stood by the table.

"You've got an appointment," Sandy stated.

"Afraid so," Linda acknowledged. "A lady who sits on the Buchanan Charity Trust. We're going over funding for some special projects."

"It's just as well," Sandy concluded, rising from her seat. "I've got to get back to the hospital. It's the late shift tonight."

The sisters embraced, each hugging the other tight.

"Take care," Linda said.

"You do the same. And please," Sandy urged, "ask him."

Leaving Linda to her business appointment, Sandy took

a detour from the elevator, walking to the left instead of the right. She approached Clay's outer office with a confident smile on her face and a scheme in her heart.

"Excuse me."

An older woman with perfectly coiffed iron gray hair sat behind a large desk. She looked up from her keyboard, brown eyes sharp. "Can I help you?" she inquired, giving Sandy a frank glance.

"Hi." Sandy stepped into the spacious room. "I'm Sandra Douglas, Linda's sister."

The other woman's face softened. "Good day, Miss Douglas. What can I do for you? I believe your sister's in a meeting right now. If you'd like, I can check with her secretary to confirm that."

"There's no need, since I just left her," Sandy said, pulling a thick vellum envelope from her oversize purse. "I only stopped by to drop this off in person. Would you see that Mr. Buchanan gets this?"

Mercedes Vega inclined her head, accepting the envelope, scanning its handwritten label.

"It's very important."

"And you don't want your sister to know, am I correct?" Mercedes's glance was direct.

Sandy's lips curved into a smile. "Exactly. It's nothing sinister, I can assure you. Just an invitation to my wedding."

Mercedes nodded her head. "Yes, I do remember Miss Douglas mentioning she had a younger sister getting married."

Sandy's glance fell to her simple diamond ring and she smiled. "That's me."

"I'll give this to Mr. Buchanan personally."

"Thanks. I'd really appreciate that." She turned to

leave and stopped for a moment when she heard the older woman's voice.

"Good luck, Miss Douglas."

Sandy smiled and continued on her way to the elevator, whistling a happy tune. If her plan worked, luck would have nothing to do with it.

"What's this?" Clay demanded as Mercedes handed him the envelope that Sandy had left for him, along with some papers that required his signature.

"Miss Douglas's sister left this for you."

"Interesting," he mused, placing it on the desk. He proceeded to rapidly sign his name across the documents and hand them back to his very able secretary.

"She said that it was an invitation to her wedding."

"Hmm," Clay murmured as he slit the heavy envelope open with a brass knife, an heirloom piece that belonged to his great-grandfather.

He pulled out the invitation, along with a note addressed to him.

"Shall I pick out something and send it to her in your name?" Mercedes inquired.

"That won't be necessary, Mercedes. I'll do it myself. As it's Linda's sister and Ethan Douglas's granddaughter, I want to give the matter some careful thought. A few questions to Linda might help me discover what they could use."

"Whatever you decide, I'm sure it'll be the right choice for them." Mercedes and her family had firsthand knowledge of just how generous Clay could be when it came to gifts, no matter what the occasion.

She left him alone and Clay opened the smaller envelope that had been tucked inside the larger.

Dear Mr. Buchanan,

You're probably wondering why you've received an invitation to my wedding, since we really don't know each other all that well. Actually, it's for my sister and grandfather's sake. I know how highly each regards you, and I thought that if you weren't previously engaged at that date, you'd come and join the celebration. They'd both love to have you there, as would my fiancé and I.

Sorry that this is such short notice, but what with our schedules at the hospital being so hectic, this was the best time for us.

And, you'd be doing Linda an enormous favor as she's such a workaholic—which I'm sure I don't have to tell you—that she hasn't had a chance to find a date.

Linda dateless? Clay found that hard to believe.

Yet, what did he really know of her personal life? She was like him in that respect, someone who loved her work and who accepted that this was a demanding life. Sacrifices had to be made. Usually this included relationships.

But not for this event.

Clay quickly flipped through the leather-bound planner on his desk, checking dates. With a little bit of rearranging, he could possibly make it. But he wanted to check with Linda first. If she needed an escort, he'd be happy to volunteer. Family weddings could be tough enough without flying solo.

About an hour later, Clay knocked on the connecting office door. When he heard the feminine voice tell him to enter, he did.

Linda looked up from her desk and greeted him with a

smile and a sweet-voiced hello. Not just any smile, he thought, but one filled with warmth and welcome.

Funny, he'd never considered before how much he enjoyed watching her wide mouth curve or the sparkle in her long-lashed moss green eyes. Strong Texas sunlight bathed the room, painting her reddish gold hair with a touch of copper.

It occurred to Clay that he'd never seen Linda wearing it down. At work she maintained a sensible style, drawn back in a sleek chignon. What about after work? he wondered. Did she let her hair down then?

"How long is it?"

Linda blinked. "How long is what?" she asked, not having a clue as to what Clay was asking about.

"Your hair," he answered.

She stared at him as if he were a stranger masquerading as her boss. What in the world was going on behind those steel-rimmed glasses he wore? "Why?"

It was Clay's turn to smile, an action that was guaranteed to melt butter. "Humor me."

Linda sighed softly and decided to do just that. "About midway down my back," she replied, then leaned into her comfortable, old-fashioned chair, her eyes still focused on the tall man who stood a few feet away from her. "Was that the reason you came in?"

"No." Clay stepped closer, taking a seat opposite her. This room was smartly decorated, maintaining a sense of individual style. In contrast to his office, this was softer. Solid maple desk and fabric-covered chairs instead of the walnut and leather that occupied his province. Splashes of color here and there in the carpet and drapes. Rich jewel-tone shades of burgundy and gold. His walls were hung with hunting prints; hers held still lifes. Ripe fruit ready

to burst, plump with color and looking almost real enough
to eat.

"I received an invitation today to your sister's wedding."

Linda bit back the groan that threatened to spill from
her throat. She wanted to die. Or kill her sister. How could
Sandy embarrass her like this?

"I'm sure she was just being polite. Please," Linda
said, trying to make amends, "don't feel obligated."

"I don't," Clay replied.

"I'll relay your regrets—"

"You won't have to," he interjected, cutting off her
words. "I've decided that I'd like to go. That is, if you
don't mind?"

"Mind? Why would I mind?"

One of Clay's golden brown brows arched. "Would it
be presumptuous of me to ask if you're going with anyone?"

Linda hesitated in answering his question. She could
say yes; however, he might still decide to come, thereby
catching her in an embarrassing fib. And besides, she'd
never lied to Clay before and didn't want to start now.
"It wouldn't be and, no, I'm not."

"Then," he asked politely, leaning closer to the desk,
"would you consider my coming along as your escort?
For moral support. I know how trying things can be, especially at family gatherings, when you're a maverick and
everyone else there is wearing a brand."

Maverick. Truth be known, she hadn't been one since
she was sixteen and first looked into those dark blue eyes.
In her heart, Linda already bore the mark of Clay's influence. Emotionally he'd stamped his brand on her back
then as surely as if he'd done it with a hot iron.

She accepted graciously since there was no other way.

Refusal might raise suspicions. "Thanks. I'd appreciate the favor, not to mention the company. You're quite right. It can be awkward at times when you're the single person in a roomful of couples." She wanted to let Clay know that she understood the reason behind his offer. He was being kind, a consummate gentleman, helping a friend in need. Nothing more. She shouldn't read anything deeper into the gesture.

Clay found himself making a much more personal observation. "That's probably more your choice, am I right?"

"What is?"

"That you're still unattached."

She wet her lips. "Yes."

"I thought so."

"You did?" Now it was her turn to raise a brow in consternation.

"Of course. You're smart, attractive, independent and earn a good living. That's quite an impressive package. I don't know a lot of men who wouldn't find that appealing."

"You'd be surprised then, Clay," she said. "Some men find it too intimidating."

He snorted softly. "Their loss, believe me. Any man worth the name would be proud to have a woman like you in his life."

Except, Linda thought ruefully, the one man she wanted above all others. Clay's was the solid testimony of a dispassionate, satisfied employer. His words stroked her ego while they scratched her soul.

"Thanks."

"None needed. It's the truth." He leaned back in the comfortable chair. "This trip will give me a chance to see your grandfather again. It's been far too long since I've had a chance to talk to Ethan. My fault, of course.''

Hearing that Clay was coming to Sandy's wedding would make her grandfather both happy and proud. "He'll be thrilled to see you again, as well, Clay. Since he retired from the bank, he doesn't get out and about much. He teaches a class at the local community college one day a week, mostly for something to do.

"Our family is scattered, so that's the reason Sandy wanted to hold the ceremony at Granddad's farm. It'll be good for him to have family around, if only for a weekend. Mama lives in Beaumont with her husband. Daddy lives in Denver with his wife and her children. Sandy's a nurse in Galveston. So, Granddad's by himself in the old house that he shared with my grandmother, who as you know passed away three years ago. He's been, I think, marking time till he can join her.''

"Yes," Clay said, recalling happier times in the past with Ethan and his wife. "He adored Miss Clara.''

"Just as she did him," Linda stated, softness relaxing her features. "From the first moment she met my granddad, I recall her telling me, there was no other man for her.''

Adored. Clay imagined the possibilities contained in that single word as it temporarily lingered in his mind. His mother and father certainly *adored* each other. As did both his brothers and the women they'd chosen. What about him? Could he ever adore any woman in that same deep-rooted way? Did he even want anyone to adore him in a similar manner?

No! came the swift answer. Because if you didn't adore you didn't risk and if you didn't risk, then you didn't get hurt. Adoration wasn't part of his checklist for a suitable future wife. It would only get in the way of a convenient marriage, a convenient life. Strictly speaking, it wasn't an option that he was looking for.

"You know, you remind me of her."

"I do?"

"She had a way of making people comfortable," he explained.

Linda smiled in gratitude. "I'll take that compliment."

"You should," Clay insisted. "More people could use that trait. Miss Clara had it naturally, along with a wicked sense of humor."

"She and Granddad laughed quite a lot," Linda recalled. "She once told me that if you can't share a laugh with your man, then you can't share a life."

Clay remarked, "I'm sure that's very true." He flicked a glance at his watch as he rose from the chair. "I've got a meeting in thirty minutes, so I'll talk to you later about what to get your sister and her husband as a wedding gift. By the way, where are they going for their honeymoon?"

"Sandy loves the water, but what with footing the bill themselves for the wedding, she and Rick aren't able to go far, so I'm sure that it will be somewhere close. I offered to give them the money for a nice trip as a wedding gift, but they wouldn't take it."

Clay smiled. "Perhaps you should have given it a fait accompli, my dear. That way they couldn't refuse."

Linda recognized the keen sparkle in his blue eyes. "What are you thinking?"

"I'll let you know later. Maybe together we can give them a gift to remember."

Together.

She savored that word as she went back to her computer screen and ran through the series of numbers, checking second-quarter projections on one of the diverse holdings of Buchanan Enterprises.

Together.

Linda cast a sidelong glance at the closed door between their two offices. Hers seemed emptier somehow for his leaving, as if a certain high-voltage charge of electricity had been snapped off by an unseen hand.

Forcing herself to concentrate on the work she had to do, Linda let go of her fanciful thoughts.

Together.

While waiting for the documents he keyed in to appear on his laptop screen, Clay turned his head and gave a lingering look at the door that stood between them.

They were a team. A damned good one. Better than he'd ever thought possible. Their styles blended flawlessly, each bringing something different to the mixture.

He returned his gaze to the words printed on the screen, staring at them until they became a blur.

Something was missing.

Clay's head lifted slowly and he looked around his office. Everything was the same. Nothing out of place.

Then it hit him.

The scent, or lack of it.

That's what was missing in here. The gentle aroma of the fresh-cut red roses that stood on her desk. The intoxicating fragrance of the brand of perfume she wore.

By comparison, his office seemed stale, oddly barren.

Strange, he thought as he went back to perusing the pages, he'd never noticed that before.

Chapter Three

"Miss Douglas will be joining me for lunch, Lettie," Clay informed his housekeeper-cook as she set down a tray and handed him a fresh cup of coffee. He was working at home today, trying to get a few things cleared off his desk so that he could spend the weekend in the Hill Country with no pressing concerns to mar his time there. Though he understood and accepted that business concerns were apt to occur at any time, no matter what the circumstances. When you controlled or oversaw as many facets of an enterprise as Clay did, there was usually an occasional glitch that had to be sorted out right away. Linda handled a great many items, to her credit, but some things demanded his personal attention, such as the deal he was working on.

"Would you like anything special?" Lettie asked, placing a small china plate, which contained two warm scones topped with strawberry jam, beside the china cup.

"I'll leave that in your very capable hands."

Lettie beamed and as she went to leave, Clay stopped her. "Wait."

"Yes?"

"I've just thought of something."

Lettie waited patiently for Clay to explain.

"Set up the table in the greenroom," he instructed. "Nothing too elaborate, but fresh flowers are a must."

Lettie smiled. "The garden should yield a nice selection, sir. Do you have anything in particular in mind?"

"How about primroses?"

Lettie nodded. "That should do quite nicely, sir. Combined with one or two other flowers, it will be just what you want. Would you like wine with the meal?"

"Tell Basil to uncork a bottle of the chardonnay that I brought back from Australia. That should be fine with whatever you decide to fix."

Lettie left to see to the arrangements and Clay took a break, biting into the fresh-baked scone. He and Linda had had lunch before. Many times, in many different places, from four-star restaurants to roadhouse cafés. But today was different. Today it was in his house, prior to their leaving for the wedding that would take place the following day.

Clay pushed back his chair and walked across the room to the glass door that opened onto a small brick patio. He stood there, hoping that Linda would approve of his wedding present to her sister. He'd planned to tell her what he'd done, then changed his mind. It would be more fun if it were a surprise to all, including Linda.

Especially Linda.

As Linda pulled her car into the private driveway of the housing development in one of Houston's most exclusive areas, she smiled and gave her name to the man on duty at the security gate. He returned her smile after checking his list. Seconds later the massive steel gates swung open and she drove through, heading for Clay's address along the oak-lined street, which was filled with one-of-a-kind custom-built homes.

She'd only been to Clay's new house once, for a formal holiday dinner party last Christmas. It sat at the end of the winding road, a large two-story Tudor-style. Spacious. Elegant.

She parked her luxury sedan, leased by the company for her use, another perk of working for Clay, and got out, walking along the brick driveway. Before she went to the front door, Linda stopped and gazed at the structure with a satisfied look on her face. The house suited Clay. There was nothing flagrant or overly showy about it, nothing that shouted or screamed. Just simple class, dignity, warmth and charm.

All it really needed, she decided, were a few dogs running about the grounds to give it the final touch. If she lived in a place like this, there would definitely be dogs. At least two. Maybe Labradors. Perhaps a collie. Or even an Irish setter.

She'd had a dog when she was younger. A mutt, nothing special, except to her. When her parents divorced and she went to live with her mom in an apartment in Beaumont, she'd had to leave the dog with her grandparents.

Linda could easily visualize Clay with a dog. It would fit the picture she had of him as the proverbial country gentleman, albeit one who lived in Houston.

Her knock had no sooner fallen upon the wide oak door with its panels of stained glass, than it swung wide-open. A tall, slim, bald man in a black suit stood in the doorway. "Good day, Miss Douglas," he said, his mellifluous voice warmly greeting her, stepping aside so that she could enter. "Mr. Buchanan is expecting you. He's in his study."

Linda stepped across the threshold.

"Is your luggage outside?"

"It's still in the trunk of my car," she replied.

"If you'll give me your keys, I'll transfer it to Mr. Buchanan's car straight away."

Linda unsnapped the lid of her compact purse and gave Basil the key ring, indicating which one he needed.

He couldn't help but exclaim over the craftsmanship of the piece. It was no ordinary key chain. "This is really quite lovely, Miss Douglas."

Linda smiled broadly as the butler examined the object, a solid gold Celtic cross. "It was a Christmas gift from Clay."

"Mr. Buchanan has excellent taste."

"I couldn't agree more, Basil," Linda concurred. "It's something I treasure."

"I can well imagine why."

"I'd better go and find Clay. He doesn't like to be kept waiting."

Basil interjected a personal comment. "For you, Miss Douglas, I think he would make the rare exception."

"How nice of you to say so, Basil."

The older man inclined his head. "My pleasure."

Linda made her way along the hall toward the back of the house, thinking about this trip. She'd planned on going by herself, but at the last minute, Clay had invited her to ride with him. As her grandfather's farm was less than an hour from the Buchanan family ranch, it made no sense, he'd said, to take two cars. He would drop her off at Ethan's and he would return the next day for the wedding, meeting her at the church.

Feeling churlish if she refused his generous offer, Linda

accepted. It meant she would be spending more time alone with Clay, for it was at least a three-hour drive to her granddad's place. Three hours in which to revel in his company, savoring the journey. Unlike other trips that they'd taken together, this wasn't business oriented. She suspected, however, that work would occupy the majority of their conversation as it normally did; however, that wasn't really important. Having this extra time with him was the real bonus. One that both excited and frightened her.

Clay added a few notes to the file on his laptop screen from papers that had been just faxed to him. He dropped the originals into a dark cherry tray for filing later. As he did so, from the corner of his eye, he caught a glimpse of someone standing in the doorway.

He raised his head. It was Linda, looking very cool and relaxed in a pair of white chinos and a navy blue short-sleeved cotton top that clung to her shapely form. What caused him to smile was her hair—she'd worn it down in tumbling waves of red gold around her shoulders.

"Your hair, it's lovely," he murmured, saying the first words that popped into his head.

Linda touched it self-consciously, glad now that she had decided to wear it loose. "Thank you." She stepped into the room, smiling as she did so, thinking how good he looked himself when he stood up as she approached the desk. Instead of his usual three-piece suit, he wore a short-sleeved white polo shirt and tailored khakis.

"None needed," he said, coming around the width of the desk to her side. He stood so close that he caught a provocative whiff of her perfume. Unlike some women, she obviously didn't feel the need to ladle it on, for which he was grateful. And she'd changed her makeup today, as well. In the office it was more polished. This afternoon it was simple—just, he guessed, a touch of mascara to complement her lovely green eyes and a hint of color to her soft, full mouth. A mouth, he noted, the shade of ripe peaches in summer, waiting to be tasted.

"It's the truth," he continued. "You know me better than to think I'd waste my time in idle or insincere flattery. I respect you too much for that."

"Yes, I do know that," Linda responded. It's not as if she'd been expecting the lavish compliments of a lover or anything like that. Clay was honest and that honesty touched her with its frankness. It enveloped her like a warm blanket on a frosty morning.

"Please," he offered, indicating the couch to one side, "take a seat and I'll be with you shortly."

Linda walked over to it, her eyes drinking in the wonderful palette of autumn colors in the tapestry fabric that covered the piece of furniture. Without thought, her hand stretched out to casually caress it. "If you don't mind, I'd rather take a look about the room."

"Be my guest," he said. "Just give me a minute to clear this up and we can have lunch." Resuming his seat behind the desk, Clay watched as Linda moved about the room, her head tilted to one side as she scanned the titles of the books on several of the shelves of the built-in cherry bookcases.

"Take your time," she responded. "I'm in no hurry." And she wasn't. It was fun finding out what his tastes were in books. Nary a novel in sight. Most of the volumes were business tomes, economics mainly, with a few on management and sales.

Then, Linda's eyes were caught by the sight of something very different on the lower shelves. She took a few steps to the right and stopped, bending down. Instead of books, the wooden shelves held LPs, old vinyl records. Intrigued, she picked several up at random and examined them.

Linda looked so different with her hair down, Clay thought, finding it difficult to keep his eyes focused on the screen in front of him. With her casual clothes and long locks, she seemed much more vulnerable, younger, less the unflappable top-flight executive. Seeing her like this, he could well imagine what she'd looked like as a college student. Eager. Earnest. On the brink of a new life. Ready to take on the world and all its challenges.

He shut the lid. "Done," he pronounced, shifting the machine to a leather briefcase.

"Planning on getting more work done this weekend?" she asked over her shoulder as she flipped through his musical interests.

"A few minor details to work out on the Madison contract. I want to get it done so that the buyout can go through smoothly."

She replaced the sleeves, turning to face him. "You're making me feel guilty," she teased. "I didn't even bring my pager or laptop." Buchanan Textiles, a division of Buchanan Enterprises, was taking over a century-old woolen mill in New England. She'd been instrumental in bringing the faltering company to Clay's notice. "Have they thrown up roadblocks?"

"A few minor glitches. Nothing that will stand in the way of our acquiring the mill and setting about making it work again."

Linda was pleased with Clay's decision to keep the operation open. Instead of looting the factory and selling off the machinery piecemeal for a quick profit, he'd chosen instead, on her recommendation, to keep it alive, remodeling and repairing what had been allowed to fall into disrepair. Jobs would be kept and a town salvaged from economic ruin. Because of him. Because he could see the wisdom in long-term.

If she needed another reason to love him, it would be for the foresight and compassion he showed in giving this business a second chance. She'd wanted to brag, to exclaim her pride in him to everyone and anyone who would listen. But that wasn't possible, let alone practical. So Linda confined her remarks of muted delight to her grandfather, who'd reminded her of something he'd once said to her.

"Remember, Linda, that boy's been brought up to believe that wealth brings with it responsibility. Privilege has its price. That's a valuable lesson to learn, so don't you ever forget it. There's too many of them today that does."

How right you are, Granddad, she thought as she picked out another LP, a smile on her mouth as she recognized the singer.

Clay crossed the room and moved closer to her.

"My mom loved his music," Linda stated, referring to Nat King Cole, aware of Clay coming close to her as she stood up. She kept her focus on the record, glancing at the list of songs included. All love songs. "She played it a lot when I was young. LPs, just like this." She placed it carefully back on the shelf, then faced him once again. "Where'd you find this stuff?"

"The occasional flea market. Some in estate and garage sales."

Linda lifted one delicately arched eyebrow, giving him a skeptical look. "You want me to believe that you personally scoured tag sales and the like for these items?" She could well imagine her surprise had she run into Clay while she was checking out some of the buys at a few of the bigger flea markets.

His mouth kicked up into a wicked grin. "I don't," he replied honestly. "Remember, my mother's in the interior design business, so when she sends one of her assistants to some of the sales, or she goes herself, she keeps an eye out for me. And auction houses here in Texas and several in New York send me catalogues on a regular basis. They keep me informed if there's anything that I might be interested in."

Linda glanced back at the shelves. "It's quite a collection."

Clay chuckled. "These are only a small part of my personal favorites. The rest are upstairs in the music room. If you'd like, I can bring along a couple of Cole's albums on CDs for the trip."

Nat King Cole singing love ballads while she was confined in a car with Clay? It was a temptation that was too delicious to pass up. "Yes, I'd like that."

"Anyone else?"

"I'll leave that up to you," she replied, tilting her head back slightly so that her hair fell back across her shoulders in long waves.

He almost reached his hand up to touch that cascade of hair, curious to see if it was as soft as it appeared. He recalled seeing a selection of art deco jewelry that was to be auctioned off in the near future in a catalogue for one of the famous auction houses in New York. Among the pieces were five barrettes of various sizes and shapes. All done in platinum, diamonds and emeralds. In her hair they would look marvelous.

But, he belatedly realized, they were not the items one gave a colleague. They were gifts for a wife, or a lover.

Still they would look damn fine with her coloring. Fire blending with fire.

Removing his thoughts from risky ground, Clay shifted his focus. "What type of music do you like?"

"Well," she started to say, moving slightly away from him, closer to the French doors—he was too dangerous to be near in so intimate a setting. It didn't matter that they'd been closer on numerous occasions as they worked. This was his home, his personal domain, and the stakes were different. "When I get a chance to listen, which isn't often, I prefer the classics, as well as Broadway show tunes and torch songs.

"Though," she added, taking a deep breath, "I must confess a sneaking fondness for operettas. I had a friend in college who was a musical theater major. She introduced me to it."

"Did you ever perform?"

"Just once," she confessed, laughter in her voice. "I was in the chorus of *The Desert Song*."

"And you weren't bitten by the bug?"

"Good God, no," she stated clearly. "It was just for fun."

"Is your friend on the stage?"

"In a manner of speaking, yes."

Clay regarded her, a perplexed look on his features. "What's that supposed to mean?"

"Jolene's a teacher. She runs the drama department of a high school."

"Locally?"

Linda shook her head. "In Killeen, her hometown."

"Do you still keep in touch with her?"

Linda admitted, "Not as often as I'd like. We talk occasionally, but she's busy and so am I." It was one thing that Linda regretted. With her job, she had no real time for many close pals, for chitchatting hours away discussing problems. Besides, it wasn't in her nature to talk much about her life.

Clay nodded in understanding. "I know what you mean. Our kind of work doesn't leave much room for friends, which is why my family is so important to me."

"So is mine. We're a lot alike, aren't we, Clay?" she asked softly.

He thought for a moment. "I imagine we are." So many little connections that he was just becoming aware of. So many common threads in their lives.

A discreet knock sounded on the open door.

"Lettie has luncheon ready, sir."

"Then," Clay said with a smile, "we'd best not keep her waiting."

Linda felt restless. The rehearsal for the wedding had gone off without a hitch. Dinner afterward had been fun and by rights she should be exhausted.

That's just it, she was. Very. Unfortunately not enough to go to sleep.

Tired of lying there, Linda tossed back the well-worn white sheet and got out of bed. Gathering the thin navy cotton robe from the wicker chair, she drew it on over her man-tailored white-and-navy pajamas and padded, barefoot, toward the kitchen. She was too keyed up, her mind going in several directions at once. Maybe, she thought, a glass of milk would help her to relax.

Pouring herself a large glass of the ice-cold milk, Linda sat down at the table. She ran one hand over the surface of the bare wood, feeling the knicks and bumps of age. Her grandmother would never hear of replacing it—the table was part of Clara's life. It had been passed down through several generations, an heirloom intended one day for Linda.

"She never could bear the thought of parting with it," said the male voice behind her.

Startled, Linda splashed some of her milk upon the surface.

"Sorry." Ethan Douglas came out of the shadows. "Should've known better than to sneak up on you. Damn fool thing to do."

Linda relaxed and, after rising, she kissed the old man on the cheek. Then she got a cloth to wipe up the spill. "I'm sorry if I woke you."

"You didn't," he assured her. "I was awake. Heard you roaming about. Besides, at my age, you don't need much sleep anyways."

Linda resumed her seat, joined by Ethan, who took one opposite her. "Sandy's still asleep, isn't she?"

"Walked by her room and didn't hear a peep. Guess she's ready to get hitched. No doubts to keep her up and about." Folding his hands one atop the other, he gave his elder granddaughter a keen look. "How you doing, sweetheart? What with all the fuss today, I didn't have a chance to ask."

"Fine, Granddaddy."

Ethan shot her a suspicious glance. "Honey, that's one big load of manure you're tossing my way."

Linda laughed, putting one hand to her mouth to muffle the sound so as not to wake her sister. She could always count on her grandfather for plain speaking. "Really," she said when she regained control, "I'm fine."

"That for certain?"

Linda sobered as she read the concern on his weathered face. She stretched out her hand, covering his arthritic one with her own. "What could be wrong?"

"Maybe that you ain't married yet?"

"Granddad!"

"Don't *granddad* me, young lady," he admonished. "And don't be telling me that I'm way too old-fashioned for these times. Love is love, no matter what the year, or the fashion."

She wanted to allay his worries, so she tempered her response. "I haven't found Mr. Right."

"I can see that pitchfork full of bull coming my way again," he said. "Nonsense. You found him ten years back."

"What?"

"You heard me, girl. Just because I'm old doesn't mean I'm stupid. Or that I'm deaf, dumb and blind."

"I never said—"

"Hmm," he scoffed, his voice gruff. "Did you really think I couldn't see it in your face that day? Or hear it in your voice?" His expression softened. "You love that boy, don't you?"

It didn't take a mental giant to figure out who "that boy" was, though Linda suppressed a smile at the notion of anyone calling the thirty-eight-year-old Clay Buchanan a boy.

She couldn't look into Ethan's lined face and tell him a lie. It wouldn't work. And, she admitted, it would be nice to share it with someone, especially someone who cared for Clay. "Yes."

"I knew it. You never could fool me, sweetheart."

"No, I never could, could I?"

"So what are you gonna do about it?"

"Nothing."

"What do you mean *nothing?*"

"Just what I said, Granddad. And," she warned him,

"I don't want you saying anything to Clay at the wedding."

Ethan had the grace to look affronted. "Like I would."

Linda leveled her own frank glance at him. "Promise?"

"I give you my word I won't tell Clay that you're in love with him."

"Good." Linda drank more of the milk, hoping that her grandfather would let the subject rest.

"High time he was married, too. He's the right age."

Obviously her wish wasn't being granted. "He'll get married when he's ready."

"Well, he ain't ever gonna find someone who's as right for him as you are. He learned that lesson when he tried to get engaged a couple of years back. It failed because he picked the wrong woman."

"You don't know that for a fact, Granddad."

"Of course I do," Ethan protested, barely keeping his voice in check. "Known him since he was a pup. Trust me. You'd be good for him."

Linda discovered that she liked hearing that. "In what way?"

"In every way that counts for a man, sweetheart."

Linda replayed her grandfather's words later when she was back in bed. *Unfortunately, it doesn't matter what you or I think, Granddad, only what he thinks.*

Clay blew smoke rings into the air, watching as they floated away. It was relatively quiet here at the ranch, no extraneous noises of the city pounding away in the background.

He took another puff of the expensive tobacco, his mind not on the quality of the product but on the hours past. Hours spent with Linda.

A half-empty snifter of brandy rested on the low coffee

table in front of him. He'd had a wonderful, relaxing dinner with his family after he'd dropped Linda off at her grandfather's home. He was amazed at how much his nephew Sam had grown in such a short time since his last visit. Jessie too, who was such a poised young lady now. His father had mentioned over brandy and cigars—casually to be sure, but with definite purpose—that Clay should think about settling down. Noah delivered only the broadest of hints, of course, but Clay understood the implied message.

His mind had wandered back to luncheon at his own house earlier with Linda. The meal had been served in the conservatory room, with sunlight pouring in all around them. Surrounded by plants, potted or in hanging baskets, it had felt as if they were in a private sanctuary. Over glasses of chilled white wine and a superb quiche, they'd talked about matters other than business, actually getting to know a bit more about each other. Exploring likes and dislikes, Clay found that they had many things to talk about that didn't include their careers.

Strange to work closely with someone and realize that there was so much more to them that you didn't know. Or hadn't stopped to consider. Humor. Confidence. Strong opinions. Like opening a door that led to many rooms. Always another door, a new choice.

Linda saw life through a fresher, younger, less cynical eye. After all, he considered, there was a twelve-year difference in their ages. He'd swum in shark-infested waters a hell of a lot longer than she had.

Clay wondered why some smart man hadn't snapped her up before now? It had to be more than she'd indicated, that she'd met some jerks who had a problem with her salary and her devotion to her job. He knew there had to be many men who'd jump at the chance to date someone like Linda.

He crushed out the cigar and finished the rest of the brandy, wondering what tomorrow would bring.

Maybe, he mused, another door to open, another threshold to cross.

Chapter Four

Linda literally took his breath away.

Clay sat in the second pew of the church, behind the parents of the bride, Ethan by his side, and watched as the wedding party gathered at the altar. Sandy Douglas was a lovely bride and looked all that she could be on her special day. But it was Linda who captured his interest, Linda who made him sit up and take notice with her strong face and unconventional beauty.

She was like a woman from another era. A kinder, gentler, softer time. Someone removed from the mundane everydayness. Her long reddish gold hair was artfully curled, falling in waves over her shoulders. Around her long, slender throat was a multistranded pearl choker that matched the triple-strand bracelet she wore on her left wrist. Her dress was an eye-catching off-the-shoulder taffeta in the purest rose shade, with a wide swath of ivory-colored lace banding the neckline, swirling down around her ankles, cut and draped to show off her wonderful figure. Her skin, he noted, was a healthy color mixture of fresh cream over apricots.

Ethan, a deep grin on his face as he watched Clay all but drool over his granddaughter, said, sotto voce, "Doesn't she look fit to dance with angels?"

Angelic wasn't quite the reaction Clay was having to seeing Linda in this new and different light. His feeling was much more temporal. As she'd walked past him down the aisle she'd smiled. A look that he was sure included her family, but somehow, Clay could almost think that it had been for him alone. Sweet. Promising. An invitation.

To what?

Investigate? Sample? Taste? Enjoy? Cross the line and break the boundaries?

Or had it been merely a trick his imagination played upon him, seeing something that existed only in his mind? Mistaking the obvious for something forbidden?

"Ethan," he answered, also in a whisper, "right here, right now, angels would pale in comparison."

Excitement danced in Linda's veins as she took her place. Not only for her sister's happiness, but at sharing the moment with Clay. Even though he sat behind her parents, separated from her by several feet and one pew, it didn't matter. They were both here, witnessing the event.

How handsome he looked this morning in his well-cut dark gray suit. Smart. Urbane. Utterly polished. Perfection personified. Dapper, as her grandfather was fond of saying. The recent trip to Australia had tanned his skin a warm shade of gold, adding tawny streaks to his hair, as well, making his blue eyes even bluer behind his steel-rimmed glasses. What was it about Clay that made all the others in the church pale in comparison? He alone stood out. Everyone else's face, including the various members of her family, had blurred when she'd walked down the aisle. For her there was only Clay with his familiar and welcome glance.

Deeper and deeper the want for him burrowed within her. Stronger and stronger rose her love until it was impossible to tell them apart.

Fantasy interwove with reality in her head and heart as Linda listened to the vows her sister and her groom were exchanging, wishing that she was saying them with Clay. That this was her wedding day. Her chance to realize the happiness she so wanted with the man she loved.

But it wasn't her wedding. It was Sandy's. God, how she envied her younger sister at this moment. Marrying the man she adored, and one who adored her in return. Starting a new life together. Building a future. Belonging. Sharing. Holding tight to what they wanted.

Clay watched as Linda lifted her hand up to her eye, brushing away what he assumed was a tear. In this highly charged atmosphere, his thoughts wandered back along the path of marriage. He'd purposely avoided Burke and Emma's wedding, pleading pressing business, which he was sure had fooled no one in his family for an instant. For Drew's upcoming nuptials, he was to share the best man honors with Burke, a task he was looking forward to. His brothers' relationships had commitment, purpose. The promise of tomorrow.

And what did he have right now in his life?

Business. The exhilarating balancing of craft and calculation, of building and balancing.

But what about when the day was done? What about his personal time? At home an empty bed waited for him. A bed that he could easily fill with any number of women, should that be all he wanted.

It wasn't.

Quantity didn't equal quality. And that was what he was seeking, ultimately, in a relationship. Quality. Only the best of the best was good enough for him, for the future he envisioned. Clay knew he set high standards for what he wanted in a wife. Why not? He'd be the one living with her. Sleeping with her. To make the kind of marriage he wanted work, he didn't have to be in love, but he certainly had to be in like.

With those words a woman's image flashed quickly into his brain.

Clay raised his head and looked up. Slowly a smile curled his lips in recognition.

Tables had been set up under a large tent at Ethan's farm for the wedding reception. Daisies, Sandy's favorite flower, were everywhere, from bouquets that sat on the tables to specially made wedding cookies, to the linens, plates and napkins. Linda was proud of her sister, proud that in the sterile and sometimes over-the-top world of professional wedding planners, Sandy had found someone who could put it together just as she wanted. Simple. Honest. And, above all, fun.

"Everyone," she observed, leaning nearer to her boss-*cum*-date so that he could hear her over the cacophonous noise all around them, "seems to be having a great time." The band was good, the food was fabulous, the atmosphere relaxing. Clay sat next to her, so close that they occasionally touched. Each time they did it was like an electric current shooting into her flesh, energizing her with the impact. Making her even more aware of him as a man—as if she needed that. Not simply the man she worked for, but a *man*. Male to her female.

"What's not to like?" Clay remarked, sharing her enthusiasm for the event. "They've managed to make this a true Texas celebration."

Linda was happy to hear him say that, considering the difference between this kind of reception and the many others he'd attended. With a nod of her head, she signaled her agreement.

"I'm so glad to see that you aren't afraid to eat," Clay said to her as he poured more wine into her glass from the bottle that they shared, watching as she took a bite out of a thick slice of aged, farmhouse cheddar. "I never could see the reason why healthy women starve themselves to fit into some idiotic idea of what the fashion magazines think men want."

Warmth suffused Linda's skin. "I never paid much attention to that."

"Good thing, too," he observed, indicating the abundant supply of down-home Hill Country food that filled two tables almost to overflowing, "as they've done quite a splendid job at tempting anyone's palate."

"And have you been tempted?" Linda asked, her voice silky smooth, slicing him a curious glance.

His eyes met hers, and his tone was intimate. "I'm only human, despite the rumors."

Only human? she thought. He was much more than that to her. He was temptation of the highest sort. Temptation to touch him. To reach out her hand and willingly caress his. To slide her fingers through his thick waves of hair. To sample those masculine lips. To cuddle within the shelter of his strong arms early in the morning.

That last thought produced a powerful image in her mind. Clay Buchanan asleep in a big bed, a sheet draped loosely over his hips. Morning sun streaming through an open window, gilding his bare torso in a warm glow. She imagined a light dusting of golden brown hair on his lean, muscular chest. He resembled a sleeping tiger or a mountain lion—sleek in repose, formidable awake. A powerful masculine beast that you roused at your own risk.

Clay looked in Linda's direction and wondered where she'd gone? Clearly something had caught her fancy. What thoughts captivated her? What was making her remarkably sensual lips curve so delightfully?

He downed the rest of the wine in his glass, pushing back his chair, acting on an immediate desire. "Dance with me," he said as he held out his hand.

Linda blinked, so wrapped up with her daydream that she'd temporarily lost track of time. "What?"

Clay repeated his request.

Instinctively Linda moved to join him as the band played a slow and sexy number, a standard from bygone days, heavy on romance. The opening bars of "When I Fall In Love" floated to them. His arms closed around her as he stepped into the melody, taking control, melding them into one unit.

She relaxed, accepting the connection between them, aware of the marked differences in their bodies. Hard to soft. Masculine to feminine.

There was nothing stuffy or formal about his dancing. Clay could, Linda thought, steam clothes with the heat he was generating. All because he felt the music, listened to the rhythm and went with it willingly, taking her along on the journey.

She felt like Cinderella at the ball, dancing with the prince of her dreams. *Enjoy it while you can,* she warned herself. *Cherish it while you can.* All good things come to an end.

Though other couples danced around them, Clay didn't take notice. All he could focus on was the woman he held.

Linda felt so right in his arms as they glided across the makeshift dance floor that was provided for the afternoon. As if she belonged there.

Where, he wondered, had that thought sprung from?

The answer came rapidly. It was a deep, in-the-gut reaction on his part, beyond planning, beyond calculation. It simply was.

"I'm going to cut in, if you don't mind," said Ethan, tapping Clay on the shoulder.

Clay reluctantly relinquished Linda to her grandfather. "Seeing how you're kin to the lady, I guess I can be persuaded," he remarked lightheartedly. He directed his next words to Linda. "I'll go and get us another glass of wine to drink."

"No more for me," Linda declared, already drunk with excitement as one dance stretched into three. "I've had enough."

Clay fixed her with a penetrating look as he asked in his distinct Texas-flavored baritone, "Then what would you like?"

You.

Linda didn't voice that wanton thought out loud. Instead, she chose the safe and proper path. "Iced tea would be lovely."

"Then iced tea it will be," Clay said as he strode off in the direction of the refreshments table.

"You two looked plum pretty together, sweetheart," Ethan commented. "Just like I always suspected. You're a match for each other."

Linda sighed. "He's just being polite, Granddad. Don't go reading more into it than that."

"Polite, hell," Ethan muttered as he sailed her around in time to the beat of the country tune as the band sang,

"Lookin' For Love." "That boy feels something for you. Damned if he don't."

"Of course he does, Granddad," she countered, her eyes straying occasionally to where Clay stood. "Respect. Friendship. A mutual admiration. That's all."

"'There's none so blind as them that can't see,'" he quoted.

That got her attention. "What's that supposed to mean?"

"Exactly what I said."

"Which is?"

"Clay Buchanan feels more for you than that."

"He doesn't," she insisted.

Ethan shook his head. "He does. You just won't accept it."

"I accept the reality of the situation, Granddad. I work for the man."

"Work," he alleged, "has nothing to do with how he was looking at you."

Linda raised her head and stared at her grandfather's face. "What?" Her voice was low, her question delivered with surprise.

"You heard me. That boy was looking like any man does when he's found what he wants."

"No." Linda's denial was soft-spoken but firm.

"Yes," Ethan retorted. "Pretend all you want, sweetheart, but I know what I saw."

Linda didn't want to hurt her grandfather; however, she believed that he saw only what he wanted to see. "Have it your own way."

"Sweetheart, I want what's best for you, Linda. I always have. Can't blame me if I think it's that young man."

She smiled, her tone affectionate. "No, I can't."

"So, then don't close your mind to the possibility of something more between you. It could happen." The music stopped and Ethan escorted Linda back to the table. "Looks like Sandy's got hold of Clay. Wonder what that's about?"

Linda took a seat, keeping a watchful eye on her sister and her boss. "Sandy's probably thanking Clay for his wedding present, I imagine."

Sandy had taken her aside earlier in the day before the wedding ceremony to tell her about Clay's gift. Surprised and pleased by his kind and thoughtful gesture, she'd wanted to go and find Clay immediately and thank him on behalf of Sandy and Rick. It would have been easy to give in to the passion of the moment.

However, she hadn't. Linda remained calm and expressed her gratitude at an appropriate moment later, after the ceremony, in words, not deeds, never losing sight of his position or hers.

"Knowing him, I'll bet it was a real humdinger."

When Linda told him what it was, Ethan let out a long sigh. "Right generous, I'd say."

Sandy thought so, too and couldn't wait to tell Clay, who she managed to find standing in line for refreshments. "I just couldn't believe it when I saw what was in the envelope," she gushed.

Clay smiled in return. "You've got Linda to thank for that. She told me that you and your husband wanted to go somewhere warm and wet, with lots of sand."

"Yes, we did, but this is too much."

Clay shrugged his shoulders. "It isn't, really."

"A house on the beach in Cancun? Completely private. And staffed. Plus, a private jet to take us there? Get real."

He assured her, "You'd be doing me a favor. It's my grandmother's and she hasn't had a chance to spend much time there lately, so it's been vacant for a while. When I asked her about it she was thrilled that someone would use it again for their honeymoon. Besides,'' he observed, ''you're practically family. Ethan showed me the ropes when I was younger and interned with him, and your sister's one of my company's best assets. I couldn't get by without Linda.'' His smile was pure sincerity. ''As for the jet, it's not in use so why not take it? Saves you the time and trouble. This way, you can leave at your convenience.''

Tears formed in Sandy's eyes. ''Linda told me you were wonderful.'' After the words left her mouth, Sandy realized she'd said too much. Especially after she saw the questioning look that came over Clay's face.

She tried to backtrack. ''What I meant was that she thinks you're a really great guy to work with.''

''I feel the same way about Linda. I don't know,'' he responded honestly, ''what I did before she came to work for me.''

''This trip means a lot to Rick and me. We won't forget your generosity.''

''Just enjoy yourselves.''

''We will. And I want to let you know I'm glad you came. Not just because of your gift, but for yourself.'' Sandy spoke from her heart. ''You're different than I thought.''

Clay's brows lifted. ''Is that good or bad?''

''Definitely good,'' she said with a laugh. ''After I left you the invitation, I wasn't sure if you'd consider it.''

''The pleasure, I can assure you, is all mine. I've had a good time.''

''So has Linda.'' Sandy cast a glance over her shoulder to where Linda sat with their grandfather, along with their parents, who'd joined the table. She waved in that general direction. "I'm so lucky to have her as my sister."

"You're close, aren't you?"

Sandy nodded. "When our folks divorced, we got even closer. When you're faced with so many changes in your life, you tend to cling to the familiar. We were that for each other."

"You share something special then."

"There's nothing I wouldn't do for her," she stated unequivocally.

"I'm glad to hear you say that," he remarked. "Now, if you'll excuse me, I promised Linda I'd get her a cold glass of tea and if I stand here much longer, it's going to get too warm."

Sandy slipped her hand onto his arm, leaning up on tiptoe to place a quick peck on his lightly tanned cheek. "Thanks."

Linda watched as Clay tried to make his way back to their table, getting waylaid in the process by several people, mostly women. Jealousy surfaced and she tried to dismiss it. It didn't belong in her life. It had no place in the scheme of things. She had no claim on him, no hold. Any woman was free to try her luck with the handsome bachelor. Linda had already overheard several comments about him from ladies today, each extolling the praises of the Texas corporate baron. Some were blatant, sizing up his probable bank account or his potential as a lover. Speculation, in some instances, ran high on each. He was being judged, she felt, not on who he was but on what he had, or what he could possibly do.

Linda wondered if he was going to make it back alive, or whether yet another eager woman would make her move. Rather than merely sit waiting any longer, she decided to do something about it and excused herself from the table to meet him.

"Here's your drink. Sorry that it took so long."

"No problem," she said, taking the glass from his hand, downing a large swallow as she followed his lead away from the tent and toward the open acreage, strolling aimlessly. At one time her grandfather's place had been a working farm, but that was almost fifty years ago and it had since gone back to a natural state, abundant with grass and trees, covered in a carpet of colorful wildflowers. It was the Hill Country in all its splendor, the place where she felt most at home. This was where her roots were, the same as Clay's. "What did my sister want?"

"To thank me for the loan of the beach house."

Linda stopped and leaned on a weathered fence, the rays of the fading sun warm on her face. "They'll love it, I'm sure."

"It's a wonderful spot," Clay said, relaxing beneath the shade of a large live oak, its branches outstretched, its trunk wide. "Or at least it was the last time I was there."

"When was that?" She turned her head and looked at him, continually caught in the spell of her attraction. If she lived to be one hundred, she knew she'd never tire of that face. It was more than his good looks. It was the integrity that shone through, bone deep.

Clay laughed. "About ten years or so."

She could read his face, tell that he was remembering the time. "With the model?" Images of him walking with a woman along the beach flitted into her mind.

"Veronica?"

"Yes, I think that was her name."

"How did you know about her?"

"When I first met you, you were dating her."

"Didn't last all that long," he admitted, taking another

deep swallow of his tea. "We didn't have much in common."

That didn't surprise her. "She was quite beautiful, wasn't she?"

Clay's lips kicked up in a quirky smile. "Yes, she was that."

"And you haven't been there since?"

"No."

"You don't like the beach?"

Clay moved, closing the distance between them, joining her at the wooden fence. "I love it. As a matter of fact, I've got a beach house in the Caribbean."

Linda couldn't recall the property among the Buchanan company's many real estate holdings, so it must be something Clay owned on his own. "You do?"

"It's a small island," he explained, "nestled away from the usual tourist traps. Completely private. Three friends and I bought it five years ago. It was a perfect opportunity. Much too good to pass up. We all had an idea for keeping it exclusive, so it wouldn't be overdeveloped.

"Each of us has a home there, and then we went in together and renovated the old plantation house into a unique bed-and-breakfast. If your sister and her husband had had more time for a honeymoon, instead of a weekend, I would have sent them there."

"Sounds like a lovely place."

"It is. Very peaceful." Clay gazed out across the meadow, past it to the gently rolling green hills in the distance. He listened to the call of birds as they flitted from tree to tree, the buzz of insects. "Like here. You can walk along the beach whenever you want, day or night. Swim. Snorkel. Relax. Read. Ride horses. Play tennis. Sunbathe. Fish. Whatever you want, it's there waiting.''

''Paradise,'' she quipped.

''It can be.''

''Giving you just enough of a change so that you're ready to go to work again?'' she ventured.

Clay chuckled. ''Right.''

''I couldn't imagine you'd be happy playing the beach bum for very long.''

''You know me so well, Linda.''

But not as well as I'd like.

''That kind of life is okay for a week or two at most, but after that,'' he admitted, ''I'm bored. I need my work. I need the challenge.'' Clay fixed sharp blue eyes on her. ''Like you do.''

''I suppose so.''

''I *know* so,'' he declared. ''Business is our touchstone, our lifeblood. It's what we need most in the world.''

And what about other things we need, Clay? she wanted to ask. Where do they fit in? What about love? Where is that on your list of priorities? Does it even have a place?

Was that all she needed? he mused. Did anyone or anything else come remotely close to giving her that same deep satisfaction?

''I think we'd better get back.''

Clay nodded. ''You're right. You don't want to miss your sister's tossing the bouquet, I'm sure.''

Linda gave a small laugh. ''I can skip that, believe me.''

''Really?''

''Oh, yeah,'' she said, carefully making her way back with Clay at her side. She savored these moments stolen out of time. But it was time to go back to the real world. ''If it were up to me, I'd sit and leave the hopefuls to it, but I doubt that either Sandy or my mother would allow that.'' What fun was there in participating in a ceremony that didn't really mean anything to her? What were the chances of getting what she wanted? And if not Clay, then why bother? She didn't want anyone else.

Yet she had to keep up appearances. Play the game. Smile and participate, no matter what she really wanted. Ironically, her mother had commented on how very handsome her boss looked; how he was the kind of man that any mother would be overjoyed to see her daughter bring home. He was a success, unlike Linda and Sandy's father, who'd only wanted to be a cowboy. No upward mobility there, her mother had often declared.

Clay was the ultimate man of her mother's dreams. He was the man of Linda's dream, also, but for different reasons.

''Families like to see the uncoupled coupled,'' Clay offered.

Linda nodded in agreement. ''That's for sure.''

''At least I can sit out the garter toss.''

''Lucky you,'' she teased.

That all depends on how you look at it, Clay answered mentally.

They drifted through the throng of people and tables when they returned, Linda saying hello, Clay at her side. A part of her was thrilled by the envious looks she garnered from other women, especially when Clay touched her hand, her arm, her shoulder. Or when he whispered a quick word in her ear. Or when they shared a laugh or a glance.

''Time to toss the bouquet,'' Sandy announced happily to everyone. ''All you single ladies get ready.''

Linda laid her empty glass on the table. Ethan winked

in her direction. She rolled her eyes in response and he chuckled.

Sandy took note of where her sister was standing, looking as if she was waiting in line for a flu shot. A wicked grin spread across her pixieish face.

Linda recognized that look as she was joined by several members of the bridal party and a few wedding guests, all clamoring for the prize, shrieking their calls for luck in top voice.

"Here goes," Sandy shouted, and turned her back, tossing the bouquet of daisies and baby's breath with a righteous snap.

It landed exactly where she wanted it to—in Linda's hands.

Linda groaned inwardly but kept a pleasant smile on her face. Sandy gave her the thumbs-up sign, flashing Linda a wide grin. Accepting her fate with grace, Linda walked back to the table, the flowers in her hand.

Rick, a big bear of a man, took the next shot. "Now it's time for the single men here to step up." He held up a scrap of lace, recently removed from his wife's thigh. "Whoever gets this lovely garter, gets the chance to put it on my lovely sister-in-law's leg." He threw a fond glance in Linda's direction. "Doesn't that make it worth your while to try?"

Shouting encouragement, several men leaped to their feet, cheering. Sandy grabbed Rick's arm and pulled his head close to hers, whispering something.

"Aren't you participating, Clay?" Ethan asked.

"I think that I'll sit this one out."

"Chicken."

Clay flashed his mentor a puzzled look.

"That's right. Afraid of what it means if you won?"

"You should remember that I don't rise to the bait,

Ethan,'' Clay said. ''You, and my daddy, taught me better than that.''

Ethan grinned in response. ''It didn't hurt to try.''

''No,'' Clay agreed.

''One. Two. Three,'' came the call, and the silky red garter went sailing over the heads of the men assembled and landed right in Clay's lap.

''Maybe I should have warned you that my brother-in-law was All Texas in high school and college as a pitcher for his baseball team,'' Linda murmured as she realized that they'd both been set up. No subtlety on the part of either Sandy or Rick.

''Everybody's waiting, you two,'' Ethan challenged.

Clay rose, the scrap of lingerie held in the palm of one hand. Turning, he held out his free hand to Linda, going along with the tradition. ''Let's not keep them waiting.''

She pushed back her seat and they walked to where a chair was set up in the middle of the tables. Linda sat down and lifted the hem of her skirt.

''Higher!'' demanded the shouts.

Clay lifted her foot, cupping her slender ankle as he slid the garter up her calf, his hand sliding over the silky nylon-clad flesh. Upward. To her dimpled knee.

''Higher!'' the chorus of voices called.

Linda pulled her dress back farther, exposing more of her shapely leg.

Clay's hand pushed the ruby red garter up to her thigh while a photographer captured the moment for posterity.

''That should liven up the next Buchanan board meeting, should they ever see it,'' he observed dryly.

Linda's tongue snaked out to wet her lips. Clay's hand felt so incredibly good on her body. The warmth. The strength. The gentleness. The absolute rightness of it. Tingles of sensation went straight to her belly, curling inside her.

Clay released her thigh and pulled the skirt over her exposed leg. "Show's over," he whispered.

Chapter Five

Clay awoke very early the next morning, glancing out his bedroom window. He lay back against the carved wooden headboard, one hand cradling his head. As he contemplated the overcast skies, he wondered where he went from here. A nagging suspicion kept jabbing at his brain, the notion that somehow, someway, he'd turned a corner in his life.

After showering and shaving, he dressed and went downstairs, heading for the kitchen and the aroma of freshly brewed coffee.

Entering the large room, Clay spied his mother at the stove, whipping up a batch of French toast.

A smile lifted his lips. It had been his favorite breakfast treat growing up. Burke's was pancakes; Drew's was eggs and home fries; Clay's was maple syrup and thick slices of pan-fried bread. Each Sunday Santina helmed the kitchen, making each of her sons his special meal. Today

Clay was the only one of her sons at the ranch. Drew lived with his fiancée Kate Reeves at her home in Pennsylvania; Burke and Emma were in Dallas for a gallery showing of Emma's work.

"Morning, Mom." Clay leaned over and kissed Santina's smooth cheek, taking a large cup from the cupboard and pouring himself coffee, the steam rising from the hot brew. From the refrigerator Clay grabbed the china jug of cream, liberally adding it to the cup.

"Morning, darling," his mother returned, dipping another slice of white bread into the batter mix. "How'd you sleep?"

Clay shrugged his shoulders. "Fine."

Santina Buchanan arched one delicate brow. "Really?"

Clay heard the skeptical tone in his mother's voice. "Really," he assured her. "Why wouldn't I?"

"Hmm," she murmured, gently flipping over the browning pieces of battered toast in the frying pan. "No reason."

He took a seat at the wide table, watching her as she deftly scooped two pieces and added them to a plate, which she set back in the oven to keep warm. He drank his coffee as she checked the strips of bacon cooking in an iron skillet.

Clay admired his mother. She had a successful career of her own, never losing sight of her own talent while raising and caring for a family; she was married to her one and only love, a powerful man who'd helmed a global financial empire for most of his life. It couldn't have been easy to balance so many things and still find time to keep a marriage thriving and growing. There was no doubt in Clay's mind that his parents were still very much in love. It was there in every facet of their life—in little things, in touches and glances, in words and deeds. They were friends and lovers.

That's what he'd wanted for himself.

But he was a realist. Sometimes you didn't get everything you wanted in life. Business had taught him that. There were times when you did the best you could and lived with the deal you struck. Compromised. Not a word he was overly fond of, but one he'd learned to accept if he had to.

"How'd you know this was just what I needed?" he asked as he poured a generous amount of warm syrup on the thick slices of French toast.

Santina smiled at her firstborn child, joining him at the table with her own mug of coffee. "Maternal instinct." She nibbled on a piece of regular toast covered in peach jam. "I always know what my boys need. That'll never change."

Clay washed down his breakfast with a large measure of coffee. "And what's that?"

Santina favored him with a fond glance, hesitating a moment before supplying the answer. She loved her children equally, willing to walk through fire for each and every one of them; however, she suspected that Clay was more like her, a romantic, than her other two sons. And because he wanted the ideal, he might never find it, forcing him to either settle for something less than perfect or remain alone, neither of which she wanted for him. "Happiness. First and foremost."

"Then you've gotten your wish. We're all pretty happy, I'd say."

"You think so?"

"Of course," Clay said, rising to refill his cup, then returning to the table. "Don't you?"

"For the most part, yes."

"Sounds like you're qualifying that to me."

"I am."

"Why?"

She gave him a direct glance, her hazel eyes zeroing on his. "Because I wonder if you are?"

Clay removed his glasses, polishing them with a handkerchief before putting them back on. "Why wouldn't I be?"

"I'm not talking about business. It doesn't take a genius, or a mother, to see that you thrive on that. You're Noah's son, no doubt about it in that respect. What I'm concerned about is your private life. Are you happy there?"

Clay took a deep breath. "Right now I don't have a private life."

"Exactly my point," Santina admonished. "You need a woman. Not just any woman, mind you, but the *right* woman. A soul mate."

"Suppose I tell you that I've come to the same conclusion?"

Santina sat back, stunned at Clay's admission. "You have?"

"Yes," he replied. "I've done some thinking about this recently."

"And?"

"I think it's past time that I get married."

"You've found someone?"

"Possibly. I'm considering."

"Considering what?"

"If we'll suit each other."

"*Suit?*" Santina rolled her expressive hazel eyes. "What kind of word is that from a son of mine?"

"Mom, I'm a big boy now, trust me. I want to be logical when I take a wife. What I need is someone to fit into my world, the life I lead.''

"Logical." Santina stared at him, not sure if she was really hearing what he was saying. She placed her cup on the table before it dropped from her hand. "Are you in love with this woman?"

Her son's answer was direct. "No."

"Then why consider marrying her?"

"Because I think she'll make me a good wife. We have a lot in common."

"That doesn't guarantee a match made in heaven, you know," she retorted. "I don't want to see you make a mistake, Clay. One that might cost you dearly."

"Don't worry," he said. "I don't think that there'll be any problem with a prenuptial."

"Money? Do you think that I'm worried about that?" Santina reached out her hand and touched her son's. "I don't give a damn about any prewedding contract or settlement. That kind of thing is between you and whomever you marry. It's your happiness that I'm concerned about."

"I think that I can be happy with her."

"You *think*. That's the operative word, Clay. Think. Is that enough to base a marriage on?"

"In my opinion, yes."

Santina felt she had to ask the next question, no matter how intrusive it seemed to him. "Are you doing this to prove that you're over Emma?"

"Of course not," Clay denied emphatically. "That was over a long time ago. Over," he added, "before it began."

"Then why consider marrying now?"

"Don't you want grandchildren?" he asked.

"Darling, I already have grandchildren. Besides, you're

not doing this just to give Noah and me more reasons to dote and spend foolishly.''

"No," he replied. "I'm doing this for me. *I* want a family. Children of my own. Someone there for me at the end of the day.''

"You're still young," Santina argued. "There isn't a need to rush. Wait. Give yourself time to find a woman you can love. Marriage without that isn't worth anything.''

"There's where we differ, Mom. I think it can be better. If you don't have strong emotions clouding your judgment, then you can evaluate what you need better. I want a wife who's a friend. A wife I like, one whom I can trust.''

"Have you given any thought to what might happen if this woman accepts your proposal, if you marry, and then you discover one day that you're in love with someone else?''

Clay took another sip of his rapidly cooling coffee. "Yes, I've considered that and it doesn't come into play. If I marry this person, then she'll have my complete assurance that when I give my word, I mean to live up to it. Simple as that.''

"Life is rarely simple, Clay. You should know that by now. Emotions have a way of clouding matters.''

"Which is why I've chosen this path. It's best for me.''

"That remains to be seen.''

He shrugged. "Probably so.''

"Nothing I can say will change your mind?''

"No. Besides, this might be a moot conversation as I haven't spoken to the lady yet.''

"You're not sure she'll accept?''

He shrugged his shoulders. "I hope she will, as I feel we can do well together.''

"May I ask who this is?"

"I'd rather not say just yet. And, what good would that do?"

"It'd give me some clue as to where your head is at."

"Very squarely on my shoulders, Mom. You know that."

"I wonder." Santina had to respect his decision. She might not like it or understand it, but Clay was her son. Still, there was another question to ask. "What if, after she marries you, she falls in love with someone else and wants out?"

"I'll cross that bridge if and when I have to."

With a big glass of orange juice in her hand, Linda strolled onto the columned porch of her grandfather's farmhouse. White wicker furniture, along with an assortment of potted plants, covered much of the wide planks of the floor.

She eased into one chair, hearing the creak as she made contact with the flower-printed chintz seat. A light rain was falling, drops hitting the roof with a steady rhythm, making the carpet of bluebonnets that surrounded the house sparkle with moisture. She listened, lulled by the sound.

Yesterday this place had teemed with people. Today it was fairly peaceful. A few birds in a nearby tree chirped happily; a trio of ground squirrels raced back and forth, searching for the peanuts she'd tossed out earlier, rain darkening their fur.

Her thoughts floated back to being in Clay's arms, held close to his lean body. Endless memories flooded back. Dancing. Walking. Sharing. Talking.

He'd been the last to leave, which had surprised her. Both of her parents had departed not long after Sandy and

Rick, each anxious to get back to their respective lives. Other guests drifted off slowly until it was only Ethan, Clay and Linda left. The caterers had cleaned up and packed away, restoring the grounds. It's as if the wedding reception had been a dream.

Ethan had wanted coffee and invited Clay to stay, which he had. The three of them sat on the porch, talking softly, relaxing, until Ethan abruptly declared, "I can't stay up any longer. You two young folks take your time." He looked at the star-heavy sky, clouds drifting in and out, smiling deeply. He gave Clay an affectionate handshake and pat on the shoulder when the younger man stood up. "Good seeing you again, boy. Don't make it so damned long next time."

Linda rose, also, kissing her grandfather on the cheek, recognizing his ploy for what it was but unable to censure him. Instead, she whispered, "Thanks," in addition to her heartfelt good-night.

The creak of the screen door and the dimming of a lamp inside signaled that she and Clay were alone. A slightly awkward silence lingered for a few moments between them. The night was warm, the darkness, broken now only by a single overhead porch light, was intimate.

Linda recalled vividly the sudden shyness that she experienced. Alone. Vulnerable. Her heart was beating so loudly she wondered how Clay couldn't hear it.

Finally she broke the hush of the night. She inquired politely, "Would you care for more coffee?"

Clay demurred, his eyes finding hers. "I don't think so."

"Yes, I guess you do have a bit of a drive," she responded. Why had she felt so tongue-tied? Was it because she wanted to reach out to him and dared not? Because the temperature that rose and the heat that pooled in the lower regions of her body, spreading outward, had nothing to do with the weather and everything to do with him? Because she'd wanted so much to share with him and couldn't?

"It was a lovely day," he casually remarked. "I'm glad that I came."

"So am I."

"Are you still wearing the garter?"

That question had come out of the blue and startled Linda. While the coffee was perking, she'd gone inside and changed her clothes, removing the fancy dress and putting on a comfortable longish twill skirt and a cotton shirt. As she'd done so, the imprint of Clay's hands on her flesh lingered in her mind. Firm and tender. Strong and gentle. Would they be that way on a woman's body when he touched it in the heat of passion? Would he linger, explore? Would he follow his hands with mouth and tongue, recharting territory? Would he sample and relish?

Those thoughts caused the heat within her to flare up again, hotter this time. Linda wet her lips, answered his question. "Yes."

Was that a satisfied smile that curved his lips at her answer, or was it a trick of the light?

Who cared? All she knew was that she was reluctant for this night to end, to let go of him. These moments were too precious. Too magical. Once gone, they would be lost forever, consigned to the closet of the past.

But she had to let go.

And she did. Calmly. Proud of her ability to keep it together.

The worst moment had been when Linda saw Clay to his car. Across the stone-covered walk, over the grass to the nearby garage, a reconverted barn, the darkness was a protective cloak around them.

He clicked a button on his key and unlocked the door of his late-model luxury car. "What time shall I pick you up tomorrow?"

"How about after lunch?" she suggested. "That'll give us both a chance to sleep late and spend some time with our families, you with your parents, me with Ethan."

"I'll call you when I'm on my way then."

"It'll have to be Granddad's number. I left my cell phone at home, remember?"

"Guess I'm so used to being able to reach you whenever I want, I forgot. Good thing you reminded me or I would have been going crazy wondering why you weren't answering." He lingered, as if reluctant to get into the car. "I really did have a good time today," he reiterated.

Then Clay did something that caught her off guard. He stretched out one hand, cupped her chin and lightly kissed her cheek. "Good night," he whispered, and got into his car.

She'd watched as the lights from the vehicle faded into the distance, swallowed up by the darkness, the touch of his hand and mouth still evident.

The impact hadn't lessened by this morning. It was still there. Still extremely potent and fresh.

"Sleep well?" Ethan asked as he joined Linda, carrying a plate containing two slices of thick buttered toast and fluffy scrambled eggs in each hand. Giving her one plate, he took a chair next to hers, a small wicker table separating them.

"Surprisingly well," Linda answered, picking up the fork and taking a bite of breakfast.

"How late did Clay stay?"

"He left not long after you went to bed."

"Too bad."

Linda ignored that remark. "I was only surprised that he stayed as long as he did."

A wry grin curved Ethan's mouth. "Well, I'm not."

She took another sip of her orange juice. "Let's not go there."

"Why?" His bushy eyebrows knit in concentration. "Because you don't want to face the truth?"

"No, because you won't."

"He wanted to be with *you*."

"Propinquity," she retorted, biting into the dark toast with a snap.

"Don't throw those highfalutin words at me, girl. It's much more basic than that. Attraction, I would say, pure and simple, except that I don't really think either word applies."

Linda gave him an exasperated glance. "How did my grandmother put up with you?"

"She loved me, sweetheart," he answered. "Just like you love Clay."

"There's a world of difference, Granddad. You loved her, too. It wasn't one-sided."

"Well, it takes some fellas a little longer to recognize the truth," he said wisely. "He will come around. Don't you worry. Though I do think it would speed up things a mite if you was to show him you care."

"You just want to play matchmaker."

"Course I do," he happily confessed. "What's wrong with that?"

"Trust me when I tell you that I can handle my own life. I have for quite some time now. And you certainly didn't worry so much about Sandy's love life."

Ethan shrugged. "Didn't have to. That girl went about getting what she wanted with both hands. Maybe she made a few errors along the way, detours you might say, but she came up with a winner in the long run.''

''I hope so.''

''So could you if you'd just go after what you really want.''

Her grandfather's words stayed with Linda as she showered and dressed. He didn't understand her situation; she couldn't just act on her feelings. Things between her and Clay were far too complicated for that. If they were different people, she might have been able to come up with some other way, some simple solution.

But they weren't different people. And there was no simple solution.

She closed the lid on her small suitcase, checking around the room to make sure that she had everything packed. Clay had called her about a half hour ago.

Even though the rain had increased, a wide smile still curved her lips. He was on his way to her.

Clay drove his car along with winding back road. The sultry sounds of the female singer surrounding him via the car's state-of-the-art stereo system put him in a mellow mood as she sang of love and longing, a tenor sax wailing beneath her vocal line.

Flashes of images from the day before swam in and out of his mind. Some sharp, others only a fleeting impression, like a color or a scent. The common thread in those memories was Linda.

He'd almost kissed her last night. Almost pushed aside the invisible barriers of restraint and reached out to satisfy a momentary curiosity, a moment's desire.

Would that have been so wrong?

Ordinarily he would have answered yes right away. He was her boss. Her mentor. A trusted friend. A strict line of demarcation separated them physically. Lines that existed in comprehension, but not in the warm blood of lust. There lines blurred and feelings predominated.

Only if you let them, which he couldn't. It wouldn't be fair. Certainly not to her. Not to him.

Still, questions lingered, tantalizing his brain. What would her lips have tasted like had he kissed her? Hot as only a Texas summer day could be? Or cool as a Hill Country night in autumn? Fire or ice? Heaven or hell?

Clay guessed that he might never know if his plans didn't come to fruition.

Could he live with that?

Did he have a choice?

The rain was coming down harder as they made their way along the interstate. Sheets of water beat against the car's exterior as the windshield wipers tried to clear a line of sight. Lightning flashed. Thunder roared ominously. The storm's incipient darkness had turned the late afternoon into early evening, forcing Clay to slow down.

From the corner of his right eye he saw Linda sitting rigidly in her seat, her face paler than normal. That was enough to make him stop, finding a spot that could accommodate the car. He pulled over and cut the engine.

"What's wrong?" she asked.

Clay detected the slight trembling in her voice. "I'm waiting for this thing to pass. It's getting too dangerous to proceed any farther. As soon as there's a break, I'll get going again."

Linda shook her head in acknowledgment. She shivered slightly and Clay reached out and touched her lower arm. Goose bumps dotted her fair skin.

"You're cold."

"It's nothing," she answered.

"Linda, you're shivering."

"It's just a reaction to the storm," she explained. "I've never liked them. Rain I don't mind, but this…"

"Why didn't you tell me before we left Ethan's? I could have waited, or we could have left for Houston tomorrow."

"I didn't want to inconvenience you."

He gave her a tender, understanding look. "As if I would have cared."

"I would have. This is my problem, Clay."

"It's not a problem, believe me. I can understand fears."

Could he? she wondered. What could possibly frighten Clay Buchanan? What would dare?

"You'll be fine," he said in that calm, even voice she'd heard him use before. "Nothing will hurt you, I promise. Word of a Buchanan."

He sounded so sure, as if he could control whatever he had to, even the weather. Odd thing was, Linda believed him. Clay *was* a man of his word. If he said she'd be fine, she'd accept that without hesitation.

Clay reached into the back seat of his Cadillac and scooped up his lightweight linen jacket, handing it to Linda.

Linda took it gratefully, wrapping it around her shoulders. It carried the faint scent of his tangy aftershave, woodsy mixed with lime. Crisp. Clean. Like him.

Rain slashed against the car. Bolts of jagged streaks of light flashed across the sky.

As the storm beat its fury upon the land, Clay went back and forth in his head about the propriety of drawing Linda to his side, offering her what comfort he could. Would she think he was making a crude attempt at a pass?

He mentally debated a few seconds longer until he heard her soft moan.

"Linda."

"Yes?"

"Come here."

She turned her head and looked at him. He had unlocked his safety belt and beckoned her with open arms.

She shouldn't. It was far too dangerous to her peace of mind.

Thunder snapped so close that she gasped. Within seconds, she'd scooted across the plush front seat and into the shelter that he offered. Danger be damned!

"I feel like such a child."

"Nonsense," Clay retorted. "You're anything but that." Clay held her close, stroking his hand over her hair, which she'd left unbound. It smelled of flowers, sweet and subtle. There was nothing remotely childlike about the outline of her body next to his. It was female. *Very* female. Soft. Curving. Reminding him how long it had been since he'd held a woman this close in such an intimate setting, even longer since he'd really *been* with a woman. Needs arose. Basic urges long denied stirred.

Inhaling sharply, he adjusted his jacket over her. "Relax."

Easy for him to say, Linda thought, while she was caught between the storm outside and the one he was creating within her. Heat fogged up the windows, locking them in a private cocoon. The chill was gradually leaving her, replaced by a growing warmth. It was the proximity of his body that caused the change.

"Comfortable?"

"Yes," she replied. And safe. Though the storm raged outside, doing its damnedest to frighten her, here, in Clay's arms, she felt content. Longing, so strong it almost overcame her, forced down the fear, replacing it with hunger. Hunger to know, to touch, to explore. Hunger to have something more than herself. Hunger that cried out for appeasement.

Hunger that couldn't be quenched.

"Feeling better?"

"Much." Burrowed against the solid wall of his chest, Linda felt as if she'd come home to where she belonged. Unfortunately, she knew that the doors of this haven would never be fully opened to her. That's the way things had to be.

"Hopefully this will be over soon and we can get on our way." Clay tried to reassure her, keeping a level tone in his voice, though he was far from calm inside. Sparks of need surfaced. Sparks of recognition of just how elemental desire could be. Old responses flared to life in a new mix. Razor edged. Snapping like a rubber band when pulled too taut.

Once again he saw Linda in a new light. A hotter, brighter light. A sharper, cleaner light. They'd crossed another line, taken steps that slowly put them onto another path. She might not be aware, though he was.

Thoughts of seduction flamed to life, his mind driven with possible scenarios. A gentle brush of his hand against her breast, her thigh. A kiss along the nape of her neck, feathering across her jaw. Nibbling on her earlobe, his tongue stroking the delicate folds. Slipping the sweater she wore up inch by slow inch, his fingertips skimming every inch of her soft, exposed flesh. Was she wearing cotton or silk beneath? Lace—enhanced or plain? What would her breasts, freed of their garment entrapment, feel like in his palms? In his mouth? What sounds would escape her lips as he suckled them?

Another loud crack of thunder and a serrated flash of lightning caused Linda to start.

"Shh," he whispered tenderly.

Linda alternately damned and thanked the storm. She cursed it for revealing her secret weakness, allowing Clay to see her vulnerable. Afraid.

Yet, without it, she wouldn't be in this position.

In his embrace, selfish, private fantasies ran riot in her head. A parked car. A couple in love, unable to wait any longer to be together, nature giving them an excuse. Emotions given free rein. Mouths blending in harmony, unable to get enough. Bodies joined hip to hip, chest to chest, legs entwined. Her eager hands ripping at the buttons of his pale blue oxford shirt. Her eyes feasting on his torso, taking in the rapid rise and fall of his wide chest. Her lips working a trail from navel to collarbone, soft kisses covering as much of his warm skin as she could. Her fingers circling his male nipples, producing a groan from deep in his throat.

Linda pushed those thoughts aside, erasing them as if from a blackboard. They didn't belong. Not here. Not now. Especially not now, when she was so close to the object of her desire.

A break came in the weather, with the rain subsiding enough that Clay decided to get back on the highway and continue their journey. "I think we can go now."

Linda slipped out of his embrace and resumed her seat on the passenger side, his jacket still around her shoulders. Clay could never know how easy it would have been for her to act on her emotions if decorum, good sense and pride hadn't stopped her.

Restarting the engine, Clay focused on the road ahead, coolly concentrating on the task of driving the slick highway. Linda mustn't know how very easy it would have been to venture into new territory with her. Slipping past the bonds of business and exploring the rough seas of yearning.

He needed time to think.

Chapter Six

Never mix business with personal feelings.

A good maxim to live by, Clay thought as he dressed for a formal dinner to be held later that evening. He was in the spacious bedroom of his recently renovated Manhattan town house.

Too bad he hadn't been following such otherwise sage advice.

Several weeks had passed since the wedding of Linda's younger sister. Weeks in which he'd had a chance to reflect, to think about his relationship with Linda and where, if anywhere, it was going. Work had kept them both busy, and an unspoken agreement not to bring up the incident in the car the night of the storm seemed mutual.

That, however, couldn't keep it from his mind. At random moments, he found himself remembering the way she'd felt in his arms, the scent of her hair, the wary look in her eyes, the way her body had cuddled against his.

Since then he'd been cautious, weighing the pros and cons of a proposal, judging the merits as carefully as he could. He didn't want to make a mistake or misread a situation. He had to be certain before he broached the subject. Being rejected once more wasn't in his game plan.

There was only one remaining thing to tackle—how they reacted to each other physically. In every other respect, he believed them compatible. And that area would be the hardest to discover. He already knew he was attracted to her. It had sneaked up on him, little by little, day by day.

But how did Linda feel? Exploring that avenue would forever change the tenure of their business relationship. Once they traversed that path there would be no going back.

Tonight's dinner was a charity event—a black-tie affair he had considered skipping and couldn't, especially not when he was the guest of honor. Not a wise move. Besides, it had been the perfect excuse to ask Linda to accompany him. She was coming as his ''unofficial'' date.

''You won't mind helping me, will you?'' he'd asked her before they left Houston.

''Of course I don't,'' she'd answered. ''It's the least that I can do since you were kind enough to escort me to Sandy's wedding.''

Kind enough. If she only knew.

Fastening the gold cuff links into his white dress shirt, Clay thought of how much they'd accomplished this past week. Meetings had taken up a lot of their time in New York, making for long days and late nights, working most meals. Almost all of their time had been spent together, with no friction. No hassles. Everything cool and professional, with no hint of any tension.

Yesterday they'd concluded their last appointment early. When he'd invited her to dinner, Linda informed him that she already had made plans. She was meeting an old college friend who worked in New York for a night out at the theater.

Clay had wanted to ask if her companion was a man or a woman, but he didn't. He respected her privacy, even if it was tough, with curiosity burning a hole in his gut. While he sat at home, alone, catching up with a stack of paperwork and magazines, he wondered what she was doing. Was she having fun? Where had she gone for dinner? Somewhere fancy and elegant, the right place to be seen? Or somewhere more intimate, a quiet setting away from the hustle and bustle?

The only thing that he could do was wait. Clay told himself that he wasn't ready for an early night. There was too much he had to get through, so he might as well stay up.

When she returned to the town house, he'd been in the library, enjoying a cigar and brandy, listening to a jazz station on the radio, having given up all pretense of actually working. He heard her key in the lock and relaxed. Linda was home. Safe. And alone. Not that he believed she would have ever brought a stranger into his house. Still it was comforting to know Linda was back beneath his roof.

Instead of taking the stairs and going right to her bedroom on the second floor of the four-story building, he listened as she walked down the hallway, her high heels tapping lightly against the marble floor.

His eyes automatically went to the pocket door, which he'd left ajar. "Hi," she greeted him. "I saw the light on and just wanted to say good-night."

Even in the dim light, Clay noticed that her eyes appeared puffy, as if she'd been crying. Quickly he put down the cigar and brandy and got up, taking the few steps that would bring him to her side. "Is something wrong?"

Linda blinked. "What makes you think that?"

His voice was low and soft. "You've been crying."

Linda laughed softly, dispelling any notion that she was upset. "Oh that. Good thing I'm wearing waterproof mascara or I imagine I would look like a racoon, as well," she said lightly. "We went to see *Les Misérables* and the show really affected me. More than I thought it would. Even before the end I was reaching for my hanky and dabbing my eyes. And I wasn't the only one in the audience doing that. I heard outright sobbing."

Clay replied, "It's a very emotional show."

"You've seen it?"

"In London when it first opened."

"Oh."

"Would you like a nightcap?"

"I'd better not. We went to a restaurant near the theater for a few drinks after the performance and stayed to listen to the cabaret." She yawned. "I'm going to bed before I fall asleep standing here. Night.".

Clay watched her leave, admiring the handsome picture she made.

Even now, a day later, he could close his eyes and see her clearly. A longish dress of cream linen, with short, bell-like sleeves, belted to show off her waist. Open-toed sling-back shoes. Her hair was up in a neat twist. Topaz earrings, necklace and bracelet finished the ensemble.

Clay drew on his tuxedo jacket. It fit like a glove.

Would she?

Into his plans?

Into his bed?

He had to know. Tonight was as good an evening as any to find that out.

Linda dusted the scented body powder lightly over her arms. Next, she added a small amount of perfume behind her ears and along her wrists. She sat in front of the mirror at an antique dressing table, feeling pampered by her surroundings. The bedroom she'd been given was actually more a suite, a large set of rooms that were obviously decorated for a woman. It had subtle touches of elegance and comfort, a throwback to the Victorian era mated with modern sensibilities.

She checked her makeup, satisfied that she'd achieved the look she wanted. Their time here in New York had flown by so quickly. Work had been the main focus of this trip, with little room for other things. Tonight was also business related in a way—Clay was being presented with an award in recognition of his philanthropic work. Excitement thrummed through her veins at being part of the evening. His "unofficial date," he called it when he'd first proposed the idea. She'd happily accepted, thrilled to be seen on his arm.

Just as thrilled as she had been to *be* in his arms a few weeks ago. Like a constant craving that demanded satisfaction, she relived that night in her memories. Often.

Before she rose from the tufted velvet chair, she flipped the radio on, the mellow sounds of a ballad filling the air. It was a duet, a man and woman harmonizing to "When I Fall In Love." Again she was transported by the potency of the lyrics. They wrapped around her like a comforting friend.

She listened, momentarily mesmerized, before shutting off the music. What she couldn't turn off was the way the song made her feel.

A white terry robe covered her nearly nude body as she walked to the spacious armoire and drew out a silky pair of panty hose from one drawer. She put them on, careful not to get a run. As she did, her thoughts drifted back to the previous night.

She'd returned from her evening out, believing that she and Clay both needed some time away from each other. Breathing space. Luckily for her, she had a college friend who worked in the city. Linda had called her old roomie the day before to see if she was free for dinner and the theater. Meg was an attorney at a small, prestigious law firm, married to a lawyer in the DA's office and mother to a toddler. She'd jumped at the chance for a night out that wasn't connected to either her career or her husband's.

They'd spent their time together catching up, Linda going so far as to let her hair down—figuratively—and talk about Clay. With Meg, she felt comfortable and safe. And it was good to vent with one person who wasn't related to her. Meg's perspective would be fresh, unhampered by prejudice.

Linda talked and Meg listened. Then she did the same for Meg, giving an ear for her friend's life. It reenforced Linda's wish that she had more of a social relationship with others in Houston; Meg voiced the same thing about herself. Work for each took up a large chunk of their respective time.

"We're exactly where we wanted to be, remember?" Meg asked over a glass of white wine after the show.

Linda recalled their late-night conversations in college, their grand plans for the future. "How could I forget? You wanted to be with a top-notch firm in the Big Apple and I wanted to work for the Buchanan corporation."

"Clay Buchanan to be more specific."

Linda nodded.

"Take care that the dream doesn't go sour, okay?"

"It hasn't for me."

"Then you're lucky, Linda. And as to your boss, only you can decide if mixing business with pleasure is worth what it might cost you."

Meg had given her some good advice.

Linda wondered if she could follow it.

When she'd finally arrived back at the historic district house, it was after one in the morning. She figured that Clay would be asleep.

Instead, as she entered the foyer, she saw a light on in the library.

She stood there, mentally debating the wisdom of confronting the leader of the pack in his den. She should probably go right upstairs and forget about seeing him. She was too emotional, what with the show and her revelations to Meg. Probably too susceptible to his ever-present magnetism.

Yet Linda couldn't resist. Heeding the silent call, she followed her heart instead of her head.

As she approached the room, she could smell the aroma of his fine cigar. Private stock. Hand-wrapped and blended exclusively for him. He'd given her grandfather a box when he came to pick her up for the return trip to Houston.

Standing in the open doorway, she spied him sitting inside, a snifter of brandy in one hand, the aged cigar in the other, wearing a plain oxford white shirt, the top two buttons undone, tie vanished.

One lamp was on and his face was partially in shadow. When he heard her enter, Clay leaned forward and their eyes met.

Even across the space of the room, the effect of those

bluebonnet blue eyes smacked her squarely in the solar plexus.

When he spoke, his rich-timbred voice settled over her like a soft spring rain after a drought. Moments later, when he'd offered her a drink, she'd gamely fought the temptation to stay and take him up on his offer. Lingering over a brandy in a cozy setting would be like pouring the potent libation on an already lit flame. Combustible. Downright dangerous.

Where Clay was concerned, she'd never learned to coat her feelings in asbestos.

Her hand fell to the padded hanger on which her dress for tonight hung. She'd searched almost a dozen stores in Houston trying to find one that had what she was looking for. She'd seen plenty of *nice* dresses, ones that would be appropriate. But that's not what she wanted. A special occasion demanded a special outfit. One that made a statement.

"What kind of statement?" a saleswoman in one boutique had asked.

"The kind that says I'm proud of who I am and who I'm with," Linda had replied.

Linda slipped the dress off the hanger and held it up to her body. She looked at herself in the mirror that was on one side of the open armoire door. It was daring. Dynamic. Not her usual style, which tended to be more conservative. This radiated confidence in herself as a woman. It was dramatic and whispered glamour with a capital *G*.

As soon as she'd tried it on she had to have it, damn the cost.

Seeing how it fit, she knew it was worth every penny she'd paid, and then some.

But would Clay like it?

Stepping into her shoes and adding jewelry, Linda
thought that there was only one way to find out.

Clay waited downstairs for her, checking his watch,
anxious to be on their way uptown. He paced the foyer.
Standing around cooling his heels bored him silly.

Tonight he was early. A full ten minutes. He'd told her
to meet him downstairs at 7:30 and it was barely 7:20.

He glanced again to the top of the stairs and saw her
standing there on the landing, poised to begin her descent.

The impact of her dress rendered him temporarily
speechless.

"Do you like it?"

His gaze drifted slowly up and down her body as she
stood there above him.

Utterly delicious.

Wonderfully stylish.

Incredibly feminine.

Linda joined him below and did a turnaround so that
he could get the full effect of the dress. It was bronze
satin, halter necked with a modest bodice. The back, however, was far from that as it plunged low and provocative,
exposing a good amount of creamy skin. It molded her
figure lovingly, ending an inch or so above her knees.

"Yes, I like it very much," he replied, wondering why
his glasses weren't steaming up. He contrasted what she'd
worn last night with what she wore now. Sweet versus
sensual. Chic versus ultrasophisticated. Stunning. In a sea
of little black dresses, she would stand out, making an
indelible mark. Catching the eye and leaving quite an impression.

Boy, howdy, he thought, it was good to be alive.

Thankfully they hadn't had to spend all night at the
charity event. Just as he thought, Linda had made quite

an impression on the folks there, wowing quite a few. A photographer from the *Times* had snapped them while they were dancing. He looked forward to seeing the picture in the Sunday Metro section. Though the woman had taken scores of other photographs, he was sure that theirs would be the one chosen to be run.

"Are you tired?"

Linda tilted her head to the side and gave Clay a warm smile. "Not really, why?"

"How about a late-night supper?"

She recalled the food at the party, tiny portions artfully arranged so that it made a pretty picture, but it would hardly feed the appetite of the average housefly.

"You're on."

Clay smiled and gave his driver instructions as to where to go. The limo sped along the streets, heading toward the Upper East Side.

A short time later the chauffeur pulled in front of a restored carriage house.

"Where's the restaurant?" Linda asked as she got out of the car.

"Right here," Clay assured her, slipping his arm about her waist and leading her forward.

Linda looked at the brick building, wondering where the name of the place was. Then she spotted it on a small brass plate next to the beveled glass door. *Derrymore*.

She laughed, glancing in the nearby window, seeing people inside what appeared to be a sitting room. "Sort of like a private club, eh? You've got to know it's here or you'll go right past it."

"Exactly."

"How did you find out about it?" she inquired as they stepped through the doorway. Inside it was warm and cozy, the deep red walls filled with wonderful artwork, all evoking a bygone era and another country. An Irish country house.

Clay gave his name and he and Linda sat down on one of the overstuffed Victorian sofas to wait to be called for their table.

"It won't be long, sir," the Irish-accented head waiter stated. "May I get you something from the bar whilst you and the lady wait?"

"What would you like?" Clay asked.

"You choose," Linda replied.

"I'll have an Irish whiskey, neat, and the lady will have a sherry." There was no need to add, "your best of each." Clay had been here before and knew the quality of the establishment.

"Coming up, sir," the young man said, and went off to see to the orders.

Another couple, holding hands on the other couch, with eyes only for each other, sipped at fluted glasses of sparkling wine. Linda saw the girl sneak a look at the diamond on her finger and watched as the girl's lips curved in a secret smile of contentment. She whispered to Clay, "I think that they've just become engaged."

Clay flicked a glance in their direction, saw the giddy look of joy on their young faces. When the maître d' returned with their drinks, Clay bluntly asked the man, "Are they celebrating an engagement?"

The other man grinned. "Indeed they are, sir."

"When they've been seated, send them a bottle of champagne and put it on my tab."

"I shall, sir," he said, and led the couple off upstairs to a private dining room.

"That was lovely, Clay," Linda declared, reaching out her hand and touching his. The skin was warm, the fingers long. She could feel the hard metal of the big ring he wore. "A very sweet gesture."

"It seemed the thing to do."

How like him, she thought. Generous. Willing to do something nice for people he didn't know, something to make their special night even more so.

"Your table is ready, Mr. Buchanan."

They were led to a small dining room, one of three in the building. The other tables were filled, with only a large one empty, a party having just departed. The doors to the garden were opened and the sound of a waterfall was heard.

"You never told me," Linda said after she sat down, "how did you find this place?"

"A friend."

She wondered as she sipped her sherry if the *friend* was male or female.

"Actually, she's a lot more than that."

Linda thought so.

"She's my brother's fiancée."

"You mean Kate Reeves?"

Dimples formed in Clay's cheeks as he smiled. "That's her. I was here after Christmas and they happened to be in New York for a few days while Kate had meetings with her editor and their agent, so when we went to dinner, Kate suggested this place."

"She's got good taste," Linda replied.

"The best. After all, she's marrying my brother."

And so lucky at that, Linda thought. Kate was wedding a Buchanan man. A genuine Texas male—the cream of the crop. The ultimate best of the best. But then again Linda realized that she was prejudiced. She was Texas born and bred herself. Deep in her heart, she cherished the notion of being a Texan's bride. *This* Texan's bride.

She figured she had a better chance of winning the lotto or a sweepstakes drawing.

"It never fails to amaze me what some people think of as food," Clay said as he skimmed the menu. "Jackrabbits wouldn't find the meal served earlier tonight filling."

Linda laughed. "I don't think you were supposed to find it so," she remarked. "It was there to be pretty, to be noticed. To make you think it was very cutting edge."

Clay held the serrated bread knife in his hand, poised to cut off a slice of the Irish soda bread that their waiter had placed before him on an oak board. "This is my idea of cutting edge. The rest is bogus."

"I've been to some parties in Texas that were the same."

"But," he countered, "not many, I'll bet. Can you imagine any Texan worth his—" he shot a glance in Linda's direction "—or her, salt being satisfied with what pretended to be dinner?"

"No."

"I thought not," he continued. "Right now I'm so hungry that I could eat the hide off an armadillo, raw."

"I doubt that."

"You shouldn't. I'm serious."

"No way," she protested. "I can see the laughter in your eyes."

"Can't."

"Can, too."

They both laughed heartily, sharing the silliness of the banter. Clay found it fun and refreshing to simply cut loose. To enjoy the moment and the woman he was with. Linda made him see the absurd humor of certain things with flair. Ease. That's what she brought to him. He could relax with her. A good quality in a friend. Or a wife.

The waiter approached them again. "Would you like some more time to decide?"

Clay looked to Linda.

"I'm ready."

"Then let's get to it."

They declined appetizers, content to graze on the loaf of bread and warm honey-butter. From the corner of her eye, Linda spotted an older couple in the corner. She watched as they touched hands throughout their meal, made each other smile, talked intimately. Evidently in love, she envied their happiness. There was nothing stiff or remote about them. They were comfortable, secure. It made her wonder how long they'd been together. She preferred to think since high school. That suited the romance. Childhood sweethearts. Destined for each other.

It was good to think that some lovers were meant to be. Inevitable. That some people found the other half of their soul. It gave one hope.

But should it?

It had gone quiet at their table. Linda alternately sipped at her sherry or nibbled on the soda bread, her mind obviously elsewhere. Done with his drink, Clay signaled the waiter and ordered coffee.

"I'll have some, too," Linda said. She leaned closer to Clay across the width of the small table. "Would you look at the dessert that couple in the corner is eating? It's sinful."

He glanced in the older couple's direction. They were sharing a piece of the house specialty, a mocha chocolate whiskey cake. A bowl of fresh whipped cream and another of assorted fresh berries stood nearby.

"I think Lettie's got a pie or something for dessert at home if you want to raid the kitchen later," he suggested. He'd brought the English couple along with him on this trip as he found their services invaluable, and they proved a buffer for gossip regarding Linda sharing his house.

"How about the berries and whipped cream?" Linda wet her lips and shot another glance at the other table.

"I think I can persuade them to let me have a doggie bag, if I ask them nicely."

When he put his mind to it, Clay could probably persuade anyone to do anything. If he hadn't followed in his father's footsteps and taken over the running of Buchanan Enterprises, Linda thought he would have made a great lawyer. Vital. Impassioned. A believer in causes. A champion in the truest sense of the word.

Clay watched her watching that couple. What was going through her mind? One moment he thought she was sad. The next, she seemed surprisingly happy. And what was it about them that had so captured her fancy?

"You don't see many men his age wearing ponytails," Clay commented as their dinners arrived. The sizzle of well-grilled steak and the aroma of oak-smoked Irish salmon filled the air around their table.

"I think it's kind of sweet," she answered. "He's got a nice head of thick, wavy silver hair. It's very un-Texas like."

Clay chuckled as he cut into his piece of thick beef. "Pretty much."

"Sort of devil-may-care and romantic."

"Meaning Texans aren't?"

Linda flashed him an aggrieved look. "I never said that."

"But were you thinking that?"

"Of course not."

"Good. Because I wasn't going to accept that slight to Texas manhood."

"You weren't?" She lifted a forkful of the tender, flaky

fish to her lips and enjoyed the taste. "And how were you going to rebut it?"

"I'd think of something," he assured her, a twinkle in his eyes. "Trust me."

Oh, how she wanted to. With her heart, her body, her future. With all the trust that was in her to give. For as long as she lived.

Chapter Seven

It was very late when they left the restaurant and headed back to the town house.

Clay was feeling absurdly nervous. If this were anyone else sitting beside him in the back seat of the limo, he would have a pretty good idea if the woman wanted to extend their time together tonight. Certain signals in her body language would have communicated her wishes outright if she'd chosen not to verbalize her wishes.

With Linda, however, Clay wasn't sure. She was first and foremost a business colleague, not a lover. They hadn't shared the intimate connection of physical partners, or even the getting-to-know-you experience of actual dates.

On the other hand, he did know her in a very special way, just as she knew him. In the office, their communication was always open and honest, no reservations, no holding back. Both spoke their minds freely.

Tonight's proposed communication however would be on another level, held in a new arena with new rules.

They were nearing the house. Time to see where they went from here.

"Are you still up for a raid on the kitchen?" he asked, breaking the silence. A small bag sat between them, containing two plastic bowls, one of fresh fruit and another of whipped cream. Clay had kept his word and secured them before they left the restaurant.

"I'm game if you are," Linda replied. Right now she was too keyed up to go to bed. And if she did, something told her that she would regret it. An inner voice, a gut instinct, urged her to follow her heart, grab the night and hold on for as long as she could.

"If you don't mind," Linda asked as they walked up the front entrance stairs and into the hallway, making their way toward the back of the house where the kitchen was located, "I'm going to run upstairs and take off these shoes." She'd been wearing heels all day and her feet were finally rebelling.

"Go right ahead," Clay answered as he flicked on the overhead light, which set the ceiling fan into motion. Then he placed the fancy restaurant doggie bag on the table. There was another set of stairs in the kitchen that led to the upper floors, part of the original plans for the house he had restored.

He looked at Linda as she made her way across the room. "Why not get into something more comfortable while you're at it? No need," he insisted, "to stand on ceremony on my account. When you come back down, everything will be ready."

What did he mean by comfortable? Linda wondered as she climbed the stairs. How comfortable was she supposed to get? Let-down-her-hair comfortable? Wash-off-her-makeup comfortable? Remove-her-dress comfortable? What?

Entering her bedroom, Linda snapped on the light and kicked off her shoes. She debated taking off her dress and getting comfortable as he suggested. Obviously it hadn't made quite the impression on him that she'd hoped for. Clay seemed to be able to take it or leave it. So much for going for the gusto.

Unhooking the button that held the halter in place, Linda unzipped the rest of it, letting it pool on the floor. She stood there for a minute, pondering what to put on in its place.

Decision made, Linda scooped up the dress and hung it back up in the armoire, then peeled off her panty hose. She walked into the bathroom and turned on the tap water to warm, washing her face clean.

Clay wanted *comfortable*. Well, he was going to get it. Her attempt at attracting his attention with her outfit had, in her opinion, failed, so why bother to go to any lengths to come up with something else that called notice to her feminine shape. And, it wasn't as if she had an extensive wardrobe to pick from, as she'd packed only suits and a few dresses for this trip. Her choices were very limited.

She questioned her judgment in buying the dress in the first place. Chalk it up to an experiment gone bad. Lesson learned. A mistake she wouldn't repeat.

As much as he loved that dress on her, Clay hoped that Linda was changing it, because he needed a clear head. It was much too tempting, considering that he guessed that she wasn't wearing a bra beneath it. The itch to unbutton that pearl closure at the nape of her neck and let it fall was much too distracting a thought. Imagining the shape and texture of the flesh underneath was slowly eating away at him.

He'd removed his own tuxedo jacket, hanging it on the back of one of the kitchen chairs, along with his black tie. He'd cut and set out slices of the deep-dish apple crumb pie, made earlier that day by Lettie, and transferred the cream and fruit to china bowls. Silver flatware graced the table, along with summer-themed linen napkins.

Unable to resist, Clay picked up a spoonful of raspberries and ate them. The tart-sweet flavor tasted good on his tongue. He wondered if Linda's mouth would taste as piquant? Tonight he certainly meant to find out. Sooner than later.

He poured ice-cold milk into two tall glasses, each decorated with hand-painted yellow roses and bluebonnets and a fancy script *B* set amidst the entwined bouquet. His mother had found an artist and commissioned them as a housewarming gift. A reminder of Texas in the Big Apple.

Clay took a seat at the table, waiting for her. Roses and bluebonnets. They'd make an interesting wedding bouquet.

Her slippered feet didn't make any sound on the steps. One minute he was alone, and the next, he wasn't.

She'd certainly taken him at his word. Man-tailored pajamas of lightweight pale blue cotton trimmed in navy blue, flat ballet-type slippers in navy, and an oversize white terry robe were her ensemble. Her reddish blond hair was left long and loose, waving past her shoulders. Her face was devoid of makeup, freshly scrubbed.

Linda wasn't beautiful in the conventional sense. Her looks were strong and defined. *Striking* was a better word to describe her. Unforgettable. The kind of face that left an impression.

''Hope you don't mind milk?'' Clay wondered if Linda

knew that wearing those clothes could be every bit as appealing to a man as a fancy outfit? Taken by themselves, they were nothing. Worn by the right woman, they were everything.

Linda joined him at the table, her eyes taking in the sight of him, shirt unbuttoned slightly, hair ruffled as if he'd run his hand through it. "It's fine by me. One more drop of caffeine and I'll be up all night."

"Well, there's no need to get up early tomorrow," Clay stated. "We've got nothing lined up."

She added a dollop of whipped cream to the pie, along with a heaping spoonful of the berries. "I thought we had one more meeting with Ortega before we finalized the deal?"

"He changed his mind. Faxed me his acceptance earlier. It's all done."

"Congratulations, Clay. I know how much this means to you."

He nodded as he put his spoon into the pie. "It adds another significant dimension to the Communications division of Buchanan. With this acquisition, we get two regional cable stations and a magazine, all aimed at the burgeoning Hispanic market."

Linda lifted her glass of milk in his direction, noticing the design for the first time, smiling as she did so. "I guess this really ought to be champagne, but here goes anyway. Congratulations. I never doubted that you'd get what you wanted."

Clay clicked his glass against hers. "To you, too. Ortega was quite impressed by your presentation, as well." He lowered the glass, his eyes on her. "We make a damned good team, don't we?"

Softly she concurred. "The best."

"I don't want to lose you, Linda."

"You won't."

"You're much too valuable an asset to Buchanan."

Buchanan. The company, not the man. For her they were one and the same.

"Is this a good time to ask for a raise?" Linda tried to inject an air of levity in her response, because if she didn't, she was afraid that she might be forced to run away. Hide. Lick her emotional wounds in private. While his words made her happy, they also made her sad, knowing as she did that she had so much more to offer him.

"I'm way ahead of you."

Her eyes widened. "I was just kidding."

"I'm not."

"I didn't do it for the money."

"I know that."

Her silently spoken words echoed in her head. I did it because I could never let you down, Clay. Never. God, don't you know that by now? she wanted to ask.

"Talent and hard work deserve a reward. Don't you agree?"

Linda smiled. "I'd be a fool not to." And I've never been that, except for you. She spooned another bite of her dessert into her mouth.

Clay watched as she did so. He'd taken her by surprise. Completely. He could read it in her expressive eyes. Good. Bigger surprises waited in the wings. Hopefully, the kind she'd like and respond well to.

"Will we be leaving for Houston tomorrow then since our business here is finished?" she asked, reaching for the glass of milk.

"What would you think about staying on for an extra day."

She put the glass back down after swallowing another drink of the cold beverage. "And doing what?"

He shrugged his shoulders. "Whatever you'd like. Shopping. Sightseeing."

"You mean play tourist?"

Clay grinned, revealing the hint of dimples as he did. "Sure."

"What would you be doing?"

"The same," he replied. "Whatever you want, if you don't mind the company?"

"What?"

"You heard me."

"Why?"

"We've earned a day of fun."

"Anything I want?" Fun and Clay. What a wonderful combination, she thought.

"Anything," he agreed. "Do you have something specific in mind?"

Linda rose and put her dirty plate and glass in the wide stainless steel sink. "Let me sleep on it."

"Do that." He followed her, setting his empty plate and glass, along with the two empty bowls, next to hers in the sink.

She glanced at the clock on the wall. It was well after midnight. Time for the day's fairy tale to come to a close.

"Good night, Clay." As she turned to leave, he reached out his hand and took hold of her arm.

"Wait."

Taking a deep breath, she faced him. "Yes?"

They exchanged glances. Eyes locked and for a moment, neither moved. Then, slowly, he withdrew his hand from her sleeve and brought it up to her face, touching her cheek lightly before dipping his head and gently touching his lips to hers for an instant. "Sleep well."

As she lay in bed, Linda couldn't get that small gesture

out of her mind. Sweet. Gentle. The passionless kiss of a good friend.

She punched the fluffy pillow behind her head, adjusting it, trying to put the incident aside. Unfortunately, she couldn't.

Clay made it clear how he saw her. When he'd reached out and put his hand on her arm, the electricity had shot through her with the force of a bullet. When his face loomed closer, she hadn't known what to expect. She only knew without doubt what she wanted. Hoped for. Longed for.

Reality, she'd discovered, had a way of smacking you in the face and forcing you to acknowledge the truth.

Clay cared about her as a friend. Nothing more.

She had to accept that and go on with her life.

Linda smacked the pillow once more for good measure. What other choice did she have?

She could leave him. Seek employment elsewhere. Get as far away from him and Texas as was possible.

No, she thought as she settled down in the bed. That wasn't an option for her. Not now. Possibly never.

So much for the best-laid plans, Clay mused as he stood under the cool flow of the showerhead.

It wasn't the right time, he told himself. As much as he'd wanted to take their relationship to the next level, he found that he couldn't. It was the look on her face that had stopped him. The relaxed attitude she presented. Completely trusting. Honest.

Experimenting then could have backfired with disastrous results. Maybe even driven a solid wedge between them.

Coward. The word mocked him.

But, better a coward than a violator of trust.

With the removal of the dress the spell of the evening had been broken. The "date" was officially over. True, the need to sample those sweet-looking lips was still there coursing inside him. The desire to skate his palm over her soft skin from head to toe was still paramount.

What had changed the mood was Linda. Shedding the sexy dress and appearing in her pajamas had swiftly erased his plans. She'd presented herself like a sister and a barrier had gone up in his head. One that said, Look, don't touch. It was her ready acceptance of their current status as friends and business partners. She felt comfortable with him, which wasn't quite the mood Clay was aiming for.

He couldn't possibly take advantage of that. Or her.

Yet, knowing that, it didn't stop or ease the wanting. The growing-stronger-day-by-day hunger that even now held him in its grip. His body responded, a primitive, atavistic reaction to the female force within her. Luckily he hadn't gotten close enough to her to show her the power an attractive woman wielded over a man. Like a wild brushfire, acknowledging the force she could command might have scared the holy Texas hell out of her.

And he didn't want that. He didn't want to make her uncomfortable.

Time, however, was quickly running out.

Somehow, someway, if he was to make his plans come to fruition, he had to make their day together count, make her see the future as he did.

Even with their late night, both Clay and Linda rose at their usual times and met over breakfast downstairs.

Lettie, herself an early riser, already had coffee brewing and a breakfast buffet waiting when they arrived within moments of each other in the dining room.

The daily papers, the *New York Times, Wall Street Journal,* the *Financial Times* and one of the Houston papers, were left on the sideboard by Basil, who'd procured them from a nearby newsstand an hour earlier.

Clay was buried in the *Journal,* checking out a story when Linda entered the room. He looked up, a smile on his face. There was something healthy, captivating and sexy about a woman who faced the day with such confidence. Small silver barrettes pulled her hair back from her face. She wore a white shirt tied in a knot at her waist and the sleeves rolled up over a navy shell, with a blue-and-white skirt that ended a few discreet inches above her knees. Flat white canvas shoes completed the outfit. One slim wrist carried a chunky silver-and-coral bracelet, which matched the earrings she wore.

Like a chameleon, she had the ability to change her appearance and, in doing so, confuse him. Today she was cool. Collected.

She wouldn't like to be in a poker game with him, Linda thought as she collected a cup of coffee from the pot and poured in a splash of cream. This morning Clay had the relaxed, nonchalant thing down pat. Composed and self-possessed. A man in control. Unflappable. While she was far from that.

"Given any more thought to what you'd like to do today?"

Linda took a seat on his right hand, spreading thick orange marmalade onto a slice of toast. "Walk, for one thing. I love the city." She took a bite and chewed that before continuing. "That's the only way to get the feel of New York. Just go out and get into it."

"I agree." Her enthusiasm was contagious, as was her

endearing smile. It was pure Texas sunshine, potent as all get-out.

"Later, I'd like to visit a museum and if there's time, go to Central Park." She stood up and picked up one of the newspapers. "Let me see what's listed." Resuming her seat, she searched through the *Times* until she found what she was looking for.

"And the rest of the day?"

Linda looked up from the page she was reading. "Play it by ear. Okay?"

"Whatever you'd like."

Clay had been true to his word. After breakfast, they'd strolled along the city streets, examining and comparing the different styles of architecture of the buildings they passed, checking out quaint shops, watching as people hurried along.

Later they caught a cab uptown to the Metropolitan so that they could see an exhibit that was soon to close, items from both Imperial Russian and private collections of Fabergé treasures, marveling at the craftsmanship of the people involved.

Lunch was improvised at a local deli, paid for then eaten in the park, watching the world pass by as they ate their thick sandwiches and drank cold cans of soda.

Linda couldn't believe that she was actually here with him, sitting casually among the throng. It was a warm day and the park was filled with people, all ages, sizes and types. Everyone seemed to be enjoying themselves. Lines of in-line skaters buzzed by, skating fast and furious, or calm and methodical. Dogs were walked. Park animals were fed. Children scampered around, playing their games under the watchful eyes of family members or hired help. Lovers, arm in arm or mouth to mouth, strolled by, content with a chance to be together.

It was watching those couples, with their lives apparently full and happy at that moment, that brought a twinge of sadness to Linda, a taste of the wishful what-if? She had only to stretch out her hand and take Clay's. It was only a matter of inches.

It might as well be miles. No matter how much she wanted to, she couldn't.

An adorable toddler scampered over to where they sat, going after his rubber ball. Clay reached down and picked it up, handing it back to the little boy, who stood there, wide-eyed and grinning.

His mother was close behind him, a frantic look on her face. "Harry!" she cried. "Don't run away from me. You know Mommy gets frightened when you do that." She picked him up, hefting the boy onto her jean-clad hip. "I'm sorry if he bothered you," she apologized.

"No need, ma'am," Clay drawled, a friendly smile on his face. "The boy was just being a boy."

"You got some of your own?" the young girl asked as she bounced the boy on her hip while he tried to play peekaboo with Linda.

"Not yet." Clay watched as the child laughed at the face Linda made. "But I certainly look forward to having a few."

The same thought ran through Linda's mind when she heard his response. Children. *Clay's* children. Linda observed him with the child and its mother, her imagination firing up. Clay would make a wonderful father. He would raise kids with the same confidence he used to run a global financial empire. He'd be there for them. Guiding. Taking responsibility. Sharing. It was simply part of who Clay was.

He turned his head and their eyes locked. Long moments passed as the woman went on her way.

This wasn't going quite where he wanted. While it was nice having time to explore the day together, Clay was left with a feeling of time running out, of losing control of the situation. Busy Central Park wasn't the place to tell Linda what was on his mind. He needed privacy for that.

"Linda."

"Yes?"

"I need to talk to you."

"About what?"

"I can't get into it now. Not here." He rose, dumped their trash in a nearby bin, came back and extended his hand to her.

She accepted it immediately, rising from the bench. "Then where?"

"The town house."

She could tell from the urgent tone in his voice that whatever it was he had to tell her must be very important. "Okay."

A hastily summoned taxi delivered them back at Clay's New York residence less than twenty minutes later.

"So, what's up?" Linda asked as they entered the library. Clay had been closemouthed on the drive back and she found it hard to accurately read his mood. One minute he'd been relaxed, enjoying the day; the next, quiet, like a weight rested on his shoulders.

She turned to face him as he followed behind her, closing the door with a soft click. Within the darkly paneled walls of the room, they were well and truly alone.

He quickly closed the distance between them. "This," he said as he caught her in his arms.

Swift and sure, his lips captured and connected. Neither savage nor sweet, they were somewhere in between. He didn't kiss like the practical man she'd labeled him earlier;

instead, he kissed like a Texas twister, sweeping her along in its wake.

Lost in the moment, Linda gave herself up to it completely, holding nothing back. Her hands wound around his neck, pulling him even closer to her body, if that were possible. She felt his hard strength pressed close to her softness. A molded fit, as if they were made for each other.

Clay couldn't get enough of her enticing mouth. He deepened the kiss as he explored the territory presented, his tongue boldly meeting hers in stimulating, erotic by-play. Arms wrapped tightly around her, he held her secure, her body imprinted on his. Female to male. Ying to yang.

Reluctantly Clay pulled back, releasing her slowly. He'd had to, or he would have been tempted not to let Linda go. He would have taken their embrace to the next step, ready or not. Now wasn't the right time nor the library the right place for what his fertile mind so easily conjured up. Besides, letting his emotions dominate him wasn't in his overall game plan.

"I won't apologize," Clay stated bluntly, his breathing coming under control. He'd acted impulsively, going with the moment, with the achingly deep need he'd felt right then. He had no regrets. This reckoning had been building, festering almost since the night of the storm.

Linda moistened her lips, continuing to meet his eyes with her own, heat pooling in her stomach. How was it that she was still standing when her legs felt weak? "Do you hear me complaining?"

A hint of a smile lurked on his mouth, that very same mouth which only seconds before had introduced her to a glimpse of what delights could be found in the simple gesture of a kiss.

"I'd hoped you wouldn't," he said. "I've been waiting to do that for some time now."

"You have?" She raised her hand and gently touched two fingers to her slightly swollen lips.

"Yes." Clay stepped closer, touching her hair, threading one hand through the strands, catching it in his fist. He looked into her eyes, which shone with happiness. "I don't make a habit of kissing employees."

"I'm glad to hear that," she murmured.

"You're the exception, Linda. For a very good reason."

His words washed over her, delight singing in her soul. Her deepest fantasy come true. Clay cared.

"I've been thinking about this for some time now," he began, trying to find just the right words to convey what was on his mind.

"About kissing me?"

"Among other things."

"What *other* things?" If this was a dream, she didn't want to wake up.

"Changing the focus of our relationship."

"To what?"

"A more personal one." Instead of coming closer, he took a step backward, moving to his desk, where he leaned his posterior against the wood. "Sit down, Linda. Please." With one hand he indicated a chair close by.

She did as he asked, slightly confused. Where was he going with this? And why wasn't he kissing her still? Like someone who'd tasted ambrosia, she'd rapidly developed a craving for another taste.

"I want to say something and I want you to hear me out before you say anything. Okay?"

"Sure, Clay, if you insist," she replied when all she

wanted at that moment was to be back in his arms, holding that masculine body as tight as she could to hers.

"When I said that I wanted us to get closer, I meant it. We're good together, Linda. At the office we're a crack team." Clay paused, letting his words sink in. "I've given what I'm about to say a lot of thought recently. Gone over in my head every detail." He removed his glasses and massaged the bridge of his nose before he put them on again. "We have the same goals. We want the same things out of life. That's important in any partnership, especially the one that I'm proposing."

He paused again and looked at her. What was she thinking? Regrettably, he hadn't a clue. Her face was composed; her eyes, however, were full of questions.

"You're the kind of woman who'd suit me, Linda. I admire and respect you more than I can say, but you already know that, I'm sure. I trust you, too. Your judgment. Your values. That's more than a lot of couples have starting out."

Clay sounded as if he were talking about a proposed business merger, listing the good points of the deal to sway her opinion. Moments before, she'd been euphoric, believing the love that existed within her had somehow spilled over to him. Yet the words he spoke now were cool, belying the man he'd been only minutes before.

"I'd be honored, Linda, if you would marry me."

She blinked. "Did I hear you correctly?"

Clay smiled. "Yes, you did."

Linda took a deep breath, her emotions in turmoil. The man she loved was asking her to marry him. The dearest secret wish she'd harbored for so long in her heart was finally coming true, but not in the way she'd envisioned. No words of love had passed his lips. No tender glances or gestures accompanied his request.

"I know that this probably comes as a surprise to you."

"You could say that," she responded in a husky voice barely above a whisper.

"Take some time to think about it," he urged. "I don't need your answer right away. I know I've sprung this on you kind of suddenly, but I meant it. I do think we could be happy together."

When she found her tongue, Linda asked, "What *kind* of marriage do you want, Clay?"

"A normal one, in every sense of the word," he stressed adamantly. "Make no mistake about that, Linda. If you say yes, which I sincerely hope you will, I will be your husband."

Her husband.

His wife.

"Yes." Her response was given softly but with authority.

Now it was Clay's turn to be surprised. "What did you say?"

Linda rose from her chair and walked the short distance until she was right in front of him. "I said, yes. I will marry you, Clay."

Clay drew her into his arms, kissing her softly on the mouth. "You won't regret it, I promise."

Linda hoped not. Fools rush in where angels fear to go. That quote ran quickly through her brain. Was that what she was? A fool? Too blind with love for him to consider saying no.

Time would tell.

"Do you mind if I ask you to be brutally honest and tell me why you agreed so readily?" he queried. "I mean I'm flattered that you didn't have to take the time to mull it over."

Linda yearned to tell him the main reason—she was in

love with him and had been for ten years. But she didn't think that's what he really wanted to hear. To admit her love might scare him off, or worse, make him pity her, so she had to be as cool and practical as he was. "What's to consider?" she retorted. "You're the kind of man I've always been looking for, Clay. Successful. Intelligent. You know who you are and what you want out of life. Well, so do I. At the end of the day I want a man I'll enjoy going home to. Someone who I can share the same world with. Someone who wants a family. A commitment. Someone I admire. You're all that and more, Clay.

"You do want children, don't you?" Linda realized that he hadn't mentioned them specifically, so she thought she'd better do it.

He nodded. "Very much."

"I'm glad," she said softly. "My idea of marriage involves children."

"So does mine." He grinned. "See, I told you that we thought alike, that we're a match. Our goals are the same." Clay leaned back and picked up the phone, pressing one button. "Basil, open up a bottle of champagne and bring it into the library, along with four glasses. I want you and Lettie to join us. We've got something very important to celebrate."

Chapter Eight

Had Linda been out of her head to agree to this marriage of convenience?

That thought had popped up at least several times a day since they'd returned from New York last week. Less than twenty-four hours after they'd arrived back home to Houston, Clay had to leave again, this time for Europe. "Thank God, I don't have to explain where I'm going and what I'm doing, Linda," he'd said right before he'd left the office. "You know the drill by heart."

That she did. As part of their sharing work, Linda knew what to expect. Her own desk had a fresh stack of work to go over each morning. Faxes, memos, reports to read. Projects that she was involved in and plans she was developing. Her own business trips to arrange. Throughout it all, she had only to close her eyes and see Clay's face. Which she did, often. Memories upon memories. The deep, satisfying smile. The forthright look. The wave in his hair. The sexy appeal of the whole package. Most of all, how he made her feel inside. Excited. Alive in new ways that thrilled her to the very marrow of her being.

He'd called her an hour ago from the jet to say that he was on his way home and would she join him tonight for dinner at his house to discuss terms, as he called it. *Terms.* Just like the disposition of a contract, where each side put forth what they wanted and what they expected from the partnership they were considering.

Right now Linda didn't feel like a soon-to-be-married lady. Her ring finger was still without an engagement ring. Clay had promised her before he left that, when he returned, he'd have something for her to look at.

"Unless, you'd prefer to get something on your own?" he'd asked. "I can make a few calls to some shops and see that you're shown the top-of-the-line material."

Pick out her own ring? Linda was well aware that some women preferred it that way. It gave them control and let them express their own taste. But that wasn't for her. She wanted her ring to come from Clay. His choice, the old-fashioned way. It would mean more coming from him. Beyond what he said, the ring would show her. A tangible symbol. Plain. Fancy. It didn't matter to her. All that she cared about was that he chose it, that he took the time and gave it some thought.

So far, she'd told no one, not even her sister or her grandfather of her plans to marry Clay. And, as far as she knew, Clay hadn't said anything to anyone, either. Only Basil and Lettie were in on the secret.

Why?

It wasn't because she was going to change her mind. Far from it. She was committed to Clay, heart and mind, body and soul. Even if he didn't love her, she loved him.

Enough for both of them. Enough to show him what love really meant. Enough to take a risk of this size.

She was gambling for high stakes. Her future happiness rested on the hand she dealt and how she played it.

Tonight the talk was on terms, plans. What kind of a wedding did she want? Big or small? Where and when?

After they decided, then she'd tell her family.

Telling Clay's was another thing. He wanted to do that as soon as possible, she knew. What kind of ordeal would that be? His mother and father were sharp, no one's fools. Would they approve? And what about his brothers? Clay was raised in the kind of family that she'd always wished she'd had. Tight-knit. Extremely close. Would his younger siblings welcome her? Or would they think her an outsider who was marrying a rich man for gain—a smart girl who'd hit the mother lode? Exchanging a good life for an even better one?

And what about any residual feelings Clay had for his sister-in-law Emma, Burke's wife? At one time he'd wanted to marry her. Was that connection completely broken on Clay's part? She knew it was on Emma's, having been to the christening party and seen Burke and his wife together. They were very much in love.

God, would they be able to tell that Clay's feelings for her weren't as strong? And if so, would they pity her? Hold her in contempt for wedding a man who wasn't in love with her?

She hoped not. But even if they did, it wasn't going to change her mind. Nothing could do that.

Her terms were set. Terms that were carved in her heart all those years ago, terms she couldn't reveal. They were very simple: she wanted Clay's love, his name, his child.

She was prepared to welcome the latter two, hoping that it wouldn't be long before the first followed.

Linda glanced at the small bouquet of flowers on her desk. The fragrant scent of the old roses filled her nostrils; their color, a pale peach, warmed her heart. Today a card had come with them, a card for her eyes alone. ''Thinking of you'' it had read. There was no signature, but that didn't matter. She knew who they were from.

Clay opened the box and looked at the ring again, a wide smile forming on his lips. It was stunning. Just the kind of item he'd been searching for. An estate piece. One of a kind. Unique. Representative of turn-of-the-century Belle Epoque style, originally worn by the mistress of a Russian prince, he'd been told. He'd liked the ring so much he'd taken the rest of the set he was shown immediately. They would be part of his wedding gift to Linda, doled out in segments.

Clay found that the idea of presenting her with these things piece by piece was fun. Ring. Brooch. Earrings. Bracelet. Each one was marvelous, a work of art. Together, on Linda, they would be breathtaking. She could carry them off. Her hair. Her coloring. Her face. On another woman they might overwhelm. On Linda they would adorn.

Yes, Clay was quite pleased with himself. He'd chosen well, all around, the most salient being his choice of a wife.

Snapping the lid shut, he placed the ring on his dresser while he contemplated what to wear this evening. Freshly shaved and showered, rested after a nap on the plane, he checked his watch as he prowled through the walk-in closet, selecting his clothes. She'd soon be here. Ready to discuss the details of their wedding.

His lawyers had drawn up a simple agreement that he thought was more than fair to Linda. His legal and financial dealings were complicated—he didn't need his marriage to be so, also. The majority of the stock in the company was family owned and would remain so. However, Clay wanted his wife to have a stake. In addition to what she already owned through employee purchase options, he'd recently obtained a sizable chunk of public shares for her. Hers to do with as she wanted.

As for the actual wedding, the sooner the better.

There was no doubt in his mind that physically they were compatible. In bed he believed they would do just fine. The kiss in New York had wiped away any lingering questions. Her response, unguarded and passionate, had created a lingering ache in his gut for a repeat performance. She hadn't been faking it; she'd wanted him then just as much as he wanted her.

He had their honeymoon destination all planned. His house in the Caribbean. Sun. Sand. Water. Tropical breezes. A chance to get to know each other in the most elemental way. Just the two of them, alone. Man and wife.

When that finally happened his life would never be the same. Already it had altered in subtle ways. Now when he conferred with her, he added a private note to the conversation. He relished the welcoming response in her tone when they talked on the phone. Before it had been strictly professional, with nary a hint of the personal. Now her voice was softer. Warmer.

They genuinely liked each other. Love wasn't clouding the issue. Each realized that this was a match that made sense. In every way and for all concerned.

He planned to take her to the ranch this weekend, introduce her as his fiancée. Show his family that he'd successfully moved on with his life. Put the past behind him where it belonged.

Linda was his future.

And what a future it would be. Married to a smart, sexy woman who matched his goals, who saw things with the same clarity that he did. A partnership in the boardroom and the bedroom. Two trains on the same track, fueled by similar motivations, going in the same direction.

Luck was on his side and nothing was going to spoil this.

"Why don't you wait for Mr. Buchanan in the living room, Miss Douglas?" Basil suggested as he welcomed her into Clay's home a few hours later.

"Thanks, Basil."

"May I say again how pleased my wife and I are that you're marrying Mr. Buchanan. He's a good man who deserves the very best."

Linda beamed at the implied compliment from the august butler. "That's very sweet of you and I appreciate the sentiment," she said as Basil showed her into the large room. "But it's me who's getting the best."

"Shall we say that it's mutual then?" he proffered in dulcet tones, his eyes warm and sharp. "Quality deserves quality."

Linda had to smile at that remark. Living in Texas must have loosened up that famed British reserve. While in New York, she'd come to know the couple better; Lettie had fussed and pampered her with one wonderful meal after another, with extra touches of warmth. Basil, likewise, had been the essence of care and concern. It was another indication of how her life would change when she married Clay—instead of doing for herself, she'd have help. Rather than them starting a routine of their own, as many couples did, she'd have to fit into his.

"Would you like anything to drink while you're waiting?"

Linda settled on the plush couch, Basil's question cutting into her thoughts. "Clay will probably have wine with our meal, so a glass of tea will do me just fine right now."

"Coming up."

Linda relaxed, her head falling back against the material. How was it that she missed Clay now more than before? It was all she could do to concentrate on her appointments today. To read through E-mails and make coherent comments. Every minute dragged by as if pulled by an ant. Slowly. Tediously. Endlessly. All she could focus on was that she'd see him tonight. Five days away from him and she was climbing the walls.

After they were married what would it be like? After they'd been lovers would the parting be more unbearable?

Lovers.

A flush of color bloomed in her cheeks. Was Clay expecting an experienced partner? A woman who was familiar with the mysteries of the bedroom? A woman who could provide her own brand of skill and confidence?

More than likely, she reckoned.

Doubt assailed her. If so, he was going to be greatly disappointed.

She ought to tell him. Give him a chance to change his mind and back out of the marriage if he wanted. He had a right to know what he was getting.

But how did she go about bringing up the subject?

Linda got up off the couch and walked around the room, stopping at the small butler's table with the pictures of his family. In each and every photo she saw strength, a certain Texas-style grit, and grace. She wanted that for the children she would have.

"A rather impressive lot, don't you think?"

She spun around at the sound of his voice. "Clay." It was a whispered endearment, filled with longing.

"The one and only."

Linda stood there, as if rooted to the spot, conflicting scenarios running through her head at warp speed. Should she run to him and welcome him the way she yearned to, with kisses? Or, should she remain calm, aloof. Dignified?

She chucked that idea and took steps that brought her closer to him. "I missed you." There was no mistaking the warmth in her voice. It was naked and real.

"Same for me."

"Really?"

"Yes, really," he answered. Clay approached Linda, holding out his hand to her. "Come here," he coaxed, his voice low and raspy. "Let me show you how much."

His gaze slowly drifted from the crown of her head to the tips of her high-heeled pumps as she did as he requested. Lifting one hand, he feathered his thumb across her full bottom lip, back and forth until she responded, closing her upper lip around it, trapping it gently within the confines of her mouth before he slowly pulled it free.

Her hair was caught up in a ponytail. Seconds later it tumbled about her neck, the braided elasticized band tossed to the coffee table.

His eyes dropped to the two gold buttons on her nipped-in jacket. One by one he undid them, pushing it off her shoulders and down her arms. The rusty-hued linen fell to the floor, unheeded. Beneath it she wore an ivory silk blouse. His hand skirted along her spine, fingers splaying, urging her closer.

Heat soared through her body as their mouths met. Long. Deep. Satisfying. It was a kiss hungrily repeated, chasing away inhibitions. Scaling heights and plundering depths. Taking and giving.

A discreet knock sounded on the closed door and they reluctantly broke apart, their breathing slightly ragged. Basil entered the room, two glasses of tea on a tray. ''I took the liberty of bringing along some for you, too, sir.''

Clay cleared his throat. He felt uncharacteristically like a teenager caught necking with his girlfriend, except that he detected a gleam of amusement in Basil's hazel eyes.

''Good idea,'' he said as he lifted his glass to his lips. ''I could use something cool.''

Linda managed a weak smile on her face to try to hide her acute embarrassment at almost being discovered exchanging heated kisses with her boss. ''Thank you,'' she said as the butler handed her the refreshment, which she drank immediately.

''When would you like to be served dinner, sir?''

Clay glanced at Linda, who'd drunk almost half her iced tea and then placed her glass on the tray that Basil left on the table. ''Make it a half hour, Basil.''

The butler gave them both an understanding smile and an arched brow. ''I'll inform Lettie.''

Linda couldn't help it, when Basil closed the door she groaned and picked up her discarded jacket from the floor, brushing it off and then laying it gently across the wooden surface. ''I can't believe it. He almost...''

''Basil is a gentleman, Linda.'' Clay smiled, his dimples revealed, white teeth gleaming. ''Besides, I think that he's seen couples kissing before.''

''I know but—''

''No buts. He'll get used to it.''

''It's *me* that'll have to get used to it.''

Clay grinned, deepening the dimples. ''You will.'' He swallowed a large portion of the contents of his own glass in one long gulp and set it next to hers, then he seized her hand and pulled her next to him on the couch. ''We've got some things to talk about.'' He looked deeply into her face as he reached into the pocket of his trousers. ''Much as I would like to take up where we just left off, we'd better put that aside for right now. It's past time to make this engagement official.''

Linda dropped her gaze and stared at the velvet box in his hand.

Clay held out his palm. ''Open it.''

She forced her fingers to grasp the object. Snapping open the lid, she gasped softly. ''Oh, my God!'' Inside, nestled in black velvet, was a ring. Linda had been expecting a nice diamond, nothing flashy or ostentatious, which wasn't her style or Clay's. She'd seen trophy rings before on the fingers of several women and thought them vulgar.

This, however, was beautiful. A real work of art. An antique, she could tell by the setting.

''Do you like it?''

She raised her face, her eyes meeting Clay's. ''It's exquisite.''

A satisfied look claimed his face. ''I knew you'd appreciate it.''

''Appreciate it?'' She dropped her gaze again to the velvet-encased ring. ''I love it. Where did you find it?''

''London.'' Clay took the box from her hand and removed the ring, tossing the empty container to the coffee table, where it landed on her folded jacket. He gently slipped the ring on her finger. ''A perfect fit.''

Linda held up her hand and admired the way it looked there, gracing her finger. As if it were made for her. As if it always belonged there. The square-cut aquamarine, flanked by two diamonds and set in a platinum band, sparkled in the low light in the room.

Her eyes filled with moisture, touched by the beauty of the gift.

Clay cupped her chin, lifting her face. "You've got to marry me now." He touched his mouth to hers for a light exchange. "The question is when? You're not going to make me wait, are you?"

Linda owed him the truth before she gave him her answer. "There's something I have to tell you."

"Can't it wait?"

She shook her head. "No."

He recognized the importance of the moment from the tone she used. "Go ahead, then, I'm listening."

She wet her lips, going for complete honesty, cards on the table, faceup. "I'm a virgin, Clay."

"What?"

She repeated her statement. "I don't know if that changes anything between us, but I felt that you had a right to know in case it did. I know it's not hip or trendy, but it's the truth."

Clay was slightly numbed by her announcement. "You've never been with a man?"

She shook her head. "No."

"Do you mind my asking why? You're a bright, attractive woman, Linda. Passionate." He spoke that word, meaning resonating in his voice. "I know that for a fact. I can't believe no man's actively pursued you before."

"It's not that they haven't, Clay," she told him honestly. "Sure. In high school, college and grad school there were boys, men who made it quite plain that they wished to take things further than I was willing to go. I've heard the words 'I want you' before a fair amount of times. Some I believed, some I didn't. And I've also been asked what I was waiting for."

"And your answer was...?"

"That retaining my virginity was *my* choice. *My* decision."

She couldn't tell Clay the whole truth, that she'd wanted the first man she was intimate with to be the man she loved. Which it would be, if he still wanted her. "For me," she said bluntly, "it had to mean something more than a quick release of tension or a casual encounter. That's not who I am."

Linda sighed, a worried look in her eyes. How was Clay going to take the news? She had to know. "Does that make a difference?"

Clay took a deep breath, measuring his words. "Of course it does."

Linda bowed her head. He probably thought she was an outdated relic or, worse yet, a coward, afraid of life. "I won't hold you to your proposal." She started to slip the ring off her finger.

Clay quickly stopped her from removing it. "Why not? I'm damn well going to hold you to your acceptance," he insisted.

Her head shot up. "You haven't changed your mind?"

"About wanting to marry you? No. And I'm not going to. I still think we make an unbeatable team, Linda. The kind that can make a relationship work. You must agree or you wouldn't have said yes." He held her hand, interlocking their fingers, and searched to find the words that would reassure her. "I know you're giving me a very distinct gift, one which will make our first time together that much more special. I'll be patient," he promised. "I won't rush you into anything that you're not ready for, but," and he stressed the following, "I do want to make it clear that I want this to be a solid marriage."

"You don't see me as a freak?"

He tenderly caressed her face. "Of course not. You've

got guts and determination to stick to your guns. Principles if you will. Today, that's almost a lost art.''

"Casual sex never seemed right for me.''

"I'm not going to lie to you and say that I've never been with a woman before, Linda. I have. Not as many as some people think, or certain reporters have speculated upon, but enough to know my way around. And I've always been careful. That's one thing you don't have to worry about.''

She appreciated his reassurance, given the times they lived in. ''That's good to know.''

"So, now that we've got that out of the way,'' he declared, ''what say we talk about the date of our wedding. And where it's going to take place?''

"If you don't mind, I'd like it to be small. Family and friends only.'' Linda didn't want her wedding day to be a circus, with paparazzi and politicians, society mavens and sycophants crowding the ceremony.

"Okay, I can live with that. But you know we're going to have to do something later on a much grander scale for business associates.''

Linda understood the responsibilities of a Buchanan wedding in Texas. There was a trade-off. An intimate ceremony would have to give way to a social party for the movers and shakers of the state. However, she could live with that. By then she'd be Clay's wife. In addition to her job as Clay's personal assistant, playing hostess to large gatherings would become a part of who she was.

"I don't have a problem with that. A formal reception at one of the larger hotels in Houston should suffice. Leave it to me and I'll make all the arrangements.''

"We still haven't set a date,'' he reminded her.

"I checked both our calendars before I left the office today and anytime within the next two weeks would be fine. If not then, we can schedule it for the fall, maybe late September.''

''Efficient as ever, Linda.''

''I try.''

''Good. I don't see any reason to wait,'' Clay stated. ''Neither one of us wants a long engagement, am I right?'' He waited for her to either agree or deny his question. She agreed with a nod of her head. ''So let's do it sooner rather than later. Is that enough time for you to get things taken care of on your end?''

''Yes.'' Linda had confidence in her organizing skills. With help in certain areas, she could pull it off.

''Now, next question, where?''

She'd given the matter some serious thought and had come up with what she thought would be the perfect spot. ''Do you think your folks would mind if we used the chapel at the ranch?''

The corners of his mouth kicked up. ''I think they'd like that. What made you think of it?''

''When I was at the christening of your nephew I remember how lovely it looked all decked out in autumnal flowers. So warm and welcoming. I thought then that it was the perfect place for a wedding.''

Clay recalled the event, the care and detail that had transformed the old place into a wonderland of color and beauty. ''Yes, I think you're right. It'll be the perfect place to take our vows. Very fitting.'' He smiled again. ''Considering that Burke and Emma got hitched in San Antonio with a justice of the peace and Drew's planning on getting married in Pennsylvania, this'll be a real family event.''

''Speaking of which, how do you think your family's going to take the news of our plans?''

''In stride.''

"Gosh, I certainly hope so."

"Don't worry. They'll love you."

They'll love you. Clay's words reverberated in Linda's mind as she got ready for bed. *They,* he stated with confidence. Still, he hadn't included himself in that remark. He could easily have said, "They'll love you as much as I do." But the truth was that he didn't say that because he wasn't in love with her.

How much heartache, she wondered, was she letting herself in for?

The answer came quickly. A lot. Especially if he didn't come to return her feelings. Yet, she couldn't turn back now. Wouldn't even if the opportunity presented itself. Clay was the man for her. She knew that at sixteen. She believed it even more so now at twenty-six.

Was she the woman for him?

Her grandfather thought so. Linda smiled as she dried her face and applied moisturizer. Telling him would be a pleasure. It was on his arm that she wanted to walk down the aisle to Clay.

She bent over and ran her brush through her hair. It would be only fitting since Ethan Douglas had been the one who introduced them all those years ago. He'd led her to Clay once before and would do so again.

They'd come full circle.

Tomorrow she'd called Sandy and tell her the good news. Linda could only imagine what her sister would say. Probably that Linda owed it all to her and her scheme to get her older sister a date to the wedding. Yes, in a way, Sandy had been the catalyst. Spending personal time with Clay, discovering more about him that weekend, had been wonderful. Maybe it had even given him the idea.

Whatever, she was grateful, in her own way to Sandy.

Linda padded across the room to her daybed and pulled back the cotton duvet cover, folding it and placing it on a nearby chair. In a short time she'd be sharing a much bigger bed with her husband.

Linda lifted the top sheet and tossed it back, sitting on the bed and drawing her knees up, hugging her arms around them.

What would it be like? His offer of marriage might have been lukewarm, filled with practical considerations, but his kiss was anything but. Spicy as the hottest salsa. Sweeter than a pound of peanut butter fudge.

How would it be the first time? She knew the particulars. In this day and age she'd have to be deaf, dumb and blind not to. For all that she was aware of the mechanics, it would be a different story once they were together. Really together. She wasn't afraid. Linda could never be afraid of Clay.

In truth she couldn't wait. She wanted to know. She wanted to be a part of something more than herself, her body and his joined as one.

A small smile tugged at the corners of her mouth. Clay had handled the news of her lack of sexual history with aplomb, as she'd secretly hoped he would. No recriminations, no reproach. He'd accepted her virginity as part of who she was.

Her glance fell on the ring she wore. He'd told her about its history. A romantic tale of love lost and found, and ultimately lost again.

An omen?

Linda couldn't let herself think that.

She already was a winner. In every way that counted. This ring may not have been given to her *in* love, but it would be worn by her *with* love. When she spoke the words before God she'd mean them, with all her heart.

* * *

Clay removed his watch and glasses, set them on the night table and slid between the cool linen sheets of his large bed, the same one he'd soon be sharing with Linda.

A *virgin*.

What were the odds? One in a million?

This information did change things for him. It added an accountability on his part to their eventual lovemaking. A sense of responsibility. He was the man she'd chosen to open the door and show her the way through. To help her cross the bridge of ultimate intimacy.

Her first lover.

He linked his hands behind his head. Politically incorrect as it was, Clay had to admit, if only to himself, that he actually felt good about that, which surprised him. He'd certainly never given the notion of sexual innocence much thought before.

He was damn well thinking about it now.

As he'd taught her the ropes of the company, all the inside details, so he would happily teach her the intricacies of physical communication. Tutoring her in pleasure.

A deep grin spread across Clay's mouth. Linda had always been a fast learner, a quick study.

Something, most likely the gut instinct he relied on, told him that she'd be an apt pupil for this subject, too.

He was counting on it.

Chapter Nine

"Anyone have an idea what's up with Clay?" Burke posed the question as he joined his family for dinner in the ranch's spacious kitchen. Before he took his seat at the large oak table, he leaned over and kissed his wife, then ran his tanned hand over his infant son's head, who sported the same dark hair as his father. He did the same thing to his daughter.

"All I know is that he's bringing along a guest," Santina Buchanan, the matriarch of the clan, announced. "A *female* guest," she added with some emphasis.

"A woman?"

Santina glanced at her daughter-in-law, Emma Cantrell Buchanan, who had made the inquiry, as she handed her youngest son the heaping platter of fried chicken. "Uh-huh."

"Interesting," Emma said with a smile, drawling out the word.

"I'd bet that she must be someone special," Burke offered as he took a plump breast from the pile of golden brown chicken before passing it back to his father. He didn't need to add that his older brother had only brought one other woman home recently to meet the family, the same woman who was now his wife.

"He didn't say," Santina replied, "but I would hazard a guess that you're right."

"Do you know who it is?" Emma inquired, spooning some applesauce into her son's mouth, while he gurgled happily.

"Let's say I've got a good idea."

"Is Uncle Clay serious about her?" Jessie, Burke's daughter, asked as she helped herself to another leg from the dwindling platter.

Santina nodded in her granddaughter's direction. "I think so."

"Well," Jessie stated, "if she's his girlfriend, then she must be someone extra special. Maybe he wants to tell us that he's gonna get married finally, just like Uncle Drew."

Across the length of the table, Santina exchanged a look with her husband, Noah.

"Is that it?" Burke demanded softly, his dark eyes alive with curiosity, catching the silent exchange between his parents.

"Why don't we let Clay tell us himself, if there's anything to tell," Noah stated. "No use speculating."

"You gotta admit, Dad," Burke replied, "that it's a good occasion tomorrow, it being the Fourth of July, for an announcement. Plenty of the family's gonna be here for the barbecue."

"I wonder what she's like?"

Burke turned his head and sliced a glance at his wife, sitting across the table. His voice was warm and low as he answered her question. "Knowing my brother's taste in women, I'd guess she's fabulous."

His wife responded, "I hope so, for Clay's sake. He deserves a woman as wonderful as he is."

"And someone who'll make him as happy as you've made me," Burke countered.

"We may be jumping the gun," Santina warned.

"But you don't think so, do you?" Emma observed with a twinkle in her eyes.

"Honestly? No."

Emma wiped the dribble of applesauce from her son's chin with the edge of her napkin. "Good. It's about time he settled down. I can't wait to meet her."

Santina debated about telling her family that she suspected that they had already met the woman, but she decided to wait. Maybe she was wrong. Clay hadn't named names, nor told her outright that he was getting married. She assumed, since their talk the previous month, that he'd made up his mind and found the woman, asked her and she'd accepted.

"When are they coming?" Jessie asked.

"They're flying up early tomorrow morning," Noah stated. "Probably around eight or so."

"Want me to drive over and get them?"

"If you wouldn't mind, Burke, that'd be great."

"Can I come along, Daddy?" Jessie begged.

Burke looked at his daughter, love shining in his eyes for her. "Are you sure you can get your pretty little self out of bed that early?"

Jessie threw him a simulated affronted look. "Of course I can."

"Okay. If you're not ready, I'll go without you."

Jessie laughed. She knew her daddy would do no such

thing. He'd make sure she was awake and ready to go.
"No, you won't," she insisted.

Burke laughed softly as he helped himself to a large
glass of iced tea. "You're right, darlin'."

"Cool. I can't wait."

"Neither can I."

"What's the saying?" Burke asked his wife later that
night as he emerged from the shower, a towel draped
loosely about his lean hips. Droplets of moisture clung to
his lean chest. "'Déjà vu, all over again'?"

Emma laughed at the reference, glad that they both
could find humor in what had once been a tricky situation.
Burke had been waiting with his car the day she'd first
arrived at the ranch with his older brother. That meeting
had been electric, with she and Burke falling helplessly
in love with each other, fighting it as best they could until
circumstances forced them to face up to the truth, their
feelings too powerful to ignore.

Emma couldn't resist throwing a teasing remark his
way. "You'd better not fall in love with this woman or
you're dead meat, Buchanan," she warned with a raised
brow. "I don't share." Emma glanced down at the child
in her arms; she was feeding their son before putting him
down for the night. "Besides, I'm not done with you yet."

Burke hunkered down next to her, his index finger
stroking his son's cheek as the boy hungrily nursed.
"You're not?" he asked, his voice deep and sexy, his
brown eyes meeting the intense fire in her blue-green
eyes. "When do you think you will be?"

"Not for a very, very long time." With her free hand
she reached out and stroked two fingertips across his wide
mouth, then brought her hand slowly down his neck,

across the broad width of his shoulders. "It'll take me the rest of my life, I think."

"Good," Burke replied. "That's about how long I figured you'd hold my interest. Till the day that they put me six feet under, and maybe beyond." His eyes went back to his son. "Are you okay with this?"

"With Clay, you mean?"

"Yeah."

Emma smiled. "You bet."

"I could understand if…"

"What?" she asked, reading her husband's mind, hastening to reassure him. "If I were a little jealous? I'm not. But am I curious?" she asked. "Oh yes. Very much so. Aren't you?"

He nodded his head. "Naturally. I can't wait to see what she looks like."

"As long as she's good for him she'll get my vote, for what it's worth," Emma stated, rising out of her rocker, Samuel fast asleep. She went into the adjoining room and placed her son in his crib.

"Now, cowboy, I think we have some unfinished business," she said when she reentered their bedroom.

"And just what would that be, ma'am?" he asked innocently, arms akimbo.

Emma padded softly across the bare wooden floor, her hips swaying gently beneath the knee-length cotton nightgown. "This," she said, grabbing the white towel and pulling it loose.

"Oh my!" She feigned a gasp, her gaze dropping low and direct. "What a big—" she paused for effect "—paintbrush you have there, Grandma."

"All the better," he said, and chuckled, "to stroke your canvas, my dear." Burke hastily scooped his wife up into his arms.

"Paint away, then," she whispered in a throaty voice, her arms about his neck. "I'll do anything for the sake of art."

It was a good thing Clay had hold of her hand as the jet approached the field, ready to land. Linda was nervous and it had nothing to do with flying. Closing multimillion dollar deals were nothing compared to the anxiety she was feeling now at the prospect of meeting the Buchanan family as his intended bride.

"Burke's there," Clay said, casting a glance out of the Gulfstream's window.

"One down, lots more to go," she said.

Clay laughed. If he hadn't seen it with his own eyes he would never have believed it. His very competent assistant appeared worried about her meeting with his relatives.

He leaned over and kissed Linda's cheek. For a split second, seeing Burke waiting by his Jeep brought back a bittersweet memory of another time, another woman.

But the outcome this trip would be different.

"I see he's brought Renegade along, too."

"I don't mind," Linda said, turning her head in his direction. "I love dogs."

"Do you?"

"Uh-huh."

"Any specific breed, or do you like them all?"

"I've got my favorites," she responded, glad that he was taking her mind off this upcoming event. "Most dog people do."

Clay chuckled at the reference. "And they are?"

"I'm sort of partial to Shetland sheepdogs or Border collies." A grin spread across her mouth. "There are those adorable pups I've seen in a dog food commercial. Some sort of new breed, I would imagine. A cross mix of Border and something else, with a stump tail. I'm not sure. Whatever they are, they're so cute.'' She opened her handbag to check her lipstick, adding a touch-up of color. ''You like dogs, don't you?''

''Yes.''

''I'm glad.''

The jet eventually came to a stop and Clay and Linda disembarked as soon as it was allowed.

''Welcome home, big brother,'' Burke called out as he walked toward them, Jessie following.

Clay stood there for an instant before embracing his younger sibling. Each slapped the other's back heartily. ''Always good to be back, Burke.''

Linda watched the scene, observing the deep affection the brothers felt toward each other. They looked like mismatched bookends, one fair, the other dark. One a land baron, dressed in faded denim; the other a financial king, top-quality designer clothes adorning his similar tall frame. Each handsome in a different way.

''Jess, I swear you get prettier, not to mention taller, every time I see you.''

Clay's niece hugged her uncle, grinning at his remarks. ''You say that every time.''

''And I mean it every time,'' Clay reiterated. ''You both know my assistant, Linda Douglas.'' He took her left hand in his and interlinked their fingers. ''I want you both to be the first to congratulate me. This lovely lady's agreed to marry me.''

Burke smiled, something he did a lot more of since his own marriage. He offered Linda his hand. ''Congratulations, Linda. And welcome to the family.''

Linda took his hand and shook it. He had a hearty grip, like Clay's, but the resemblance ended there. Burke's skin was harder, forged by life on the ranch. ''Thanks.''

Jessie was less formal than her father. She stepped forward and embraced Linda. "Great," she remarked. "I get to have another aunt. Way cool."

Linda smiled in return, her anxiety fading. "And I've always wanted to have a niece."

"You'll have a nephew, too," Jessie proclaimed, who, at fourteen and a half stood as tall as Linda, who was five foot nine. "I've got a baby brother."

"Even better."

"Let's get you two back to the house," Burke said, grabbing one of the small weekend cases that the pilot had deposited while they were all talking. "Breakfast's waiting, not to mention the rest of the family."

Jessie strolled with Linda, peppering her with questions while Clay walked with Burke. Renegade stood watch by the car's hood until Burke signaled the animal and he came running.

"Does Drew know?"

Clay hunkered down and ruffled the dog's fur. "I called him last night. He and Kate are going to fly in for the ceremony."

"When's that to be?"

"In two weeks."

Burke sliced a glance in his older brother's direction. "Kinda sudden, eh?"

Clay's direct gaze met his brother's. "Why wait if you know what you want."

Burke shrugged. "Guess you're right."

"Damn straight." Clay stood up, the dog retreating to his master's side.

"Then I wish you both all the happiness that's possible." He added softly, "I mean that, Clay."

"I know you do, Burke." They took the few steps that brought them to the Jeep.

"Daddy, you ought to see Linda's engagement ring. It's totally awesome."

"Is it now?" Burke asked, one sable brow rising above an equally dark eye.

Linda proudly held out her hand so that Burke could see the ring. "Mighty pretty, indeed."

Noah and Santina Buchanan had the same reaction when they saw the ring about a half hour later. "Beautiful," Santina exclaimed.

"Well done, son," Noah stated.

The Buchanans' welcome had been warm and unreserved, which further relieved Linda's anxieties. Collectively and individually, his parents' reaction to the announcement had been positive.

"This bit of news gives us another reason to celebrate today," Noah stated as he poured steaming fresh coffee into large cups for Clay and Linda. The smell of fruit pies, warm from the oven, wafted through the kitchen as Mary, the Buchanans' housekeeper, took four out of the oven and replaced them with four more.

"As if we ever need an excuse to have a good time on the Fourth," Burke chimed in, giving an anticipatory look toward the pies, accepting a refill of his mug.

"I made you both something light," Santina stated, fixing two plates with scrambled eggs and toast. She placed them in front of Clay and Linda, along with a bowl of fresh fruit for each. "We'll be having fixin's set up outside from noon on, but I figured you could use something to tide you over till then."

"Thanks, Mrs.—"

"Santina," she insisted. "You're part of the family now, Linda, and we don't stand on ceremony around here. We're pretty informal."

"Not to mention the best family a girl can marry into," Emma said from the back stairs, the baby in her arms.

Burke jumped up from his seat at the table to take the child from his wife, placing a quick kiss on Emma's lips. "Mornin', sweetheart."

"You were supposed to wake me when you left," she scolded him gently, helping herself to a cup of coffee.

"You were sleeping so peacefully I didn't have the heart to," he said in excuse, rejoining the group at the table.

"May I?" Linda asked, indicating that she wanted to hold the baby.

"Certainly," the proud papa replied.

The baby felt good in Linda's arms when Burke placed Sam there. The child was wide-awake, staring at her with his father's dark eyes, a grin on his tiny lips.

Behind his glasses, Clay fixed his gaze on Linda and his nephew, thinking that they looked so right together. Some day soon, he hoped that she would be holding their son or daughter as tenderly as she was holding Burke and Emma's.

"Do you want to have kids right away, Uncle Clay?"

Linda's head snapped up and eyes widened at that direct question. She shot Clay a glance, startled by his niece's query.

"Honey, we've got to get married first. Give us a little time to enjoy being wed before we give you cousins to spoil."

Burke stood up, draining the coffee in his cup with one swallow. "Jessie, come with me. I want to check on how everything's coming along outside."

Jessie jumped up and followed her dad out the back door.

Emma reached for her son and noted the sparkle of the

ring on Linda's finger. She immediately looked at Clay. "Is this what I think it is?"

He answered without hesitation. "Yes."

"Congratulations, Linda. You're getting a wonderful man."

Clay gallantly interceded. "I'm the one who should be receiving your congratulations, Emma," he stated. "I'm getting a terrific woman."

"I stand corrected," she said as she placed her son in his high chair.

"No need," Linda hastened to add pointedly, aware of the history between these two. "I *am* getting a wonderful man."

"I think I can safely say that any woman who marries one of my boys is getting the best," Santina offered.

Noah laughed, a twinkle in his blue eyes. Linda could tell where Clay's charm, not to mention his striking eye color, came from. "See, we're all impartial here, Linda."

"Impartial, hell," Santina replied, her hazel eyes glowing with pride. "I'm their mother. If I can't brag about my sons, who can?"

Linda thought of that later in the day when she'd been congratulated numerous times on her good fortune by the assorted relatives and friends who'd come to attend the famous Fourth of July barbecue at the ranch. She'd been greeted by various people, made to feel welcome and accepted, especially by Santina's mother and brother, by Clay's cousin Vicky, Santina's partner in the interior decorating firm, and Vicky's husband, Joe, who'd extended an invitation to get together for dinner as soon as she and Clay could manage.

All this went to making Linda feel a part of a wonderful whole. She loved the closeness, the camaraderie of belonging that was the Buchanan clan. Growing up, this had been one of her dreams.

Most of all, she loved being able to walk hand in hand with Clay, to touch him whenever she wanted, to share comments. Her engagement gave her license to indulge her stored-up daydreams.

And it had altered Clay in some ways, too.

He'd surprised her earlier when they were walking in the garden by pulling her down to the enclosed wooden swing. There, amidst the trellis roses winding around the structure, he'd shown her that he was more than the cool corporate executive. His kiss was wild and wonderful, drawing her into another world, a place where only they existed. Sounds evaporated, smells faded. The only reality was his mouth, warm and possessive on hers, his hand tunneled in her hair, holding her close, deepening the encounter.

Her fingers wove their way through the soft hair that curled about his neck, lost in the sensations he evoked so easily.

"Clay." That was followed by the noise of a throat clearing loudly.

At the intrusive sound, they broke apart, each breathing hard.

"Sorry," Burke apologized, amusement dancing in his brown eyes. "I was asked if I'd seen you. Dad's going to make a toast to the happy couple and he wanted you both there." A smile curled his lips. "I'll go tell them you're coming."

"So much for privacy," Clay murmured as he rose, helping Linda up.

As they'd woven their way through the garden to rejoin the party, Linda thought it was probably a good thing that Burke came just when he did. She was feeling out of control. Spinning into another realm, one completely sensory. The day was plenty hot already, and Clay's kisses made it ten times more so. The air was sticky, thick with humidity. But that's not what made her feel limp, as though each breath were an effort. It was him.

The party, more like a fiesta, was in full swing. Fireworks were promised for later that evening. Buckles came undone and buttons unbuttoned as everyone there made an ample dent in the large quantity of food displayed.

As the mood of the day mellowed, Linda took the opportunity to sneak away from the festivities. She drifted from the crowds, wandering along a stone walk that led to the chapel. Oak and pecan trees, along with wildflowers, lined the pathway.

Opening the carved wooden door, Linda stepped inside. When she did, a sense of tranquility swept over her. Light spilled into the interior of the structure from the side windows and from the redesigned roof.

In her mind's eye Linda envisioned it redecorated for a wedding. Flowers were everywhere, spilling from containers, petals strewn along the aisle. She could imagine Clay standing there, at the other end, waiting for her, flanked by his two brothers, a look of longing in his face.

The only thing that darkened that vision was that her husband-to-be didn't love her. Longing on his part was her fantasy. For him, it was a simple marriage of convenience. She saw the wedding through eyes of love—he saw it with eyes oblivious to love.

"It's a lovely place, isn't it?"

Linda spun around at the sound of the voice behind her. "Yes," she replied, staring into the face of her fiancé's mother.

"Clay told me that you wanted to get married here."

Linda lowered herself to one of the polished wooden pews. "If you wouldn't mind?"

Santina took a seat in the pew opposite. "Why should I?"

"There's something very compelling about this place," Linda stated. "A sense of peace and serenity. I've never been overly religious, but the feeling I get in here is very special. Cherished. Protected." She looked at Santina. "Does that sound funny?"

"Not in the least." Santina tilted her head and looked around the room. "This little chapel has seen many happy times. It's celebrated triumphs and withstood tragedies. A wedding performed here would be especially blessed, I think. Love sanctioned by the memories of the past." A small smile curved her lips. "Good vibes people call it today."

"Positive energy," Linda said with a smile.

"Exactly. I assume that you'd like to make a few minor changes around here for the wedding?"

"With your permission?"

"No problem," Santina assured her. "Just how did you see this place?"

"Very simple." Linda explained the vision she had. "Quiet. With a large quantity of flowers, mainly roses. Warm colors, like yellow, gold, orange, apricot. And candles. Votives, tapers, whatever. Lots of them as I'd like the ceremony to be held at twilight.

"Music. There's got to be music. Clay's a jazz buff, but I think classical would serve us best that day. I'd like everything to be elegant without being overwhelming."

"If you'd let me," Santina offered, "I'd like to help. Would you trust me to see to the chapel? That it's decorated as you wish?"

"Would you? That'd be a big help, but I don't want to burden you. I know that you have a full-time job, too."

"It'll be my pleasure," Santina insisted. "Besides, this is what I do. You don't have much time and I'm sure you have plenty of other things to handle in order to be ready. Now, do you have a dress?"

"I do have something in mind." Linda's eyes lit up as she thought about the dress she'd seen last week in a small boutique in Houston. Totally distinct and different.

"From the look on your face, it must be something very lovely?"

"It is."

"Good. I love it when people know what they want. Saves time, trouble and, hopefully, heartache in the long run. You have that in common with my son. Clay's always known what he's wanted." Santina changed topics. "What about a guest list?"

"It's small. We want to keep this intimate. Family and friends only. There'll be time later to do the big party. Clay wants to have a fancy reception in Houston after we get back from the honeymoon."

"Get used to that, my dear. He's a social animal."

"I know," Linda agreed. "That's not a problem for me. I enjoy going out." She took a deep breath and wet her lips, wanting the other woman to know the truth that was in her heart, feeling that she could confide in Clay's mother and that the older woman would keep her secret. "I love your son."

Santina smiled and said softly, "I know."

"You do?"

Santina nodded her head. "As a decorator, I have to size up prospective clients pretty quickly—to get some kind of idea what will suit them. A style that they'll be comfortable living with. Over the years, that's enabled me to see past the obvious. To be able to cut to the chase, as Burke would say. I could see how much you cared for Clay when I saw the two of you together today. It was, to use another clichéd phrase, written on your face.''

''I plan to make him happy.''

The older woman's eyes were kind. ''I sincerely hope that you can, my dear. My son is a good man, one who doesn't do or take things lightly. When he stands with you and pledges himself, he'll mean it. He's like my husband in that respect. Clay takes care of his own. Whatever he starts, he sees through.'' She rose. ''Now, what say we get back to the party before someone sends out a search party?''

''Thank you.''

Santina regarded the younger woman. ''For what?''

''For giving your blessing. It means more than I can say.''

Santina impulsively hugged her future daughter-in-law. ''You're welcome.''

''Linda seems like a fine lady to me,'' Burke said to Clay before he took a deep swig from a long-necked bottle of beer.

Clay, puffing on an expensive cigar and leaning on the smooth, well-worn fence, gazed out into the paddock, watching several horses frisking about in the close-cropped grass. ''She is.''

''Right genuine, too.''

''It's in the blood. Remember, Linda's Ethan Douglas's granddaughter.''

Burke sliced a glance to his right in Clay's direction. ''Good stock.''

Clay laughed. ''Spoken like a true rancher. It was he

who introduced me to her right here ten years ago, at another one of our barbecues.''

''Damn. Small world.'' One of the horses ambled over, looking for a treat, which Burke supplied.

''Isn't it?'' Clay stretched out his hand and patted the colt's neck. ''What goes around comes around, sometimes in the strangest ways.''

Burke took another swallow of his beer as the animal suddenly galloped off. ''Any reason for the rush to get married?''

Clay took a long drag on his cigar, blowing smoke high into the air. ''Besides the fact that we don't want to wait, no. Guess I don't hold with long engagements.'' He smiled. ''I'll leave that to brother Drew.''

Burke smiled. ''Yeah, that's too long for me.'' He finished the rest of the bottle. ''Things worked out for the best, didn't they?''

He knew what Burke was asking—if things were finally back where they belonged between them, before matters had gotten so complicated. If Clay had forgiven him without reservation for marrying Emma.

Clay reached out his hand and squeezed his brother's shoulder. ''Yeah, they did. I know now,'' he added in an attempt to ease any lingering doubt in Burke's mind, ''that Emma and I wouldn't have been right for each other in the long run. She's your kind of woman, just as Linda is mine. She and I—we speak the same language, think the same way about a lot of things.''

''When did you know?''

''That I wanted to marry her?''

''Yeah.''

''I think I knew before, but it was after her sister's wedding that it really hit me.''

''Love's kinda funny like that, ain't it? One minute

you're going along, comfortable with your life, and the next—bam!'' Burke slapped his hand on the fence. Several of the horses reacted by snapping up their heads and looking in the brothers' direction. ''She's there, filling a place you didn't even know was empty. Opening up your eyes and your heart.''

The normally laconic Burke was positively poetic, Clay thought.

''That how it was with you, Clay?''

Clay didn't want to shatter his brother's illusions as to why he was marrying Linda. Better, he rationalized, to agree. It would save time and an argument about his motives. Burke wouldn't understand, loving as he did. Neither would Drew, nor his parents. Love was their ultimate foundation for marriage.

Clay disliked lying to any member of his family. Sometimes though, it was the best and only course available. The reasons behind his marriage were no one's business but his own. His and Linda's. So he wasn't deeply in love? Then again, neither was she. Like the Tina Turner song proclaimed, ''What's Love Got to Do with It?'' He and Linda were better off, their marriage more secure, without the entanglements of love. They had what counted: friendship, honesty, caring, respect.

A smile tugged at Clay's mouth. And their relationship had an unexpected bonus—passion. Sexual heat, slow and simmering. Each encounter took it a step further, a degree hotter.

''Yeah, Burke, that's how it was for me.''

''I'm glad.''

''So can I count on you to stand up with me?''

Brown eyes met blue as Burke took the olive branch handed him. ''I'd be mighty pleased, big brother.''

''I was hoping you'd feel that way.''

Burke chuckled, any lingering tension dissolved. "Guess that means I'm gonna have to get out my best suit."

"Hmm," Clay said, "I think we'll talk about that."

"Later," Burke insisted. "I don't know about you, but I'm ready for another go-round with the chuck wagon. There's a piece of peach pie that has my name on it."

"Sounds good to me."

Chapter Ten

"Am I making a mistake?" Linda asked anxiously as Sandy helped her into her wedding dress.

Her sister gave her a solid hug as she buttoned up the back of the dress. "You're following your heart, aren't you?"

Stunned by that remark, Linda turned her head and looked at the younger woman.

"Yes, Linda, I know," Sandy said softly. "I've known for quite some time."

"Known what?"

Sandy shrugged. "That you're in love with Clay. That you have been since we were teenagers."

Linda was astonished by her sister's perspicacity. "You can't have known since then."

"Not then, I was too much into myself at that time. It was much later that I saw the clues that were there. He's all you talked about after you went to that party with

Granddad and I thought it was just a crush. I mean he was handsome, rich and plenty sexy. Hey, what wasn't to like? From one of Texas's oldest and best families." Sandy located the embroidered high-heeled ivory shoes Linda was searching for while she was speaking.

Sandy continued as her sister slipped the shoes on. "I started to put the puzzle together when you were in college. When I asked you where you wanted to work when you graduated, you named his company right off the bat. Never hesitated."

"I wanted to work with someone I respected." Linda lifted a tall plastic bottle of water from the nearby dressing table and took a long drink. "I guess I've always known who I am and what I want out of life."

"And you're sure it's him?"

"Why wouldn't I be?"

"Does he love you as much as you love him?"

Linda checked her makeup in a small mirror. It was a way to avoid Sandy's ultrasharp glance. "And what if he doesn't?" she asked, hoping that the claims of the lipstick manufacturer for a kiss-proof mouth would prove true.

"You're my big sister, Linda, and I want you to be happy. That's all I care about."

"I *will* be," Linda insisted. "Stop worrying."

"Sometimes I used to wonder if it was Mama's continual harping on being a 'success' that might have forced you into a career you didn't want."

"She had nothing to do with it," Linda stated adamantly. "Actually, I'd say Granddad was more of an influence than either of our folks. When we spent summers with him and Grandmom in the Hill Country, I used to pester him to teach me about banking and about finance. What was great was that he never treated me like a kid. He encouraged me. And when he took me to that picnic at the Encantadora where I met Clay, I thought it was an omen, that I was on the right track.''

"God, I hope Clay knows what a prize he's getting.''

Linda smiled in a confident manner. "I intend to make sure that he does. Every day for the rest of our lives.''

"I know this is kind of awkward and really none of my business, but have you ever been with anyone?''

Linda shook her head.

"I didn't think so.''

"It's all right," Linda said, "Clay knows.''

"That must have surprised the hell out of him.''

"Let's say that he wasn't expecting that bit of news.''

"When was that?''

"While we were in New York, things were getting pretty intense between us.''

"So was it great?''

"Great?'' Linda realized then what her sister was asking her about. "Oh, you want to know what it was like with Clay? I'll let you know.''

The truth dawned on Sandy. "You mean you're getting married and you haven't slept together yet?''

"Uh-huh," Linda acknowledged. "That's what our honeymoon's for.''

"Whose idea was that?''

"It was a mutual decision.''

"I gotta hand it to you, sis, I don't think I could have waited that long to be with the man I love. If for no other reason, curiosity would have killed me.''

Linda confided, "Actually, I don't think I could have waited much longer. When I'm in his arms and he kisses me, all I want to do is have it last for hours.''

"Honey," Sandy said, and chuckled, "I don't want to break it to you but no man, not even a Buchanan, lasts for hours.''

Linda giggled at her sister's saucy comment. It broke the intensity of their conversation. "Even I know that. What I meant was that I wanted to be with him for hours. You know, to be close. Without phones or faxes. No beepers or pagers. Just us. You don't know what it's like when he kisses me."

"Pretty good, I'd imagine."

Linda scoffed. "That doesn't quite cover it. I feel electricity, heat, magic. All at once. The kind of sensations you pray for, or read about."

"Hot damn!" Sandy exclaimed. "If you two have that kind of chemistry going for you, then you're already ahead of the game."

"I hope so."

"I know so. When I first met Clay, he struck me as a man who likes and expects the best that life has to offer. He's getting that in you, Linda. And if, God forbid, he doesn't know it yet, then I'm sure he will and soon. Love like you have for him is the kind that changes lives. Alters the person who receives it for the better. It has to." Sandy looked her sister up and down and then hugged her tight. "Now, have you got everything? Old, new, borrowed and blue?"

"Blue's covered." Linda pointed to her bridal bouquet, a mixture of pale yellow roses and bluebonnets. "I'm wearing the old." She indicated the gorgeous pair of earrings that matched her ring. Clay had given them to her last night, totally surprising her. He'd knocked on her door after she'd retired and when she opened it, he stood there.

"What's this?" she'd asked. Her hair hung in a hastily gathered ponytail and her face was freshly scrubbed, clean of makeup. Moisturizer and her cotton pajamas were all she wore.

"A little something for the bridal tradition. This fits into the old category."

She accepted the box, opening it up. When she saw what was inside she said, "You shouldn't have."

"*I* wanted to," he'd insisted, "which is good enough for me." He crossed the threshold of her door for only a moment as he cupped her chin and put his mouth to hers for a tender kiss. "Until tomorrow. Sleep well."

Linda's heart had soared with happiness. There was hope, she thought. There had to be.

"What about new?" Sandy asked, bringing Linda back to reality.

"My dress and shoes are new," she answered. "All I need is something borrowed."

"May I supply that?"

The sisters turned in unison as they heard the female voice from the open bedroom door.

Emma stood there, a smile on her face. In her hand she held a lace-edged silk handkerchief. "Santina gave this to me when I married Burke. It's been in this family for generations."

Linda willingly took the linen handkerchief from Emma. It was lovely, thin with age, delicate, with a set of the entwined initials *VRB* artfully embroidered into one corner. She recognized the initials immediately. The first American Buchanan bride had owned this keepsake.

"That's very kind of you," Linda said. "Thank you."

"No need." Emma kissed Linda's cheek. "Think of it as passing the torch from one Buchanan wife to another. Now we share a special bond, one of the heart. Love for two very different, very special men who happen to be brothers."

"I'm going to go check on the transportation," Sandy said, leaving the two women alone. "Be right back."

"I'm very fond of Clay," Emma stated sincerely. "We share a close friendship."

"I know."

"You also know that I hurt him a few years back. It wasn't intentional, but I did nonetheless."

Linda sharpened her gaze on the other woman. "That's in the past."

Emma smiled. "Good. I'm glad to hear you say that. I was afraid that you might have some doubts or questions."

"I don't." That was the truth. Before she'd accompanied Clay home to make their announcement, Linda had had some lingering doubts about Clay's feelings for Emma. Being at the ranch that weekend had erased them from her mind. He was relaxed and happy about Burke and his wife. There were no sad looks, no wistful glances in Emma's direction. Everything was out in the open, no hidden agendas as far as she could tell.

"Well, I just wanted you to know that I'm happy for you. And, I'd like to give you my wedding gift now."

"You didn't have to get us anything," Linda said. "I can't imagine what else we could use. You should see the gifts stacked up in Clay's house so far. Unbelievable."

"This is more on the personal side. I left it in the hallway. If you don't mind, I'll bring it in."

"Please do."

Linda wondered briefly what it was. When she saw, her eyes widened in amazement.

Emma stood behind the huge framed canvas, holding it aloft so that Linda could see the picture.

It was a portrait of Linda and Clay. "When did you do this?"

"I started it the day that you left. I made sketches of the two of you while you were here that weekend and then I studied several of the photographs that Jessie took. From all that I found what I was looking for."

"It's wonderful." Somehow, it also made her wedding seem more real, more like a continuation of a tradition. Like they were a part of history, reaching back and stretching forward.

"I hoped that you'd like it."

"Saying I like it would be an understatement. Has Clay seen it?"

"No. I wanted you to be the first. Outside of Burke, of course." As it was heavy, Emma placed it against a large, plush chair in the room.

Linda stepped closer, scanning the painting. She remembered the pose captured there. They were pictured outside, the hot Texas sun depicted in the scene overhead burnishing their hair. Clay stood in back of her, clad in a cotton polo shirt in terra-cotta, a smile graced his mouth, with the hint of dimples creasing his cheeks. Linda loved that look, which Emma had successfully captured. She stood in front of him, wearing a camp shirt in royal blue. His left arm was around her shoulders and her left hand, with the ring capturing the light, was atop his. Her head was tilted slightly back, a smile on her face.

A brass plaque on the bottom of the elegantly carved cherry frame revealed how Emma had titled the portrait. *The Claim,* and Linda and Clay's names were inscribed, along with the date.

"I'll cherish this." Tears formed in Linda's eyes and she made quick use of the borrowed silk hanky to capture them before they could fall. "But why the title?"

"Simple," Emma stated. "The way Clay was holding you represented, to me at least, a man staking a claim to a woman quite loudly."

"You think so?" Linda didn't quite believe that; however, it was gratifying to hear it from Emma's lips.

"Yes, I do."

Linda reached out and squeezed the other woman's hand. "I appreciate your stepping in at the last minute to take my friend's place as bridesmaid." Emma looked beautiful in the turquoise tea-length dress of georgette that floated around her legs. It went well with her reddish brown curls.

"I was happy to do it," Emma responded, "though I do hope that she's doing better."

"A little. I called New York this morning and talked to Meg's husband."

"You said that she had an accident?"

Linda nodded her head. "That's what her husband told me when he called the other day to let me know why she wouldn't be coming. He said she fell down the stairs in their apartment, breaking a couple of ribs and her left arm. She had a concussion, too. Luckily it wasn't worse. She could easily have been killed or paralyzed."

"Life is so precious," Emma remarked. "When I look at Burke, my son, or Jessie, I thank God for each day with them. I can't imagine if anything happened to them."

"I know what you mean. I couldn't imagine my life without Clay in it."

"Let's hope you won't ever have to." After making that declaration, Emma checked her watch. "Oops. I'd better go downstairs and see what's keeping your sister. Are you okay by yourself?"

"Fine. Go ahead. I'd actually like a few minutes to myself anyway."

"See you downstairs then."

When Emma left her, Linda took another swallow from her water bottle to ease the dryness she felt in her mouth.

Soon she'd be married. A bride. A wife. She'd add Clay's name to hers. Forever linked.

But that's not what the paper she'd signed the other day had stipulated. It was an "in case" document. In case the marriage didn't last, she would get *X* amount of money. In case they dissolved their union, she'd get a fair share of his life. As if money could compensate her for a broken heart should they break up.

She hadn't wanted to sign it. Not because it wasn't generous with terms. It was. Overly. It was the cold, calculating nature of the language. Written in legalese, it detailed every possibility, every contingency. Clay had urged Linda to let her own lawyer have a look at it.

Right then and there she had wanted to scream, "I don't need your money, Clay. That's not why I'm marrying you. And if it fails, I don't need you to take care of me. I can do that for myself."

But she hadn't. Linda knew the rationale behind the document. No one with his money and standing even considered not having his assets covered in any deal, and this was how he looked at their wedding—as a deal. She understood the need while mourning the loss of trust it represented. For Clay, love came with a price tag. It was the smart thing to do.

So, after carefully reading the pages of paper, she signed the document, for his peace of mind. To refuse would have roused his suspicions. She'd been unable to tell him how much she loved him. If she declared that her love came without cost to him, that it was a gift, free and clear, she feared he wouldn't believe it. So she'd kept quiet, hugging the secret to her heart.

"Are you certain?" he'd asked.

She'd looked up from the desk in her office where he'd presented her with the papers. "I trust you, Clay. What's listed here is more than fair. A good contract all around, I'd say.'' Still it had hurt Linda to sign her name on the spaces indicated by the little tabs. Like admitting defeat before it even happened.

It brought to mind their reasons for getting married as she adjusted her flower-trimmed hat and pulled on her lacy gloves.

He was marrying for a wife.

She was marrying for love.

Eventually, she prayed, he would come to feel the same.

''Not too long now, big brother,'' Drew drawled as he helped Clay on with his jacket. ''Only a short time left as a carefree bachelor.''

Clay shot his younger-by-two-years brother a glance. ''Then you're next.''

Drew grinned, his full lower lip curled. ''Can't wait.'' He checked out his appearance in the bedroom's full-length mirror, adjusting his tie.

''Satisfied?'' Clay asked wryly.

''As long as Kate is,'' Drew countered, referring to his fiancée, ''then I'm happy.''

'''And then there were none.'''

''How about that?'' Drew asked, brown eyes twinkling. ''Who would have thought that we'd all find the women we weren't even looking for?''

Clay laughed at his brother's remark while a sultry jazz-pop singer sang in the background, her voice coming from the radio singing ''Smooth Operator.''

The song sobered his mood. That was him all right. He had everyone fooled, all except his bride. She knew the truth. He wouldn't lie to her, not now, not ever. This wedding was a convenience, for both of them.

He listened to the lyrics as he took a linen square and wiped off his glasses. Heart of ice? No, he preferred to think he possessed a heart of steel, forged hard as a Toledo blade, invulnerable to the follies of love.

"Do you have the ring?"

Drew tapped his pocket. "Safe and sound. I was surprised that there was only one in the box."

"That's because I already wear one. That's enough for me."

Drew, who wore a similar signet ring to Clay's, looked askance at his brother. When no response to his comment came, he let it slide. Clay was a man unto himself, never one to follow the herd. A maverick. Then again, he supposed that all of them were in their own ways.

A big, booming baritone voice asked, "There's a rumor that there's a wedding taking place 'round these parts today? Think it's true?" Noah Buchanan walked in, followed by his youngest son.

"I'd heard that, too," Clay responded with a welcoming smile.

"Then I suggest that we get a move on. It's getting near to dusk and you should be to the chapel before your bride, son." He held up a 35-mm camera. "But first, a picture. All of you together."

Burke joined his brothers and posed for a snapshot, their arms linked about one another's shoulders.

"One more just to make sure," Noah ordered as he brought the camera up and focused, getting the shot. "Perfect." He set it aside on the nearby dresser top. "Before you go, I just want you all to know something," he stated. "I'm very proud of each of my sons. You've all enriched my life and Santina's more than we ever thought possible. I can only wish you each similar joy with your own children.

"As for love, I'm grateful you've all found it. If you only discover half of what your mother and I have experienced in our life together, you'll be blessed by heaven in ways you won't believe. Love in all its forms is the glue that holds this family together. It makes us stronger, braver, better people. Able to handle whatever life throws our way."

Noah grinned, his teeth showing white against his salt-and-pepper close-trimmed beard. "Okay, end of speech." He went up to where his sons stood together, kissed and embraced each of his boys.

Burke reminded the room, "Time to go, fellas. We wouldn't want the bride to beat us there."

Clay took a last look in the mirror. "I'm ready," he said confidently.

Burke had come up with a wonderful idea to ferry the bride the distance from the house to the chapel without her walking. He had several of the ranch hands set to cleaning one of the old carriages, which had been in storage, polishing the worn leather and sprucing up the interior. It was decked out with ribbons and flowers, white paper bells trailing from the back, pulled by a team of matched grays.

Linda adored the idea. A link from the Buchanan past to her present. Burke's thoughtfulness touched her deeply, as did the warmth shown by all the family toward her. She couldn't wait to show Clay the portrait that Emma had painted of the two of them. And she knew just where she wanted it hung—in her office at Buchanan Enterprises. There she would be able to look at it whenever she wanted.

"Nervous?" Sandy asked as they climbed, with assistance, into the open-top vehicle.

"A little," Linda confessed as she settled in.

"So was I. You'll get over it." She smoothed the skirt of her soft peach dress over her crossed legs.

Linda broached a subject that she and her sister hadn't mentioned before. "You do understand why I didn't want our folks here, didn't you?"

"Linda, this is your day."

"I just didn't want them to spoil it for me. They were barely civil to each other at your wedding. Clay understands, thank God. He was there and saw firsthand what happens when they're in the same place for more than a few minutes." Linda took a deep breath. "I'll send them both an invitation to the reception. That ought to keep Mother happy. And it'll be big enough that they don't have to bump into each other as they would have here."

"I can hear it now," Sandy remarked without rancor. "She'll be able to tell all her friends that her daughters married well. One to a doctor, the other to a gazillionaire."

"And not one word about how well we've done on our own with our respective careers," Linda added.

"Not her style," Sandy commented wryly.

"Which is why I didn't want her here to put a damper on things."

"What about Dad?"

"He and Stephanie are visiting with Josh and his family in Seattle. He told me of his plans when I called to tell him about my engagement."

"It's kind of fitting to have Granddad walk you down the aisle anyway, I guess."

"That's what I thought. You and he are the only family I want or need here today. Besides, after the ceremony, I'll have Clay and all his kin." Or as much of himself as he'll allow me to have. It's not as if I didn't know that coming into this marriage. He's been honest and up-front.

"Almost there."

Lanterns had been staked out along the path, throwing a warm glow onto the early evening. The day was warm, but not as hot as it had been earlier in the week. A thunderstorm the night before had knocked down the temperature and pushed aside the excess humidity, granting them a reprieve.

"There's Ethan." Linda's mouth curved into a relieved smile. Her grandfather was waiting to escort her to Clay.

Excitement zipped through her veins. She'd been forbidden to enter the chapel this morning to see what Santina had accomplished. Her soon-to-be mother-in-law wanted the decorations to be a surprise so Linda humored her. Why not? She had every faith in Santina's ability to turn out a wonderful scenario.

The driver halted the carriage in front of the chapel. He jumped down from his seat and held open the door so that Sandy and Linda could alight. Emma was already inside, as she'd left the house with Burke and their children.

"You ready, sweetheart?" Ethan asked, coming down the two stone steps that led to the entrance while Sandy hurried inside to meet her escort, Drew.

Linda replied, "Since I was sixteen, Granddad." She noted that the steps were strewn with a bevy of rose petals in the colors she'd requested.

The old man chuckled at her statement. "That's my girl." He gave her a quick, assessing look. "Your grandmother would have been so pleased if she could have seen you today. You're every bit as stunning as she was on the day that I married her. Yes, sirree, you've got the same look about you that she had. Like Lauren Bacall in 'To Have and Have Not.' Sultry. One hundred percent genuine.'' He patted Linda's gloved hand and kissed her cheek. "I love you, girl. Don't you ever forget it."

"I won't."

"Now I imagine that Clay's kicking up his heels inside, so we'd better get started."

As they entered the chapel, Linda blinked slowly. It was just as she'd asked for. The scent of the various arrangements of roses floated in the air, their shades blending to form a warm bath of color in the muted light of the multitude of candles.

She looked to the right and heard the soft sounds of a chamber group as they played Vivaldi. The assembled friends and relatives stood, their glances locked on to her. She recognized her secretary and Clay's, along with Basil and Lettie as they lifted their cameras for a picture. At the far end of the flagstone aisle stood her sister and Emma, along with the trio of Buchanan brothers.

It was Clay who temporarily stole the breath from her throat. Everyone else dissolved away, as if swallowed by fog. There was only him. Standing there, waiting, a deep, welcoming smile on his face, looking extraordinarily handsome in his charcoal gray lightweight wool cutaway jacket over a pearl gray vest and striped black-and-silver ascot tie over thin-striped trousers. He wore a single white rose in the buttonhole.

Linda wet her lips with the tip of her tongue. This was it. The moment she'd waited for. Finally.

The chamber group struck up the wedding march and Linda started down the aisle toward Clay.

She looked incredible. Unlike brides he'd seen before who went overboard with frills and tons of fabric, Linda kept it simple. Classic. She wore an ankle-length dress, a layer of lace over an underdress of creamy ivory satin with see-through lace sleeves that dipped to her elbow. In her gloved hands she carried a small, compact bouquet.

Clay approved wholeheartedly.

His eyes met Ethan's and the much older man smiled broadly as he led Linda to her groom. Clay gave him a slight nod of his head, acknowledging the debt that he owed.

"Dearly beloved..." the minister began.

Chapter Eleven

"What are you thinking about?"

Linda glanced up at her husband, her lips curving in a smile. *Husband.* That word sounded so beautiful, especially when coupled with the name Clay Buchanan.

"How everything went off without a hitch and what a great job your mother did with the chapel," she replied. "It was like something out of a fairy tale. Extraordinary."

Clay handed her a fluted glass of champagne and took a seat opposite her in the jet. "My mother's not one to do a job less than a thousand percent. And with this, it was for love." Most of the interior lights in the cabin had been dimmed so that the passengers could sleep if they wanted to as it was after one in the morning.

Linda sipped the bubbly liquid, the muted light giving a feeling of intimacy in the luxury plane. "What about Basil and Lettie?"

''They're fast asleep up front. Which is where I thought you'd be, asleep.''

''Too wired to sleep, I'm afraid.''

''I know what you mean. We could have simply gone back to the house in Houston and put off the trip until tomorrow.'' He rephrased that as he realized the time. ''Or rather later today. There was no real hurry.''

''Why not?'' she asked, a hint of excitement in her voice. ''After listening to you describe how stunning this place is, I can't wait to see it.''

''Trouble is in leaving this late, we'll be arriving just as the sun comes up.''

''What's wrong with that?''

''You'll be too tired to really appreciate it,'' he cautioned. ''Sunrises there need to be savored. Over a lingering cup of coffee, a bowl of fresh fruit and the view from the bedroom terrace in my—sorry, force of habit—*our* house. Sunlight hitting the water, streaking it with color. White clouds so puffy they look like balls of cotton floating in the sky.''

''Sounds perfect.''

''It's paradise.'' He sipped from his own glass, like her, too wired to sleep right away. ''All the more so because my visits there are so infrequent.''

''Maybe we should rethink that?'' It crossed Linda's mind to wonder if he'd been there with any other women. Would she find touches in the house from a previous girlfriend? Would there be ghosts of past lovers in his bed that she'd have to deal with? Comparisons that she might not measure up to?

She couldn't help the doubts, much as she tried to ignore them. They would pop up at odd times and when they did, Linda had to tell herself that she was his wife now. The rest didn't matter.

"I think that's what makes me appreciate the house so much, I'm not there frequently enough for it to get stale. A little bit of hedonistic heaven goes a long way for me."

She teased, "All work and no play…"

"Makes Buchanan Enterprises' board of directors very happy," he quipped in return. "Why don't you try and get some rest? I've got to clear up something and I might as well take care of it now as later."

Clay leaned over and gave her a quick kiss on the cheek, got up and walked to the back of the cabin where a desk had been installed, sat down and went to work on his laptop.

He was driven to keep occupied. If he and Linda had been alone in the plane he would have gladly sacrificed work, but with Basil and his wife aboard, that put a damper on spontaneity. This was their wedding night and she was spending it alone. Or at least unattended while he tried to keep busy.

In the soft light Linda glanced at the rings she wore. Her girlhood dream was now a definite reality. A platinum band had joined her engagement ring, making this a binding contract. Signed, sealed and delivered. Her true-love Texan's bride.

She had to confess, if only to herself, that she'd been disappointed that Clay hadn't chosen to wear a wedding band. What to her was a symbol, a token of exclusivity and pride, obviously hadn't meant the same thing to him.

Well, she'd tackle that later. Other memories floated into her brain. Lively, happy moments at the ranch after the ceremony. Total joy at being surrounded by friends and family. The cherished tokens of the happiness everyone was sharing. Clay's obvious delight with the portrait that Emma had given them. Their shared joy at the gift from his parents of several items from the family's collection of heirlooms. A silver dressing table set for her; a matching silver shaving set for Clay. They'd brought them along for good luck. From his brother Drew and his fiancée Kate they had received a large antique blanket chest, overflowing with items. Burke's held an element of surprise; he'd promised that their gift would arrive when they returned from their honeymoon.

His family had showered them with presents. It wasn't the number or the type that touched Linda's heart—it was that each was given with so much love and genuine affection.

As were the wedding cakes made by Lettie. Four in all, each one unique in style and ingredients, each a marvel to behold and an even better one to taste. Samples of all four were packed and set into the refrigerator on the jet. Linda wanted time later to have more of each, hopefully sharing them in an intimate setting with Clay.

In bed?

Anticipation brought a catch in her breath, a tightening in her stomach. She'd waited for so long. What would it be like when they finally made love?

In one of her suitcases she'd packed a nightgown she hoped would please Clay. When she'd seen it she knew she had to have it, especially to wipe away the memories of her tailored cotton pj's from his mind. This confection would heat the blood, inflame the senses. Or so she thought when she glimpsed it on the model in the lingerie store. Long and clinging, a testament to femininity. It was confident, sexy and daring. When she'd slipped it on in the dressing room, she'd felt empowered. Bold. Ready to put it to the test.

Maybe making love was routine for him, she thought as she drifted off, but it was hardly that for her.

Clay had trouble keeping his mind focused on the business sites he was scanning in an effort to hold his rising hormones in check. So much for the calm, cool exterior he was presenting to his bride. If only they'd been alone. He would have cheerfully abandoned any pretense of working long ago and given in to the need to show her what the phrase "mile-high club" meant. Discretion put a cap on that idea. It was his wedding night and he was surfing the net for company, eager for something, anything, to take his mind off the woman sitting not far from him. The smell of her perfume. The curve of her lips. The feel of her in his arms. The look in her eyes. The thought of what she'd be like in his bed.

He'd slept with other women before but couldn't recall one who'd made him hungrier to sample her. Aching, with a burning need to explore.

Was it the lure of being first? Or simply the lure of her?

The latter, he answered quickly. Her passion was real. Her responses fresh and charming. A crackerjack mind and a personality to boot.

Clay congratulated himself on a choice well made. If he'd designed a blueprint, he couldn't have come closer to what he wanted in a wife than Linda.

His family had taken to her immediately. Her warmth had won them all over and, in doing so, removed any lingering doubts in anyone's mind that he wasn't getting on with his life.

He recalled the look on her expressive face when he'd given her the earrings. It was alive with delight. Her eyes had sparkled like the gems, their color incandescent. He imagined her reaction when he eventually gave her the bracelet and the necklace. She took such abundant joy, no matter what the gift.

As if drawn by an unknown force, Clay raised his head and gazed in Linda's direction. She'd fallen asleep, her red gold hair tumbled about her face and shoulders. Soon he would see it spread upon the linen pillowcase in his bedroom. Soft shoulders would peek out from the top sheet. Maybe one leg would have escaped from the material and he'd glimpse a trim calf or a hint of thigh.

Was he anxious?

You bet!

Was he eager?

Damn straight!

A trace of a smile curved his lips. Soon he'd know the sweet rewards of his bargain.

Linda stepped onto the terrace, sniffing the early after-noon air with its fragrant scents of frangipani and spices. Red bougainvillea trailed along the wrought-iron grill-work and down the side of the house. The villa was mod-eled after a Spanish-style hacienda, giving Linda the feel-ing that she'd stepped back in time.

Clay had been right about the view. It was spectacular. Mountains in the background, miles and miles of sea all around. The colors of the water ranged from deepest sap-phire to resplendent turquoise to shimmering aqua. Gentle waves lapped upon white sand beaches.

It wouldn't surprise her to see a pirate crew sail into view at any minute.

She'd woken refreshed from several hours of sleep and had to see for herself exactly what Clay had described. Paradise, he'd called it. It certainly looked the part.

She leaned over and glanced at the terrace below. Flow-ers of all sizes and types abounded. They graced the walk-ways, followed along the stone steps that led to the beach or were gathered in colorful beds.

"Mrs. Buchanan, you're awake. Care to join me?"

Linda spied Clay, sitting under a large-umbrella-covered white iron table, flashing her a big Texas grin in greeting.

"Give me a minute, Mr. Buchanan and I'd be happy to," she answered, dashing back inside. She pulled open a drawer to the wide bureau and removed a pair of cuffed shorts and a cotton top. She'd fallen asleep in her bra and panties, being too tired to remove them when she'd arrived. Tossing off her cotton robe, she hastily removed her underwear, replacing it with fresh, then finished dressing. She pulled her hair into a simple ponytail and slipped on a pair of white canvas shoes and left the room, eager to join Clay.

He sat on the terrace, enjoying the feel of the breeze as it played over him. Trade winds kept the island from becoming unbearably hot. Here they blew gently, balancing out the warmth of the sun.

He sipped a large mixed-fruit beverage, chilled to perfection. A plate of fresh fruit, cut into bite-size pieces, was set before him, along with a flaky croissant.

Earlier when they'd arrived, he'd played the gentleman, insisting that Linda take the master suite for herself, while he would make do with a guest room, at least for the time being, which he hoped would be of short duration. Clay wanted to get this marriage started and that meant being husband and wife in all senses of the words.

"You were right, Clay, this place is wonderful."

Linda joined him and sat down in the chair that he held for her. As she did so, he bent and kissed her mouth.

It was soft and sweet, clinging momentarily, hinting at suppressed passion. Automatically Linda lifted one hand and circled his neck, holding him close for a moment before they broke apart.

"That's a great way to start the day."

She laughed softly, finding it easy to slip into the role of wife. "Dare I say breakfast of champions?"

"Whatever you'd like, darlin'." He took his seat. "Would you like something to eat?"

"I'm starved." She cast a covetous eye on what he was having. "That looks pretty good."

He picked up a portable phone and pressed a series of numbers. "Yes, Lettie, my wife would like one of the same."

"Ask her to add a cup of coffee, too," Linda said.

Clay nodded and gave the request, replacing the phone. "It'll be right out. Now, what would you like to do after we eat?"

"How about a walk along the beach?"

Clay took her hand in his and kissed her palm, moving slowly down to her wrist. "I think that can be arranged."

Warmth surged through her body at the contact of his mouth to her skin. Linda wondered if he could feel the increased beat of her pulse?

Basil broke the spell of the moment when he appeared, wooden tray in hand, carrying her food.

"Good afternoon, Mrs. Buchanan," he said with a friendly grin as he placed the items in front of her.

A pleased smile was her response. "And a very good day to you, Basil."

The butler nodded and returned to the house, leaving them alone once more.

She tasted the juice and sampled the fruit. "Heavenly."

They ate their meal, content without the necessity of conversation. Occasionally they would steal a glance in the other's direction, smile and return to their food.

A half hour later they were strolling along the white sand, shoes abandoned near the entrance of a nearby cove.

Clay's hand reached for hers and Linda gladly entwined her fingers with his. Clay's grip was strong yet tender.

"How much of this is yours?" she asked, the silky-soft grains of sand warm under her feet.

"See where that far mountain is?" He pointed to a spot a few miles along the beach.

"Yes."

"That's where my property ends."

"And the B and B?"

"That's on the other side of the island."

"So it's completely private here then?"

"Very." Clay's response was low and intimate. His voice wrapped around her like the salt-tinged breeze, warm and caressing, with a hint of tang. "What did you have in mind?"

She looked around the area, pretending not to get the implied nuance of the question. Linda wasn't totally comfortable yet bantering with him about wants and needs. Hers were too close to the surface.

"This'd be a perfect spot for a picnic or a late-night supper. A swim. Maybe a fire." An unexpected yawn escaped her mouth. "Sorry," she apologized.

"Look, why don't we go back to the house and we can both catch up on our sleep? As for your idea, what about later this afternoon, when the sun isn't quite so strong?" Clay didn't want his wife's pale, creamy skin being burned by the sun. If something was going to set her skin ablaze, he'd rather it was him with his touch that did the igniting. "Lettie can fix us up something. I think there's a large hamper in the kitchen that can hold everything we'll need. Game?"

"It's a date."

Clay smiled at the incongruity of making a date with his own wife. And he couldn't resist putting his mouth to hers and taking her lips in a deep, slow kiss that fanned his ardor and hers. They clung together, like sea and sand.

Minutes later he released her, brushing the pad of his thumb across her kiss-swollen lower lip. "A preview."

The wooing had begun.

Like windsurfing—diving off a cliff and letting the force of the wind carry you along where it wants to take you—that's what Clay's kiss felt like to Linda. A strong, powerful current in its own right. Liberating. Exhilarating.

She pulled the soft linen sheet over her naked body, easing her hand beneath one of the pillows, as she prepared to take a nap.

Had he felt that kiss searing through him as it had through her? Had he lost touch with everything around him and felt only that—as she had?

Hard to tell with Clay. He wasn't a newcomer to romance, unlike her. He was the seasoned pro, she the rookie.

Linda sighed and, scrunching the pillow, drifted off to sleep with Clay Buchanan on her mind and in her heart.

The cool shower he'd just taken hadn't helped Clay erase the memory of Linda's touch, the scent of her skin or the feel of her mouth. It was all there, painfully, vividly alive in his mind and in his body. He lay supine on the queen-size bed, one hand behind his damp head on the down pillow, the windows open to capture the fresh air, its scent ripe with the tang of salt mixed with floral and spices.

He closed his eyes and listened to the rhythmic pounding of the surf, picturing the beach where they'd just been. Only now stars hung low in the sky, almost touching the water, a half-moon hanging low and bright.

Just then, a silvery female figure emerged from the waves. Slowly, revealing one area of skin at a time. Head. Shoulders. Lush breasts. Neat waist. Flaring hips. Long legs. Wet and seductive. Water dripping from pale ivory skin in rivulets. Easy and comfortable, the water nymph moved onto the cool sand, reveling in the caress of the breeze, like a lover's hand skimming along her body.

She smiled then, as he knew she would. For him. Always and only for him.

Damn! Clay swore. What the hell was ailing him? He was mooning about his wife like a sick calf. Or, to be more blunt, like a randy stallion after a mare. Solid proof of his desire for her was evident; his navy blue silk shorts rubbed against the rising heat of his skin.

That kiss on the beach had only been a prelude. An appetizer to what would come next.

There was no denying the obvious. He wanted Linda in his bed. And soon.

Their plans had changed. Dinner was eaten at the house instead of the beach. The more Clay thought about it, the better he felt at postponing that rendezvous until after they'd had a leisurely meal. Tonight he wanted to take the night slow and easy. Dessert, he told Linda, would be better served under the stars.

That in mind, he'd chilled another bottle of champagne and given Basil and Lettie the rest of the evening off. This time was for him and Linda, alone. He'd built a small fire on the beach, then set up the large blue-and-green plaid picnic blanket close by while Linda unpacked the contents of the hamper.

As she did so, her belly quivered and the potent sensation fluttered through her body. He was everything she wanted in a man—and more. So much more that she trembled with awareness, and a slight vestige of trepidation. All through dinner she'd longed to reach across the table and touch him, give in to the need to express the rising tide of her desire for him. Just to experience the warmth of his skin, or the curl of his hair would have been enough to sustain her.

Or maybe it wouldn't have. Once freed, could she call back her emotions, emotions that had been held in careful check all these years? He was the catalyst for going past the point of no return, for sailing over the edge into the ultimate pursuit of pleasure.

The time had more than come to chart the course.

She settled on the blanket, accepting the glass of champagne Clay gave her. "What shall we drink to?" Linda inquired, the small boom box he'd brought providing background music. The hot sound of a tenor sax spilled over the relative quiet of the beach with a sweet clarity.

"How about to today?"

"And tomorrow?" she tacked on.

"Even better."

Linda loved the sound of his voice. It was an interesting blend of honey and steel, strong and smooth. She might go so far as to say evocative—with all sorts of images coming to mind: the power needed to command a boardroom, coupled with the rich, sexy quality that could make a woman fall under his spell as he led her to the bedroom.

They clinked their glasses and drank deeply, their eyes on each other as seconds ticked by until he suggested, "Dessert?"

Linda nodded, watching as he spooned the fruit into a bowl for her. "Lettie told me that you insisted that she have strawberries on hand."

He shrugged. "Guilty."

"Well, I'm grateful. I love them."

"And lots of whipped cream, right?" Clay remembered her fondness for it when they'd raided the kitchen that night in his New York town house. He topped the berries with the cream and handed the bowl to her. "Here, allow me." He selected one of the biggest berries and held it out to her, the tip covered in a thick cloud of white foam.

Linda bit into it, chewing slowly, the sweet, ripe taste of the fruit and the cool perfection of the cream mixing in her mouth, tantalizing her taste buds. She smacked her lips in delight. "Perfection."

"I agree," Clay said, popping the rest of the morsel into his mouth.

"My turn," she remarked, repeating the gesture for him, and, when he'd taken his bite, slightly larger than hers, she took what was left for herself. Sharing this with Clay was a sensual experience; for her, it crossed the borderline into the erotic.

Then he dipped her index finger into the bowl of cream and brought it toward his mouth, sucking off all the sweet substance.

Copying his moves, she did the same, her mouth capturing his finger, her tongue licking it clean with sweet strokes.

More champagne flowed as they worked their way through most of the strawberries.

What was it about her, he wondered, that made him want to experiment, to try new things, explore new pathways, tackle new challenges? The expectant look in her eyes as he'd held out that first strawberry? Or the swift catch of her breath when he'd licked the cream from her finger? Or the flush of charming pink that raced across her cheekbones as he wiped off a stray dab from her upper lip and brought it to his own?

"What's wrong?"

Clay smiled. "Nothing, darlin'."

"You seemed so faraway all of a sudden."

"Just thinking, that's all."

She turned her head away from him, staring at waves as they lapped at the shore. "I thought you might be bored."

Was that fear he heard in her tone?

Clay reached out and stroked her cheek, his hand skimming down and cupping her chin, gently turning her back to face him. "With you? That's impossible." Bored? Hell! He was trying hard to hold on to control. His mind urged caution and pacing—he had all night and then some; his body pushed for satisfaction, swift and sure, like a wildfire about to break loose and burn unchecked.

But he wasn't a green kid. He was a man, one who'd been there before; however, not with Linda. With her, it had to be good. No, it had to be better than good. As close to perfect as it could be.

At the winsome look on her face, Clay knew he couldn't wait any longer to kiss her. Removing his steel-framed glasses, he placed them on the blanket, out of the way. He carefully set aside his champagne glass and pushed the remains of their dessert to one side.

Her mouth was a mixture of strawberries, cream and champagne, the tastes all blending to form a sweet combination as her lips parted and his tongue gained entrance.

His kisses were deep and soulful, sweeping her along in the wake, drawing her closer to him. Their bodies strained as they melded, the plaid blanket their temporary sanctuary. For a moment Linda rested atop him, her body learning the solid flesh beneath the expensive clothes; then she was spun over and her curves cradled him.

Her agile hands roamed from his hair to his shoulders and down his back, until she could stand it no longer and searched for his skin. Burrowing beneath the lightweight sweater he wore, her fingertips slid along warm, smooth skin.

Her reward was the sound of his breath, caught in a swift, deep intake before he expelled it slowly.

Their eyes met and held, each understanding the message written within.

His lips nibbled along her neck, tugged gently on her lobe. "Remove it," he whispered huskily.

His words came to her out of a sensual fog. Slightly dazed, she asked, "What?"

"My sweater."

Linda complied, shoving the material higher and higher, until, with his help, it was gone. She took the opportunity to look. Lean, sculpted muscles ridged his torso. A light dusting of golden brown hair feathered across his chest. Of their own volition her fingers reached upward, spreading out across his flesh.

A woman's touch had never driven Clay so close to the edge before. It was as if Linda's caress superceded all others in his memory—wiping the slate clean of past experiences, charting a brand-new path.

His heart beat faster. The blood ran hot in his veins. He captured her hand and held it pressed against his heart. "Feel that?" he asked in a husky tone. "*You* do that to me."

The rapid leap beneath her fingertips echoed her own. This was power, the kind she'd never known before.

Clay leaned over her, his lips making contact again with hers, sending them both into a savage eddy of rampant desire, like a whirlpool spinning out of control. Hunger ravaged them, their mouths meeting, coupling in unabashed glory. This wasn't gentle or genteel—it was all too human, all too real, all too wonderful.

His hand smoothed its way along her curves, getting to know the territory. Flesh yearned for flesh, intimately. With skill at his command, Clay quickly unbuttoned the small tan buttons that held her shirt together, slowly peeling it apart. Her breasts were covered by a silky half bra, barely holding the mounds within. A quick snap and it fell open, giving Clay the opportunity to see what he wanted.

Linda felt the sweeping glide of his hand across her skin, his wide palm cupping her breast, his thumb rubbing her nipple to a stone-hard point. She'd been so wrapped up in the kisses they'd been sharing that she wasn't aware of what else was happening.

She was aware now. Heat snaked deeper and hotter in her body, pooling in her belly. The sensations Clay brought forth in her body were new, fresh, intense, galvanizing. Like a flower blossoming in the sun, she was coming alive.

Shockingly cognizant of the texture of his hands, she gasped in pleasure when they were replaced by the laving of his tongue, the gentle pull of his mouth. She arched her back, pressing herself against him, inviting Clay to prolong his ministrations, all the while her hands were reaching for and finding his back, his broad shoulders. Her short nails anchored there, grasping him tighter and tighter, as if afraid to let go, riding the crest of this wave.

Then suddenly something cool was plopped onto her breast.

Her eyes flew open. A dollop of whipped cream covered one nipple.

"I couldn't resist," Clay murmured in a raw voice as he bent his head to remove it. That done, he ran his tongue over his lips, as if prolonging the relished achievement and he smiled. "Darlin'," he drawled, "that's what I call the icing on the cake."

Linda couldn't help it, she laughed.

Clay liked that sound. It was rich and sweet. He enjoyed the fact that they could share laughter along with passion.

"I want you, Linda." He leaned on his arms and looked into her eyes. "But not here. Not the first time." Clay pushed himself into a kneeling position, his body aching for hers. He owed her the best. A memorable night. There would be time later for new places, or for quick fulfillment. Tonight was for her. She deserved soft sheets instead of sand. Candles and perfume.

He'd almost lost total control tonight and that wasn't like him. It was as if she'd thrown some heretofore unknown switch on inside him and Clay wasn't sure he appreciated that. No other woman had gotten under his skin as quickly or as deeply as she had.

How come?

He pushed that thought aside for right now. "Let's go back to the house."

Secretly Linda was glad Clay had called a halt when he did. This was all too willful and crazy, definitely not like her, rolling about the beach on a blanket, giving in to the wildness this man brought out in her. Wildness born out of want. Want for Clay alone. With a hunger that started like a small seed within her until it grew and filled every inch of her, begging to be let out.

Trying to appear calm, she did up her clothes and, when she started to gather the other things together, Clay said in a tone that resembled a growl, "Leave it. We'll take care of this tomorrow." He stood up and held out his hand. "The night belongs to us. Let's not waste another minute."

Chapter Twelve

Clay sat in a chair in the guest bedroom, exhaling the cigar smoke upward. He wanted to give Linda some time before he joined her, a chance to do whatever it was that women did on their wedding night.

And, damn it, he wanted to give himself some time, too—time to quell the small surge of apprehension that had arisen since they'd entered the villa.

He drew another deep puff on the cigar. You'd think it was his first time with a woman the way he was feeling. Excited. Eager. Wanting to please. Anxious to make their first time together memorable.

Because Linda had nothing to compare it to, Clay wanted to make it immeasurably incomparable. Seductive. Sensual. Tempting. A journey into a world of pure pleasure. Like Adam and Eve—first man, first woman, first mating.

Swift and sure, want rose in him as images of her

floated into his brain. Sharp and brilliant, they formed a pattern of loveliness. Eyes as warm and deep as the sea. Hair the color of a new-minted penny in the sun.

He slipped one hand into the left pocket of his silk robe, grasping the item there. The bracelet felt cool to his touch. It needed the contact of her skin to make it come alive. On her wrist, against her skin, it would shimmer as it was meant to.

Clay checked his watch; enough time had passed.

He inhaled his last drag of the cigar and rose, grinding out the remains in the heavy glass ashtray on the nearby small table.

He took a deep breath. His bride awaited.

Linda stood on the terrace with the silver brush in her hand, gazing out into the distance, finally finished with her several dozen strokes. The moon was high; the stars, it appeared, were close enough to pluck.

She'd used the exercise of brushing her hair to try to take her mind from the events unfolding. If she concentrated on that task, then she wouldn't think about Clay.

Or so she thought. Wrong.

He was there, an enduring, immutable presence, with her forever. The guiding light in her life.

Stepping back inside, Linda placed the brush on the bureau and picked up a bottle of perfume. Dabbing it on her wrists, she closed her eyes and thought of him. His touch. His kisses. His sheer presence. When she was walking down the aisle, she was struck anew by his quietly commanding figure. *Star power,* it was called by entertainment writers. You were either born with it or you weren't. While all three Buchanan brothers had it in spades, it was Clay who had the charismatic touch of the natural-born leader.

And tonight he would lead her to a place she'd never been.

Linda looked in the mirror, staring at her reflection there. Would Clay like what he saw?

She fervently hoped so.

Linda almost laughed at her insecurity. Here she was, a woman who could go toe-to-toe with the roughest and toughest of them in business negotiations, who could handle the best and the brightest on an equal footing, and she was frightened. Not of Clay, but of what he could make her feel.

Or worse, what he could force her to reveal, the true nature of her emotions. The depth, the breadth, the heights. He was, she understood, capable of bringing her joy beyond measure and heartache beyond recognition. To keep her end of their bargain she would have to keep the most private part of herself just that, private. She couldn't let him see how much he meant to her. He wanted no hassles, no frills, no complications.

How hard would that be to do?

She'd know soon enough.

"Linda."

She turned and faced the now-open door where Clay stood. His hair was slightly mussed, as if he'd been running his hands through it repeatedly. That observation brought a sense of perspective to her, along with a smile. He wasn't as blasé about this as she might have expected given his experience.

Her eyes were drawn to him, unable to break the contact. All he wore was a navy blue silk robe that ended at his knees, loosely tied at his waist. Beneath it she could see a flash of tanned chest, hair-dusted legs and bare feet.

Mesmerized, Linda looked her fill. She'd seen male models in ads wearing much less; however, they didn't possess the panache of Clay Buchanan. Pound for pound, he had it all over them. They were representations of dreams; he was the real thing. Enticingly so.

As Clay stood there, his gaze took in all of her. From the crown of her head to the ankle-skimming hem of her peignoir set. Heavy white satin and lace, it flowed around her body.

He strode forward, coming to within inches of her. "If you've changed your mind, tell me now."

Linda tilted her chin upward. "I haven't, Clay. This is what I want."

His smile was beguiling. "Good." Reaching into his pocket, he withdrew another part of his ongoing gift to her. "Give me your hand."

Linda held out her left arm and watched as Clay fastened a bracelet around her wrist. She felt the weight of it and noted that it was a perfect match to her earrings and engagement ring.

"What can I say?" A voice inside her head mocked that she could tell him that, as much as she loved this gesture, it would mean more to her if he were to say simply, "I love you." For those words she would happily forsake all else.

Instead, she added, "I'm overwhelmed." She lifted her arm and Clay took hold of her hand, kissed the back of it, gallantly, like a knight saluting his lady. Or a prince his princess.

His mouth drifted lazily higher up her arm, sending darts of fire under the skin, spreading to every corner of her body.

Next his hands were at her waist, deftly undoing the sash that held her robe in place. Slowly, with infinite care, he loosed the item, pushing it off her shoulders and sliding it down her arms and onto the floor.

He dropped his gaze, taking in the rapid rise and fall of her breasts beneath the satin that covered them. He lifted one hand and skimmed the strap, stroking the material, then moving it past her shoulder. Then Clay followed the line of the nightgown, from where it covered her full breast, to the lace insert that dipped to her waist.

Satin molded to skin; his hand molded to both, warming and inflaming. Gliding his fingers along the curves and dips, he could feel her trembling response to his touch.

That brought him a small measure of satisfaction. If she'd remained unresponsive, it would have been a sad indication of the direction the night would take. This reassured him that she was on the same physical wavelength as he was.

His long-fingered hand was warm, spreading fire in its wake. Every second that ticked by brought her closer to true knowledge. Like a hungry, constant craving, Linda longed for the promise his touch provoked.

And burning inside her was the need to explore on her own. To see and feel for herself the texture of his skin. Luckily his robe was loosely tied, as well, and she had no difficulty removing the knot, slipping her hands against his warm flesh, her palms flat.

Clay quickly shucked off the silk, tossing it in the direction of the bed so that she could continue.

Linda breathed deeply as she spread her hands wide across his chest. Beneath one hand pumped the steady beat of his heart. Her fingers stroked through the whorl of hair, enjoying the crisp feel.

Next came masculine nipples that begged to be examined. She gave in to the need and heard his swift intake of breath when she touched them.

She raised her head and looked into his beloved face. "Shall I stop?"

Clay's reply was a groan. "No."

Following the example that he'd set earlier, she bent her head and touched her lips to one of his nipples. Opening her mouth, she flicked her tongue around it.

He groaned again, deeper this time. Clay felt her action like a brand. Red-hot, it burned his skin, leaving an indelible mark.

Need warred with patience within him.

Experience battled with innocence.

Unable to stop himself, he fantasized about her mouth covering his whole body, making every inch of skin tingle as much as that which she'd already covered.

Clay's hands grasped her arms and pulled her gently back. When she'd lifted her head, he could see that passion glazed her eyes. They were wide and haunting, mirrors to the wonder of the sensual journey she was experiencing.

Dipping his head, he took his turn at her mouth, capturing it with his own, sending them both into the swirling mists of ecstasy.

One kiss was not enough; others followed, stronger and hotter than the one before.

One touch couldn't suffice; more ensued, each bolder and more intimate.

His lips worked a path along her collarbone, tasting her skin. "Do you," he asked, his voice raw with desire, "know how much I want you? Do you have any idea?"

Linda, her own voice husky, answered, "If it's as much as I want you, then it's tearing you apart."

Her honest confession sliced through him like a scalpel, cutting through remembrances of their old, easy camaraderie, expunging them totally. They ceased to exist. All that was important was the here and now. Him and her and the heat that burned with every caress, every look between them.

Clay bent and swung her up into his arms, the satin draping across his body as he carried her to the bed, where he gently placed her upon it.

"You're beautiful," he whispered as he joined her, running his palm down her body from her neck to her calf.

Even though he sounded so sincere, Linda had to ask, "Am I?"

His eyes met hers. "Trust me," he said, sliding the fabric up her leg, exposing her skin to his touch.

"I do, Clay." With everything, she added silently. With my heart. My love. With everything that's in me. Don't you know that I'd walk through hell for you?

He took the satin gown higher and higher, exposing her thighs. "I want to see you, Linda. All of you. As much as I love this delightful item, right now it's in the way."

Linda acquiesced to his request, aiding him in removing the garment. When that was accomplished, she lay there, aware of his blue eyes taking in every inch of her skin. She fought her natural modest urge to throw her arms across her breasts and belly. Instead, she watched him watching her, taking pride in the fact that he seemed quite happy with what he saw.

She had the body most men dreamed about. Curves where it counted. High, full breasts he couldn't resist cupping and kissing. Long legs that could hold a man tight in their grasp.

Linda gasped and arched her back, her eyes fluttering shut as Clay proceeded with his study, analyzing each nuance, each breath. Her skin was smooth and his fingertips trailed a path from her breast to her waist, skimming, smoothing, loving along the trail, moving to the apex of her thighs.

He felt the sharp dig of her nails in his back, the weight of the bracelet as it pressed into his skin. Clay smiled at the sounds coming from her throat. Pleased, contented sounds. A woman surrendering to her basic instincts.

He was driving her crazy. With each brush of his hand, each stroke of his tongue, each erotic kiss, he was taking her closer and closer to the edge. Linda could feel herself slipping into a secret garden of delights, blossoming under his tutelage. Clay was a master of his craft. Skillful. Passionate. Completely in charge.

Then, when he gently pulled away from her, she started. "What's wrong?"

"Nothing," he assured her, his own breathing as ragged as hers. "Just taking care of something I almost forgot."

Linda watched as he removed a foil packet from another pocket in his robe, realization hitting home. He was searching for protection.

Her eyes widened farther when he deftly removed his silk shorts, revealing himself to her. Before her was the long, lean body of a man in his prime, all there for her to see. Sculpted by a divine hand, chiseled in living marble, a testament to male beauty. Sleek. Powerful.

"Clay." It was a plea, an invitation, a command.

He responded.

Once again their mouths blended into one, need raging through their bodies, straining them, joining them.

The journey was taken.

Untold pleasure was the reward.

So much for no complications, Clay thought as he stood on the balcony and watched the sunrise.

Raking a hand through his hair, he turned his head and

looked in the direction of his wife, who was sleeping deeply. He'd been the same way until a half hour ago.

Their time together had been magic, refreshing his soul and revitalizing his ardor. Sex had always been an activity that he enjoyed participating in. Last night, however, had been beyond the best sex he'd had. It was a revelation.

Linda's response to his possession of her was abandoned. He regretted any momentary pain he caused her, swallowing her cry with his kiss when he breached the barrier of her innocence.

"I'm sorry."

"Don't be," she'd said.

"It's over now, darlin'. From here on in it just gets better, I promise."

He could still hear the echo of her husky-voiced reply, "Show me."

And he had.

Linda had proved herself to be an apt pupil, grasping the fundamentals instantly, adding her own flourishes as she adapted to his lead.

What had surprised him most about last night was how she'd made him feel, as if he'd soared to another level, a place he'd never been before. While it was memorable, he wasn't sure he was comfortable with that. Clay was used to being in control of his emotions, keeping the reins tight. He'd compared it to bustin' broncs. He'd done it before when he was younger on the ranch just to prove to himself and everyone concerned that he could. He rode the high-spirited animals, not the other way around, taming them to his hand. It was the same way with feelings. He held them in check, because a cool head was his objective.

Last night he hadn't been cool. Last night he'd abandoned control and achieved the most satisfying sensual experience. It shattered all his previous encounters with the force of a storm, washing them all away.

Clay stepped back into the room, careful not to disturb Linda as he slipped back into bed.

She slept like a child, completely trusting. But she wasn't a child. Linda was a woman. A beautiful, loving woman.

She snuggled up against him.

Damn, he wanted her again, his body reacting instantly to hers. If possible, more than before. Who would have thought that a made-to-order marriage would provide satisfaction on all levels?

Linda opened her eyes slowly, feeling a delicious sense of languor steal over her. The pillow she slept upon was warm and breathing. Shifting carefully, she tilted her head back to get a good look at Clay's face. He was relaxed. Seemingly without a care.

A deep smile curved her mouth. She hadn't known how close she could get to another human being until last night. Beyond all expectations, he'd taken her on a sensual excursion that defied description. Moved from boss to husband to lover, and in the process, showed Linda a part of herself before unknown. Degrees and shadings of emotions that opened her eyes in new ways.

The hardest part had been keeping a leash on the love that lay just beneath the surface of her every gesture. Holding her tongue when she wanted to shout out loud the depth of her love, a love he didn't want. At least not yet.

Soon, she hoped.

The urge to pinch herself and prove that all this wasn't a dream was almost overwhelming.

However, she didn't need to do that. The ache in her

muscles, the vivid recall of his kisses and caresses was enough to convince her of the truth. She was indeed Linda Douglas Buchanan, wife to Clayton.

How could she love him more today than she did yesterday? It defied logic but the truth was she did.

Linda was also glad that she'd waited to experience the special moment of surrender with Clay. That intimacy, that acceptance, had been worth the long delay. Sharing it with him had forged a bond between them. Or at least she prayed that it had. A bond he wouldn't want to lose. A bond he'd want to build upon for a future that included love.

Her hand slid across the width of his chest. Linda followed that with her mouth, laying kisses here and there.

"Don't start anything you don't plan to finish."

Linda halted, raising up her head. She looked into the blue eyes of her husband, her mood changing. "What makes you think I don't have plans to see this through? I've been taught by the best never to leave a job undone. Especially not when it needs the personal touch."

There was laughter in his voice. "And who taught you that?"

Her eyes twinkled. "Oh, someone whose name escapes me right now."

"Must not have been all that great, darlin', if you can't recall."

"I think that he was a Texan."

"Well," Clay said, "that puts him on solid ground."

"And I seem to remember that he was formerly the most-sought-after bachelor in the state."

His arms held her close. "Someone catch him?"

"A very lucky lady."

"Could be he thinks he's lucky, too."

"You reckon so?"

"I *reckon* that to be a fact, sweetheart." Clay maneuvered Linda so that she lay under him as he brought his face close to hers and whispered, "Let him show her how much."

They didn't leave the bedroom until dinnertime.

"What must Basil and Lettie be thinking?" Linda asked Clay as she picked up her perfume bottle, getting ready to add a dash more to her body.

"That we're newlyweds and doing what most couples do on their honeymoon—enjoying themselves." He crossed the room and stood behind her chair. "Let me," he insisted, taking the green glass bottle from her hands.

Linda met his eyes in the mirror. Without breaking contact, she quickly swept her hair into a twist and anchored it so that he could have access to her flesh. That accomplished, she closed her eyes and said, "Go ahead."

Removing the stopper, Clay stroked it slowly around her ears, a dab to one, then the other. Next came the nape of her neck, which he had to sample first with his lips.

She was wearing a honey-colored slip that clung to her body and plunged deeply in front.

That was his next target. Hunkering down, he took the perfume and drew it between the hollow of her breasts, gently following that up with a puff of his breath along the same path.

Linda shivered, gripping the delicate handles of the chair.

His hand covered the bone of her knee, fingers splaying to either side before he slid them to cup her calf while his other hand dotted the fragrance on her bare skin.

She inhaled sharply.

He lifted her foot, dabbing the scent along her ankle. "All done."

Her eyes flew open. Her thank-you was managed in a small, somewhat shaky voice.

"No need, darlin'," he insisted. "I enjoyed it as much as you, maybe even more."

The twinkle in his eyes and the curve of his mouth told her as much.

Linda slipped on her dress and stepped into a pair of high-heeled sandals. "I'll find a way to return the favor."

He slipped on his dinner jacket. "Don't think I won't hold you to it."

"Deal?"

"Deal, darlin'. You always did have a knack for negotiating."

"And you've always been smart enough to recognize a very good offer when you hear it."

Linda returned the favor in her own way the next morning.

When she woke up, Clay was missing from the bed. How quickly she'd gotten used to having him beside her. Warm. Sexy. A skilled lover who showed her what it meant to surrender to desire. True, she had no one to compare Clay with, but she didn't have to. She went on instinct and the sensations he evoked. She'd read articles, heard women talk. Knew what was expected of a generous man in bed.

He fulfilled every criteria and then some. Encouraged her. Challenged her. Teased her.

Tossing back the single linen sheet, she got out of bed and reached for his robe, which he'd nicely picked off the floor where she'd tossed it hours earlier. Tying the sash around her bare body, she padded into the adjoining bathroom, searching for Clay.

Light washed over the room. Tile gleamed on the floor

and in the oversize shower, a magnificent shade of blue green. It was the same shade that she'd seen from the bedroom window when looking out to the sea. Haunting in its beauty.

An old-fashioned pedestal sink stood by itself, its white bowl hand-painted with colorful tropical birds.

But the room was empty of other occupants. He wasn't there.

She crossed to the open French doors that led to the balcony and looked out. There was no sign of him that she could see.

Where could he have gone?

"Morning, Linda."

She spun around at the sound of his silky smooth baritone with its unforgettable accent.

Clay strode into the bathroom, a deep grin on his mouth. "I'd say that my robe looks better on you than it does on me."

Linda laughed softly. The silk carried Clay's scent and wearing it made her feel closer to him. "Maybe I'll keep it." She crossed the room and joined him, slipping her arms about his neck and lifting her face for his kiss. She might not be able to tell him she loved him, but she wanted to show him in every way she possibly could. If this was all she had for right now, then she would gladly use it.

He returned her hungry kiss with one of his own, pulling her closer.

"Your hair's wet." Linda's fingers were damp from the moisture in his hair.

"I went for a swim."

"You should have awakened me. I would have gone with you."

"I thought you might need the sleep more."

A sweep of pink flushed her cheeks. Clay smiled at that and then noticed the slight telltale marks of color on her face where his beard had scraped her skin. He ran a hand over his jawline. "Sorry about that. I didn't shave yet this morning."

"Then let me do it for you."

"Excuse me?"

"You brought along that gentleman's kit, didn't you?" He nodded.

"There's shaving gear included, isn't there?"

"Yes." Clay arched one brow. "Have you ever done this before?"

"No." It was Linda's turn to smile. "But since these past few days have included some memorable firsts, I thought I might like to add another to the mix."

"And I'm the guinea pig?"

"Think of it as my contribution to expanding your horizons."

"Okay," he said, giving her a grin. "Would you like a cup of coffee first?"

"You bet."

He went into the other room with Linda and got out the items she requested after pouring a large cup of coffee for each of them from the pot he'd brought upstairs.

Clay had to admit that the idea of her taking over the task of being his personal barber for the day was erotic. Putting himself in her hands and letting her have control, albeit temporary, was intriguing.

She carried her cup of coffee back into the bathroom and ran warm water in the sink, soaking a thick washcloth as she downed the caffeine.

"Here it is."

Linda pointed to a stool. "Ready when you are."

Clay handed her the kit, which she placed on a small

chest of drawers that held towels and washcloths. She
opened the leather case and took out the Georgian-style
shaving set, a soft badger bristle brush with a silver handle, the *B* prominent on the top. The razor gleamed in
silver, also; both were held by a stand that featured a
wolf's head, which matched the handle of the razor. She
removed a brown jar of shave cream and opened the lid,
sniffing the fragrance. Woodsy. Masculine.

The wet washcloth was wrung out and laid around his
face, allowing the warmth to penetrate his pores. Minutes
later it was removed and Linda dabbed the brush into the
cream and stroked it across his jawline and down his neck
in a caressing motion. "Like that?"

"What's not to like, so far?"

"The best," she whispered in his ear, "is yet to come."

Afterward, Clay had to admit that he'd never experienced a shave quite like that before. "A man could get
used to that, darlin'."

"Could he?"

"Undoubtedly. It has a definite appeal."

Linda loosened her robe, tossed it onto him with a smile
and stepped into the shower, turning on the water and
soaping her skin, leaving the glass door ajar. Loving him
had freed her underlying sensual nature.

"So does this," she said, and held out her hand.

The remainder of their coffee cooled as, after shucking
his clothes, he joined her.

Chapter Thirteen

Linda wished that the honeymoon had lasted longer. All too soon it was back to work, back to her life, except now when she woke up it was in her boss's bed, held in his strong arms. She and Clay shared a life without boundaries. At home or the office, they were a team, a couple, a legally sanctioned unit.

She glanced at the sandwich that sat on her desk half-eaten. The amount of work she had kept her too busy to finish it. One clear-polished index fingertip pressed into the bread. The air had hardened it considerably since it was delivered several hours ago. Now it was going stale.

And, she admitted to herself, so was the promise of her marriage.

On the surface, everything was fine. She and Clay got along well. Nothing had changed in that respect. And as for other details, like making love, that was *almost* totally perfect. Physically, it was grand. Solidly enthusiastic on both their parts. Emotionally, however, was another story. For her, she truly was making love when she gave her body to him. For Clay, Linda was certain he didn't share that feeling. How could he? Making love was an emotional commitment to a relationship. Having sex was based on pleasure, love didn't really factor in the scheme of things.

How damnably naive she'd been to think it wouldn't have mattered to her if he loved her when they slept together. That it wouldn't hurt deep down in her soul whenever they were close. A part of her wanted them to be closer still.

In the two months since they'd been married, never once had Clay said to her, "I love you."

Of course she hadn't uttered those words to him, either. With good reason. The same reason she'd had before—that if she told him she might lose him. Lose the respect he had for her.

But what about the respect she had for herself? Where was her pride?

For Clay, she had dared any dare, risked any risk.

Or so she thought. Linda found out that there were limits. She didn't dare to tell him the truth. She couldn't risk him knowing the depth of her love, having him feel sorry for her.

Lately she'd begun to think that she'd made a huge mistake in marrying him. A real beaut. Linda had ignored the warning of her head to follow the dreams of her heart. Hopeless didn't seem like so insurmountable an obstacle back then. She hadn't let that stop her. Confidence might have been her personal Achilles' heel.

In the interim, Linda had discovered that sometimes dreams came with a high price tag. And that sometimes the cost was more than one bargained for.

Before he left on his last business trip—he'd been gone almost two weeks—Clay had mentioned that he wanted to have a serious discussion with her about children when he returned.

Children.

That idea brought an infusion of warmth. Her hands wrapped around her belly as if she already sheltered a child within, which she knew was false. Linda wanted Clay's babies. More than anything she yearned to give him a child. A son or daughter. Maybe both.

She'd thought about it constantly since he'd dropped that comment upon her. Children had been part of the bargain he'd outlined to her when he asked her to marry him.

Now that he appeared more serious about it, the doubts crept in. They were both healthy and chances were they wouldn't have a problem in conceiving. There was money aplenty to see to their future, to whatever any child would need.

And love. They would have that. What worried her was that although any children she and Clay would have would be loved by each parent, they wouldn't ultimately be conceived in total love.

That's what bothered her now. Maybe foolishly. As a child of divorce, as one who knew firsthand the effects of living with parents who didn't love each other, she didn't want that for any child of hers.

The intercom on her phone buzzed.

Linda pressed the button. "Yes?" She'd told her secretary to hold all her calls unless it was vital.

"It's Mr. Buchanan on line one for you."

Linda hesitated an instant.

"Excuse me," her secretary's voice interrupted her

once again. "Did you hear who I said the caller was? Your husband."

"I'm sorry," Linda apologized, and picked up the receiver, depressing the flashing button. "Hello, Clay."

"Hi, darlin'."

"Where are you?"

"Somewhere over California, I think."

"Then you're on your way home." As much as she loved the house and got along well with Basil and Lettie, who spoiled her, she missed him. Funny, for someone who'd been on her own for so long, she got used to living with Clay mighty quickly. The transition from business hours to all hours was swift and sure.

"Yes." There was a pause over the line until Clay added, "I've missed you, Linda."

God, he still had the instantaneous power to affect her with his silky-smooth voice. He didn't even have to be in the same room. All Linda had to do was hear that unmistakable tone and she was ready to melt. Puddle on the floor of her office like ice left out in the sun.

"You've been missed, as well," she responded, keeping her own voice as neutral as she could make it, warm without gushing. "Would you like me to wait here for you or are you going directly home?"

"Home. And don't wait up if you're tired. I'll probably be flat-out dragging by the time I get in. I just wanted to let you know in case you were worried."

"About what?" she asked, her eyes on the bouquet that sat on her desk in a small vase, miniature roses in white and red. "You've always got things well in hand."

"And if I didn't, you'd have them that way." Clay paused, letting his words sink in. "We're a good team, Linda."

Team. As in the office, unstoppable business partners. "I know."

"Why don't you skip out early?" he suggested. "Go home and relax."

"I've got a few more things to do around here."

His voice held a teasing tone. "Work for a slave driver, do you? No time off for good behavior?"

Linda's mouth kicked upward into a smile. "Up at dawn, toting that barge and lifting that load."

"All the more reason to leave while you have the chance. I won't tell if you won't."

Going along with the verbal game, she asked, "What will your silence cost me?"

"Hmm," he drawled. "Now that could be interesting. *Very* interesting. Let me think about it."

"Take your time."

"If that's the way you want it, darlin', I'll be happy to oblige. Keeping the pace slow and easy can be—" he paused for effect, letting his words sink in "—entertaining, shall we say?"

His words conjured up just the images she was sure he wanted her to think about. Languid, early-morning sessions in bed. Measured kisses and all the time in the world to linger.

"See you soon, sweetheart."

Linda hung up the phone and stared at it, as if willing it to ring again. What was she expecting to hear? "Oh, by the way, I forgot to tell you something important, Linda. Don't know how I could have forgotten to tell you that I love you, sweetheart. You mean everything to me. I've found that I'm only half-alive without you."

That wasn't going to happen. Certainly not anytime soon.

What was she going to do?

She didn't have a clue, except that she was going to take his advice and leave early.

Linda scooped a stack of papers into her briefcase and shut down her computer. Clay was right. She needed a break. Some downtime. A long, leisurely soak in a warm tub sounded just about perfect to her right now.

Clay hadn't lied when he admitted that he'd missed Linda. He had. More than he realized. In the short time that they'd been married, he'd come to depend on her in odd ways that went beyond the scope of her job or what he envisioned of a wife. He expected that when he woke, she'd be there. If not in his bed, then close by. That when he went to sleep, it would be with Linda in his arms.

The hunger for her hadn't subsided, either, since their honeymoon. If anything, it had grown stronger, feeding upon itself. Since their wedding, they'd only been separated a night or two at most. This trip, which required him to crisscross the Pacific, paying calls on clients and investment partners, was unavoidable. It had been on the schedule for weeks. He had planned on asking her to accompany him, but something held him back.

Need for space?

Perhaps. His own desire to prove that just because they'd got married, they didn't have to be yoked together behind the corporate plow.

This time apart would provide perspective, clarify the situation.

Which was what?

That his marriage was succeeding beyond his wildest hopes and plans? That marrying Linda had been the smartest move he'd made in a long time?

Damn right!

Returning to an empty suite night after night in city

after city had driven home the point that Linda had changed his life, for the better. Whereas before he would have been content to relax, or catch up on work, now he prowled around the rooms as if searching for something he'd lost. Or misplaced.

He would lie in bed, wishing that she were there beside him. And not just to make love to. He wanted to talk to her, share observations, discuss whatever he felt like. Doing that in short phone calls or E-mailing wasn't the same as being alone and conversing. Privately he could say what he wanted, how he wanted.

Or even show that he wanted. At odd moments, the hungry urges for her would sweep over him and his imagination would take flight on a sensual journey. He marveled that for a man who'd been relatively celibate this past year, he could want a woman the way he wanted her. Strong flashes of need raced through him.

He lifted the snifter of brandy to his lips, picturing her asleep in their bed when he returned home. Perhaps she'd be waiting for him downstairs, curled up on the sofa in the living room, music playing softly in the background, eager to show him that he wasn't alone in missing their closeness. Or maybe she'd be ensconced upstairs in the den, watching a movie on the wide-screen TV, a bowl of popcorn at her side, pillows piled high behind her as she relaxed on the floor, their normally frisky puppy at her side.

That picture brought a smile to his face. Linda loved that dog, a gift to them both from Burke. A black-and-white Border collie mix named Ranger.

Clay had to admit that he was rather fond of the puppy himself, especially since the animal brought such pleasure to his wife.

He downed the remainder of the brandy. Life was pretty

good. No, he reckoned, it was better than pretty good. It was damned fine. He had everything he wanted and he was happy. Really happy. Linda had a lot to do with that.

"Is something wrong, Mrs. Buchanan?"

Linda looked up from her plate. She was eating dinner by herself in the kitchen. If Clay were home, they would be having their meal in the dining room, but as she was alone, Linda preferred a less formal setting. Ranger sat at her feet under the table, munching on a toy chew bone. "No, Lettie. I'm fine."

The older woman expressed her opinion freely. "It's just that you looked rather sad just now."

"It's been a very long day."

The housekeeper-cook smiled knowingly. "And you'd be missing your husband, as well. That's no surprise what with you two being newlyweds and all. Don't worry, he'll be home shortly." She poured Linda another cup of hot, strong tea, brewed the English way. "Now, would you be wanting another slice of the quiche?"

Linda waved her hand, having succumbed to temptation and consumed a hearty helping of the custardy smooth ham and cheese. "Any more of that and I won't be able to get off my chair."

"Nonsense," Lettie scoffed. "You're not one of them birdlike creatures who starve themselves so that they resemble underfed whippets or greyhounds." She stored the remainder of the quiche in a container and placed it in the refrigerator in case it was wanted later. "In my day women wanted to look like women, not walking sticks."

"I'm hardly likely to be mistaken for that."

"And that's much the better, I say. And," Lettie added with a gleam in her eyes, "it suits Mr. Buchanan, as well, I'd be thinking."

"My husband likes women," Linda commented. "That's one of the reasons I..." She let her sentence trail off, about to say that it was one of the many reasons that she loved Clay. He genuinely liked women. A successful man, he wasn't threatened by someone of the opposite sex who had brains and ability and used them.

"He likes one in particular, I'd be thinking." Lettie moved closer to Linda, her voice dropping in a confiding, conspiratorial whisper. "If you don't mind me saying, ma'am, Basil and me have noticed the change that you've brought into this house since you and the mister have married. He laughs more. He doesn't spend half his day now in the city proper, thinking about business. Not so's you'd notice, him being so clever and all with money, it kind of comes natural. But many's the night he's spent hours with his laptop, locked away in his office here. Or being obliging and fulfilling his social obligations."

"He still does both."

"Of course, though it's not the same as before, I'm thinking. Basil tells me, not that we're gossiping about either of you, ma'am," she offered.

"I understand," Linda said with a smile. "Married couples talk, Lettie." She and Clay had talked about a lot of things, though never what was in their hearts.

"Well, as I started to say, Basil takes note that now when the mister is getting ready to go out, he's happier to be going about with you on his arm." Lettie moved back to the counter, lifted the glass lid from a cake dish. "Can I be offering you something sweet to finish off your meal?"

"Not tonight, Lettie. I'm going to take a bath and go right to bed."

"Then I shall wish you good-night, ma'am."

An hour later, Linda, her bath done, slipped between

the dark green sheets of the king-size bed that she shared
with her husband. She lay on her side, thinking about what
Lettie had said. Mulling it over in her mind as she shut
off the light. Nice to know that Basil and Lettie believed
she was good for him, because Linda thought so, too.
Trouble was, it could be a hollow, Pyrrhic victory.

Without mutual love, what kind of marriage did she
really have?

Without the *hope* of love, what kind of life could she
live?

Clay punched in the security code to his front door and
let himself in. It was late, just before midnight.

A light was left gleaming in the hall to welcome him
as he set his suitcase and garment bag to one side. The
rest of the house looked shut down for the night. Loos-
ening his tie, he pulled it off and draped it over the stair
rail. From the direction of the kitchen he heard the snap
of paws upon the tiled floor.

Soon enough, Ranger came into view, head cocked as
he tried to identify the intruder that stood in the hallway.
He began wagging his tail when he recognized Clay, who
hunkered down to run his hands over the dog, scratching
Ranger's ears. "Miss me?"

In response the dog licked his hand and began to bark.

"Shh," Clay said sternly. "You'll wake everyone.
Let's get you back to your bed so that I can get to mine."
He picked up the pup and carried the wriggling ball of
fur back to where the animal's bed was located in a corner
of the large kitchen.

The dog sat on his bed, head tilted to one side, eyes
fixed on Clay.

"Did you take good care of her for me?"

Ranger gave a short yap as if he understood the question.

"Then I think that deserves a reward." Clay reached for the tin of doggie biscuits and, after extracting one, tossed it in Ranger's direction. The puppy caught it and settled down happily, gnawing on the tasty treat.

Moving, Clay snapped off the kitchen light and made for the stairs.

He entered the bedroom, familiar enough with the layout so that he didn't have to turn on the light, trying not to wake his wife. Silently he crept across the floor and into the adjoining bathroom to remove his clothes.

A few minutes later, that accomplished, along with a quick washup, he walked back into the room, now lit by the soft glow of the bedside lamp. Linda was awake, hair tumbled about her shoulders. The sheet on his side of the bed was pulled back invitingly.

She debated about whether or not to pretend to be asleep. The moment he walked in the door, she was instantly awake, as if sensing him. Like a switch being thrown on, the current raced across the space that divided them and its charge sharpened her senses, alerting her to her husband's presence.

Her eyes feasted on him: tall and intensely male, he stood there, letting her look her fill.

And look Linda did. Hungrily. He was the after-dinner sweet she longed for, the dessert that she craved constantly, like a starving beggar at the feast.

Clay stepped closer. "I tried not to wake you."

"It doesn't matter." All he wore were a pair of tapered boxers in burgundy silk that clung to his skin. Her eyes lingered and she could see the effect she was having on him. She slid higher up on the pillows, waiting.

"I want you." Though his words were spoken softly,

they came across the width of the bed with the force of a trumpet blast.

They were bittersweet to Linda's ears.

The light stayed on as Clay removed his glasses and slipped into the bed, tossing the fine cotton top sheet to the foot of the bed.

How could a woman look so incredibly sexy in a pair of pajamas cut to resemble a man's? Yet look it she did, appealing in her white and pale blue thin stripes.

He stretched out his hand and brought her head closer to his, lightly feathering kisses across her face. "All the way across the Pacific I've wanted to do that."

"And every night, lying in this lonely bed without you, I've wanted to do this," she replied, taking his face between her hands, her mouth against his. Her tongue snaked out and she tasted his lips. "Brandy," she murmured. "Old and expensive. The very best kind."

He couldn't resist the temptation she presented, taking her mouth with unleashed passion. Sweeter than honey and hotter than any spice known to man—that's what her kisses were like.

Her skin was smooth and supple as he loosened the buttons that held the shirt together and placed his hand inside. He could feel the rapid beat of her heart against his palm before he eased it inches over and covered her breast. Lovingly he cupped her flesh, working his thumb across the pointed tip of her nipple.

She was drowning in the sorcery of his touch, the sure-fire magic of his lips. Succumbing to the powerful forces he released within her with the greatest of ease.

Her shirt was open all the way, giving him easy access to her. Each inch of skin knew his touch; each hill and valley felt the stroke of his hand. Familiar territory, yet always captivating. It was times like these when he wished that he was good with words, the kind poets or lyricists used. Since he wasn't, he relied on his body language to communicate to his wife the indescribable pleasure he found in her body.

Linda couldn't resist running her hands over him, re-learning all the spots that triggered a reaction in him. Clasping him close, she feasted on his neck, trailing kisses down the column of his throat, the hollow of his neck, the sweep of his chest.

She loved his mouth and returned to it, sharing a series of intense kisses that shook her to her very core. Each one deeply intimate, shockingly personal.

His hands were busy unbuttoning the side of her pajama bottoms, sliding the material down her legs, pushing it to the floor. When that was done, he stroked his palm along her thighs, then upward to her very core. Testing the damp warmth, he found her ready.

Their bodies and lips entwined, Clay set the rhythm and Linda willingly gave him back measure for measure until all around them exploded in brilliant sparkles of light, showering their senses.

Linda awoke about an hour or so later. Carefully she checked to make sure that Clay was still asleep. Discovering that he was, she got out of bed. Picking up her pajama bottoms from the floor, she hastily pulled them on, refastening her shirt, too, giving another glance over her shoulder at her husband.

Tiptoeing quietly out the door, she hurried downstairs in the direction of the living room.

Curling up on the sofa, she let her thoughts drift back to their heartbreakingly excited coupling. They'd been so intent on satisfying their overwhelming hunger that Clay hadn't stopped to use protection. Even now, his child could be taking root inside her.

That scared her. She didn't know if she was ready for that as much as she might want it. If *they* were ready.

It was obvious to her that she needed more time to think. Alone. Away from him and this house.

Tears welled in her eyes. Two weeks away and not a word of love from him. Deep in her heart she had harbored the secret fantasy that when Clay came back, he would realize that he cared about her as more than his friend, his business associate, his handpicked wife. That he loved her for who she was. That he wanted a real marriage. One based solely on love. The forever, happily-ever-after kind.

She'd misjudged the capability of her own heart to withstand the pain of loving someone who didn't love her.

How could she have been so stupid? So utterly reckless with not only her own future, but Clay's, not to mention any child they might have?

They had to talk.

But not now. Not here. She couldn't handle the heavy emotions that would dredge up. A few days away would give her a chance to sort things out and then they could see where they went from there. Forward and together, she prayed.

"Where are you going?" Clay asked as he came into the bedroom from the shower the next morning to find Linda packing a suitcase.

"Out of town for a few days."

He slipped on his glasses. "Where?"

"First to New York to see Meg. She's out of the hospital but not back to work. I talked to her the other day and I thought she might like a visit. Then, I think that I'll go and spend some time with my grandfather.''

''Why? Is something wrong with Ethan?''

Linda turned and faced him, once again her eyes feasting on the sight of him. All Clay had to do was just be and that was enough for her. She fought the impulse to run into his arms and ask him to hold her and never let her go. But if she did that then nothing would get resolved. They had to go forward because it hurt too much to stay in the same place.

''No, he's fine.''

''Then why the visit now?''

''Because I need to get away.''

''Away?'' he asked. ''From what?''

''You.''

Clay's face reflected his confusion. ''Me?'' He stepped closer to her. ''What's this all about?'' he demanded.

''It's about us.''

''I don't know what the hell you're talking about.''

''No,'' she said sadly, ''I don't suppose that you do.''

''Well, would you like to tell me?'' He couldn't figure out what was going on. A few hours ago they'd been blissfully happy, as close as two people could be.

''I don't want to get into it now.''

''Why not?''

''Because I'm not strong enough.''

''For what?''

''To talk about our marriage.''

''Our marriage,'' he repeated, bewildered by her sudden change in attitude from loving wife last night to cool woman this morning. It was like waking up with a stranger. ''What about our marriage?''

''Clay, there are some problems.''

''Problems?'' None that he could think of, but obviously something that was bothering her. "Then let's talk about them, now."

"I can't."

"That's not a reason, that's an excuse."

"Maybe you're right. But I've made up my mind."

"So that's that?" His tone had an angry bite to it.

"For now." It was the hardest thing for Linda to turn her back on him and fasten the case. "I'll be in touch."

"Don't go."

Linda turned around and faced him again. It wasn't a command he'd given; it was a request, one she wished she could honor.

"I have to."

Clay could read the pain in her eyes. Where was all this coming from? He took hold of her arm. "I won't let you go, not like this."

"Don't make this harder than it is for me," she said. "Please."

At that barely whispered entreaty, Clay released her.

Linda lifted her left hand and laid it upon his bare shoulder and, leaning close, she kissed him softly on the mouth. "Goodbye, Clay."

Chapter Fourteen

Clay prowled around his large, empty house, feeling as if any trace of color and vibrancy had abruptly vanished from his life with the departure of his wife.

Linda had only been gone for a little over a week. A week in which he hadn't talked to her personally. She'd E-mailed him at the office regarding work, keeping up-to-date with business. But occasional faxes or daily electronic communications couldn't make up for her prolonged absence.

When he finally settled, it was in the living room. Ranger sat at Clay's feet, a forlorn look on his doggie face, as if wondering, too, where his mistress was and when she would return.

Clay looked down at the puppy, whose head rested on his paws. "I know," he stated softly, "I miss her, too." And he did. Much more than he thought possible. Insidiously, she'd wormed her way into his life, deeper and deeper, into every nook and cranny, every detail. There wasn't any part that didn't have her signature stamp on it now.

He discovered that he missed her humming to herself when she was happy. He missed that quick look of triumph they shared when a project was completed. Or the way her eyes glowed when she was pleased with something, like her daily flowers. He missed hearing her dulcet voice, seeing her captivating face, listening to her talk, about anything. Missed so many little things and the total package.

Problems. She'd said that there were problems in their marriage. That was startling news to him. From his perspective, there'd been no hints, no warnings of trouble. What was so wrong that they couldn't work it out right then and there?

Clay replayed the scenario in his head constantly. There'd been no hint of discord when they'd made love that last time.

The last time. The words reverberated in his brain as he stared into space.

Had it been?

No! He refused to believe that it was the last time he'd hold her, kiss her, make love to her. To never again find the peace and solace she offered was unthinkable.

Before, when his marriage proposal had been turned down by Emma, Clay had made work his cure for what he thought had been a broken heart—discovering, instead, that it had simply been a bruised one—devoting most of his waking hours to business.

However, work wasn't quite the panacea today that it had been before. Not when so many things there made him think of Linda. She permeated the office just as surely as she permeated his life outside of it.

He raked a hand through his hair. What the hell had gone wrong? Why hadn't he known? Why hadn't he seen?

And when were they going to be able to fix it?

Obviously she wanted some space to work out whatever was bothering her. But for how long? Clay liked to meet any questions or signs of dispute head-on, tackling them right at the start before they could escalate and threaten whatever deal or agreement was pending. That wasn't possible now as she'd fled the scene, taking with her whatever it was that had precipitated the event.

The phone rang.

Ordinarily Clay would let the machine pick it up so that he could monitor the caller. This time, however, he grabbed at the portable phone quickly, hoping that it was Linda. "Hello."

"Hi, Clay. Home in the middle of the afternoon? I'm shocked, brother. I really expected to get the machine or at the very least, Basil. Am I interrupting something?" A hearty chuckle accompanied the questions.

"If you were, Drew, I can assure you that I wouldn't have bothered to answer the phone." The hopes that had been raised by the sharp ring had been dashed just as quickly by the reality of the caller's identity.

"Never let it be said that the Buchanan men don't have their priorities straight."

Clay wanted to ask if by any chance Drew had heard from Linda, then thought better of it. Why would she get in touch with either of his younger brothers—or any member of his family? If she couldn't talk to her husband, what made him think that she would be communicating with them? "What's up?"

"I thought that since I'm in the neighborhood, maybe you and Linda could join me for dinner tomorrow night?"

"You're in Houston?"

"No, I'm at the house in King William Street."

That comment brought a smile to Clay's lips. Only a native Texan would disregard the distance between Houston and San Antonio and claim that he was "in the neighbourhood" when in fact he was several hours away.

"Where's Kate?" Clay knew that their upcoming wedding was only weeks away. He and Linda had talked recently about what they were going to get the couple to celebrate the event. Clay had even considered asking Linda if she wanted to take a quick side trip, since they were going to be on the East Coast, to the Caribbean villa for a few days. It would be no big deal to fly down there for a few days of sun and surf.

Immediately, his thoughts turned backward to a heavenly night of lovemaking there on the beach while they'd been on their honeymoon. Waves crashing against the sand with the same primeval intensity as the rhythm they set.

Drew answered his brother's query. "She's in San Diego at a romance writer's conference. The keynote speaker."

Clay could easily hear the pride in his brother's voice when he talked of the woman he loved. It was right there, in your face. Drew was head over heels in love and didn't care who knew it.

"How come you're not with her?"

"Girls-only trip," Drew explained. "She's meeting with a few friends there who are going to take some time together after this for a short research trip up the coast. Significant others not included," he added good-naturedly.

"And you miss her already?"

"Damn straight, big brother. I drove her to the airport this morning—we got into San Antonio yesterday—and it was damn tough to watch her get on that plane. Any time apart for us is tough. But you must know what I mean, being a newlywed.

"So, do you two want to do dinner? I can drive over tomorrow."

"Linda's not here right now."

"Where is she?"

"She had to go to New York." Half the truth.

"Too bad. Looks like we're both bachelor men again, if only for a short time. So, what about dinner? Are you interested?"

"How about I meet you in San Antonio instead?" Clay suggested. If Linda was at Ethan's, then it wouldn't be too far for him to drive. What was another few hours of tackling the interstate and back roads if he could see her? It'd be worth it.

If Drew was surprised by Clay's suggestion, he kept it to himself. "Okay by me."

"Then I'll see you."

"Looking forward to it."

Clay placed the phone back on the end table, glad that his brother had called. He needed to talk to someone and he had no qualms about baring his dilemma to Drew, a man who'd had his share of relationships, someone who could be counted on for solid advice. While Clay did have a few close male friends, none was as close as either of his brothers. Their bond, while occasionally bent over the years, could never be broken. It was forged with equal measures of blood, pride and heritage. They were family, just as Linda was now. And family belonged together.

That led his thoughts to the topic he'd brought up with Linda before his last business trip. Children. Could that have been what caused her to leave? She'd said before that she wanted kids. Had she changed her mind?

There was something else to consider, too. What about the fact that they'd made love without protection? As far as he knew, she wasn't on the pill. Could their repeated sensual encounters that night have resulted in a baby?

Secretly a part of himself wished that it was true. He wanted to be a father. Wanted to see Linda's body grow and change as it sheltered their child. Wanted to welcome a son or daughter into their lives.

But maybe that wasn't what she wanted?

Hopefully he'd know soon. He was getting damn tired of waiting, one way or the other.

She wasn't being fair.

She'd run off without so much as a real explanation, just the vague word *problems* tossed in his direction. How could she blame Clay if he wondered what she was talking about.

Each day without actually talking to him was harder than the day before. E-mail was okay, it would do in a pinch because it must, but it wasn't the communication of choice. Nothing for her could replace hearing his wonderful voice. That sexy, drawling Texas-flavored baritone that thrilled her down to her toes and back up again.

It was a warm morning in the Hill Country and Linda had gone for a walk. A creek bisected one part of her grandfather's property and it was to there that she went, drawn by the peace and serenity it offered. Live oak and pecan trees covered the ground, along with an outcropping of rocks. More rocks were located in the creek bed, where the water splashed over the natural barriers as it flowed downstream. In another few weeks or so the leaves would start to turn, changing colors, signaling the advent of fall proper. Change was in the wind, all around.

Linda stopped to watch a couple of gamboling squirrels

as they covered the ground in a race, playing tag with each other.

This place was a far cry from her life in Houston, from her office, and especially from her husband. It was peaceful, filled with the sights and sounds of the country. Nestled here among the trees and the quiet greenery, she could almost believe that she was in another world, one far removed from the turmoil that she'd left in hers.

Trouble was, she couldn't stay away forever. Sooner or later she and Clay would have to talk. The vows they'd exchanged demanded that.

But how to bring up what she felt was wrong?

Linda and her grandfather had had a talk when she arrived. It wasn't possible to hide the pain she was feeling from him, nor did she want to. He'd seen through her pretense right away, demanding that she tell him what was going on.

She had, glad to have a chance to unburden herself yet again. Her sister Sandy and her friend Meg had both been willing listeners, but Meg had too many problems just now for Linda to be totally forthcoming about her own. Instead, Linda found herself dispensing advice to Meg.

Sandy forthrightly counseled Linda to "follow her heart," which for Linda had always been her work and Clay Buchanan; the two were intertwined.

Ethan had been a tad more pragmatic, his advice hitting hard. "You weren't raised a quitter, girl. Talk to him. Tell Clay just how you feel. Lay it on the line for him, clearly. He deserves to know the facts as you see them. After all, you two said your words before God, so they've got to mean something. Better or worse, remember. Rain or shine."

Linda had listened quietly, absorbing his words.

"You've told me that he's never said that he loves you. You tell him?"

"Not exactly."

"What the hell's that mean? Either you did or you didn't."

"I didn't."

"Then how's he supposed to know? Wait to read it in the *Wall Street Journal* or see it on CNN?"

"I had hoped that he'd guess."

Ethan rolled his eyes beneath bushy brows. "You remind me of someone who sees something and completely misunderstands the situation when all they had to do was ask the right questions. No one ever said that married life was easy, girl, or that marriage to a man like Clay Buchanan would be a picnic, but you're a Douglas. Your folks might have been quitters when it came to marriage, but then they were never right for one another. You and that boy are. Whatever the doubts, you owe it to both of you to work it out. Give yourselves another chance."

His words made sense.

Whenever she'd wanted something, she went after her goal, full steam ahead.

Linda glanced down at the wedding ring she wore. Granddad was right. Clay deserved her honesty. If he couldn't handle it, then it was better that she learned the truth right away instead of keeping them both in limbo.

After standing up and brushing at the seat of her twill pants, she took off at a run through the path, heading back to her grandfather's house, eager to get in touch with Clay.

Fifteen minutes later, winded, she stopped on the porch to catch her breath. Gasping, she took in great gulps of air.

"You all right?"

Linda's head snapped up. She nodded to her grandfather. "Yes," she said in a raspy voice.

"Good. Wasn't sure if I was going to have to call the local paramedics or not."

Straightening, Linda kissed him on the cheek. "I'm fine, Granddad. Really."

He grinned. "Damned right you are."

"Excuse me," she said. "I've got to make a very important phone call."

"Clay?"

"Uh-huh."

"Good going."

"Let's hope so." Linda hurried through the door and made her way to her bedroom quickly, grabbing her cell phone from her purse. Dialing the number of the office, her call was answered immediately by Clay's secretary.

"I'm afraid that Mr. Buchanan isn't available, Mrs. Buchanan."

"Where can he be reached? It's important that I speak with him right away."

"He left word that he was going out of town for a few days, to San Antonio. He left word that he could be reached at the family house there. Do you need the number?"

"No, thank you. I have it." Linda hung up and rummaged through her handbag, flipping open her tapestry organizer. She located the number and dialed it.

A sexy male voice came on the line. "Hello."

Disappointment hit her. It wasn't Clay's voice, though it was familiar. "Drew?"

"That you, Linda?"

"Yeah." She didn't bother with polite chitchat; instead she got right to the point of her call. "By any chance is Clay there?"

"Funny you should ask. He's on his way."

"Give him a message for me?"

"Sure. What is it?"

Linda debated a fraction of a moment on how she should word her message and then decided to be honest, whatever the consequences. If there wasn't a chance for their marriage, Drew would find out soon enough. Besides, Clay trusted his brothers. And if he did, then so would she. "Tell him we need to talk. That I'm at my grandfather's farm. I'll wait to hear from him."

"I'll make sure that he gets it as soon as he arrives."

"Thanks, Drew."

"Consider yourself lucky. I'm gonna restrain my journalist's natural curiosity and not ask what's going on between you two. Just one thing, though."

"And that is?"

"An observation, if you don't mind. You're good for big brother. We all think so, for what it's worth."

Tears misted Linda's eyes. "It's worth a lot, Drew."

"Keep that in mind then. Let me let you in on a little secret, darlin'. We Buchanans can be stubborn." He injected a tone of levity after that comment. "I know. You're shocked. Can't be helped. It's locked in the genes. Or in the denim, whichever you prefer."

Linda couldn't help herself, she chuckled at that remark.

"If it's right," Drew added, a sober note now in his voice, "then it's worth fighting for. No matter what. Burke and I learned that the hard way. Deep down, Clay knows it, too."

Oh God, she hoped so, with all her heart.

"I've changed my mind, Drew."

"About the message?"

"No. Tell Clay that I still want to talk to him. Just add, please, that I'm on my way there."

"Smart move. Why waste time waiting for him to come to you."

"You got that."

Linda snapped the lid shut on the cell phone, putting it back in her bag. She quickly gathered her things and re-packed her suitcase and garment bag, eager to be off.

Minutes later, she was standing on the porch, cases in hand. "Thanks, Granddad."

"For what?" He rose from his wicker chair.

"For being there whenever I've needed you." She gave him a quick peck on the cheek and a hug.

"You don't have to thank me," he said. "I'm happy to do it." He glanced at her assembled things. "You going to Clay?"

"Yes. He's on his way to San Antonio, so I thought that I'd meet him there. It's neutral territory."

"Then you do what you have to do. Just let me know the outcome."

"Your wife called."

"Linda?" Clay shot his brother a pointed glance. "When?"

"Unless you have another one stashed away some-where, it was Linda. About an hour or so." Drew handed Clay a big glass of iced tea. "She left you a message."

Clay took a deep swallow of the beverage before he asked, apprehension threading through his gut, "What did she say?"

"To sit tight. She was coming here. And—" he paused for effect "—that you two had to talk." Drew helped himself to another glass of the cold drink, pouring a refill from the glass pitcher. "What's going on?"

They were sitting outside in the back garden, beneath the wide branches of the live oak, each man a picture of the counterpointing sides of casual dress. Drew was in a black T-shirt and light denim jeans; Clay wore a white polo shirt and a pair of olive khaki trousers. Drew, the taller and broader of the two brothers, leaned forward, his head turned toward Clay, awaiting his reply.

"I can't honestly answer that except to say Linda left me over a week ago."

"Left you? As in walked out?"

Clay nodded.

"Why?" Drew felt no compunction about grilling his brother. His suspicion, that Clay had driven here so that he could talk to him, confirmed.

"I don't have a goddamn idea why," Clay said with a trace of anger.

"Something must have happened?"

"Well, if it did, I haven't a clue," Clay explained.

"You're sure?"

"Of course, I'm sure," he snapped. "One minute we were happy, as close as man and woman can be and several hours later, she tells me that we have problems and that she needs some space to clear her head." Clay rose abruptly from his wicker chair. "Do you know how that feels, Drew? Like a knife was stuck in my back. It came out of nowhere."

Drew could sympathize. He knew how he'd feel if Kate ever walked out on him. Devastated. Exactly the way Clay was feeling now. "And things were fine between you before that?"

Clay shrugged. "I thought so. Obviously I was wrong."

"You didn't have a fight? A disagreement?"

"No. Linda and I don't have fights, Drew. We see

things in the same light. Ours is a pretty stable relationship. At least I thought it was.''

''Perhaps not quite if she left.''

''For the life of me I can't figure it out. I've gone over
and over it in my mind. Trying to find some hint at what
she meant by problems. It was useless.''

''Forget a birthday, perhaps? Or some special date? I
would have said an anniversary, but you've only been
married two months.''

''No.''

Drew didn't like asking this next question, but he felt
that he had to. ''Is there another person involved?''

''Hell, no!'' Clay snarled the words. ''There's been no
one else for me and if there had been for Linda, she would
have told me about it.''

''You know that for a fact?''

''I *know* Linda.''

''Sorry.''

''She's like no other woman that I've been with,
Drew,'' Clay stated. ''Making love to her is like…''

''Waking up from a long sleep and discovering the true
joy of mating. Heart and soul. Body and mind. I know,''
Drew assured his brother. ''It's like that for me and Kate.
In her I found the other part of myself.'' He grinned, his
full lips curving in a deep smile. ''You must love her very
much.''

Clay heard one word louder than all the rest. *Love.*

Drew watched as Clay stood straight, ceasing his pacing across the carpet of grass. Like someone seeing light
for the first time after being in the dark, his expression
was one of wonder.

Drew probed gently, ''You do love her, don't you?''

Did he?

Clay's response was from the gut. ''Yes!''

It came as a major surprise to Clay to hear the truth spoken by his own lips. He loved Linda. Loved her so much in fact that losing her would be like ripping out a part of himself.

No wonder he'd felt truly lonely for the first time when she'd left, as if all that was beautiful had been erased from his life. She was the puzzle piece that he'd been searching for, the missing element that made life complete. Right there under his nose and he'd almost overlooked it. How foolishly arrogant.

Talk about clueless.

It couldn't be too late. He refused to believe that. She was on her way here and he meant to win her back. When Clay wanted something, or someone, he went after it with all that was in him. And he wanted her. In his life. In his bed. In his heart. Now and forever.

"Thanks, Drew."

"For what?"

"For making me see the light."

"Excuse me?"

"I'll explain some other time. Right now I want to take care of something that I should have done before."

Drew watched as Clay headed for his luxury sedan. "You're leaving?" He rose from his chair. "Linda's on her way," he reminded Clay. "What do I tell her if she gets here and you're gone?"

With a grin, he tossed his car keys into the air and grabbed them just as quickly. "Tell her to wait for me. I'll be back as soon as I can. And Drew, we'd like some privacy."

"Then use the guest house. It worked wonders for me and Kate." With a sly look, Drew added, "Trust me. I won't be insulted if you two don't join me for dinner. Just do whatever you have to to hold on to love."

"I intend to, little brother." As he walked quickly toward his car, Clay repeated the words to himself. *Come hell or salvation, I intend to.*

Linda paced back and forth in the living room of the guest house, anxious to see Clay. She couldn't believe that she hadn't received a speeding ticket in her haste to get to San Antonio from Ethan's farm since she'd put the pedal to the metal, ignoring posted speed limits.

Then, when she arrived, it was Drew who'd met her, explaining that Clay was coming back after he took care of some unspecified business.

Another indication that she wasn't a high priority on his list? she wondered.

Linda appreciated the fact that Drew was gracious in offering the use of the guest house. What she had to say to Clay was best left between the two of them. From the look in Drew's eyes, she could guess that Clay had already told his brother about their recent rift. While he said nothing about it, she knew that he knew.

She tried to sit down on the couch while she waited but that hadn't lasted long. Nervously she paced around the room.

The sound of a car in the driveway forced her to the window. Looking out, she recognized it as Clay's.

Linda swallowed the lump that had risen in her throat, watching as he emerged from the vehicle. As usual, her pulse rate jumped when she saw him. She loved him so much that it hurt.

Clay saw the woman at the window as he was walking toward the guest house.

Linda. She was here, just like she said she would be.

Determined, he made his way along the path and

opened the door. He entered the house, proceeding to where she was.

When he saw her, he couldn't believe that he'd ever thought he'd loved someone before her.

Stepping closer, Clay approached her. "Hello, Linda."

She took a step back and Clay felt that reaction like a slap of cold water.

"Clay."

He wanted to kiss her desperately but something told him that wasn't the wisest choice to make right now. Instead, he decided to let her keep her distance if that made her more comfortable and in control. "Drew said you wanted to talk to me. Well, that's good because I have something to say to you, also."

Linda took a deep breath and wet her lips. "I don't mind deferring to you, Clay, when it's necessary, but not this time. If you don't mind, or even if you do, I want to go first."

"I'm listening then. Do you mind if I sit down?"

"Go right ahead." Linda watched as he did just that, wondering where to begin. Seconds ticked by as she fought to find the right words.

"Marrying you has given me my greatest joy and my greatest pain."

Clay heard the words, took the impact of them like a body blow. "I didn't know being my wife was such a hardship."

"Wife?" she asked. "That's just it, Clay. I'm not your wife. I'm just the woman you happen to be married to."

That pronouncement stunned Clay. Linda could see it in his face.

"I wanted to be let in but you kept closing the door, shutting me out. Letting me have a little piece of you when it suited."

"That's not true."

"Yes, it is, Clay. Think about it. I certainly have. And that's not all I've thought about," she confessed. "There's something else I should have said, too, while I'm laying my cards on the table. This situation is partly my fault—I kept something from you that I should have told you about when you first asked me to marry you."

His eyes met hers. "And that is?"

"That I've loved you since I was sixteen."

"What?"

"You probably don't even recall the barbecue that Ethan brought me to, but I sure do." Her voice softened slightly. "I saw you then and knew that no other man would ever do for me. You were who and what I wanted. And not because you were rich. Your money never meant anything to me then and it doesn't now. I only signed that prenup to make you happy. It's who you were that mattered to me. Your brains, your drive, your integrity. You had everything I was looking for.

"The only thing I didn't know then was that you didn't have a heart. That's why I never told you how I really felt. I was afraid and that fear kept me silent. Fear that if I told you how much I loved you, you'd want out of this marriage.

"So I kept quiet, burying the love I had for you so that you wouldn't see it, sharing only a fraction of it until it damned near killed me to keep my emotions in such tight check.

"I can't love like this. I can't live like that. I thought, foolishly I now concede, that I had enough love for both of us. But I don't. This marriage was supposed to be a partnership, not a one-way street. If I can't have what I deserve, then I can't settle for less. No more. No way.

"Once I believed that I'd do anything for love. Now I

know that's not true. There are limits. Staying in a love-less marriage is at the top of the list—I can't, so don't expect me to. I do have some pride. Maybe not as much as I thought, but I do have it.''

Clay ached for the pain that he'd unknowingly caused Linda. He should have guessed her secret. Women like her didn't marry for business reasons alone. She had too much love to give to throw it away for convenience's sake.

''I had your body, Clay, but I never had your heart. Do you know how that felt? Like I was being used. I tried to tell myself that that wasn't true. That you couldn't have made love to me like you did if you didn't care. Kind of naive, wasn't I? I wanted to believe that what we shared was so different from what you'd known before.''

''It was.''

She ignored his comment, too wound up to slow down. ''You know what's even more ironic? I was going to tell you so many times exactly how I felt, usually after we'd made love, because then was when I felt closest to you.

''That last time, I had to leave our bed or I would have told you then and there. God knows I wanted to. So much so that I thought I was going to scream from keeping it inside a moment longer. And I was afraid that I'd lose you if I said anything, so I kept quiet.

''Only later it hit me. How can you lose what was never yours to begin with?''

''That's not true.''

''Unfortunately, it is,'' she countered. ''Want to know how I figured that out?'' She didn't wait for his reply. ''You never even bothered to wear a wedding ring.''

''You never said anything.''

''You never asked. Maybe I'm being petty but I don't care. Burke wears one. It's a symbol, Clay. Of commitment. You wanted me to wear one, which I did, gladly, but you decided not to bother." Her deep hurt was evident in the tone of her voice. "Doesn't that tell you something? It does me. Since you don't seem to give a good damn about it, maybe neither should I." Linda tried to pull the wedding band and engagement ring off her finger and found that they were stuck.

"I think that's a sign, don't you?" Clay rose and clasped his hand over hers to still her movements.

"Of what?" She looked into his eyes, getting lost all over again. When would this man cease to move her?

Never, came back the quick reply.

"That they belong on your finger, like this one does on mine." He pulled a slim box out of his trouser pocket and gave it to her. "Go on and open it. Obviously I couldn't find a match to the set I gave you, so I looked around some of the more exclusive shops in San Antonio until I found something that I thought you'd like and would have picked out, had I given you the chance. That's where I was earlier. Read what's inside."

Linda lifted up the box's lid and reached for the ring inside. Gold and platinum gleamed in a thick traditional band. Picking up the ring, she held it so that she could read what was inside. *Forever yours.* Next to it was the date of their wedding.

Clay held out his hand. "Put it on."

Linda's hand shook slightly as she pushed the ring onto his long finger and slid it over the knuckle and into place.

With his other hand, Clay captured hers and held it trapped between both of his. "With this ring, I thee wed, again," he stated in an emotion-thickened voice. "I love you, Linda. Are you willing to give me and our marriage another chance? To let me prove to you that although I was a fool before who almost lost the one thing he couldn't afford to lose, that I'm worth the effort. That what we shared is worth it?''

Tears may have blurred her eyes, but Linda still could read the truth in his. He did love her. It's what she'd wanted to hear, what she'd prayed to happen. ''Another chance?''

''Uh-huh.''

How could she refuse? She'd followed her heart before and it had led her to Clay. It always would.

''You've got a deal, Mr. Buchanan.''

Clay smiled. ''Then I suggest that we seal the bargain, Mrs. Buchanan.''

And they did, in the best way possible.

Epilogue

"Aren't we the lucky ones?" Drew asked as he and his brothers each raised a glass of champagne to toast his wedding day. They were standing in the downstairs office of the large house he shared with Kate in Chester County, PA, helping themselves while the guests assembled on the grounds outside, herded there by the bubbly blonde who was hired to handle this affair.

"That's a fact," Burke added. "We each got ourselves the best that life has to offer. Women who love us and kids on the way." Burke was referring to the fact that Emma was pregnant again, and just this past week, both Drew and Clay had found out that they were going to become daddies, too.

"To the Buchanans," Clay offered, clinking his fluted glass against his brothers'. So much had changed in his life and it was all due to Linda. She'd shown him that his heart wasn't invulnerable. She'd melted the wall of ice that had surrounded it with her patience, her concern and, most of all, her unselfish love, teaching him the art of the best deal going—to love without reservation.

To think that he'd almost lost the greatest gift that he'd received in his life. He'd almost let slip away what he should have been holding on to, the love she offered. The love that showed him that no matter how many companies he controlled, how much money he had, or how many pieces of property he owned, that without her love he was poor in what truly counted.

"Can I get in on that?" asked a decidedly masculine voice.

"Of course, Dad," Clay said, handing their father a glass, too.

"Now I propose a toast. To my boys. The best of the best." He lifted his glass in Burke's direction. "The heart of the land." Drinking, he shifted the glass toward Drew. "The eyes of the bard." He drank again, then turned and faced his eldest son. "The soul of the warrior."

"There you are," chirped a perky-voiced blonde, whose flowing thick locks cascaded around her magenta suit jacket. "We're ready for you outside. The bride will be down shortly and it wouldn't do for you all to still be here."

Drew laughed. "We surrender, Miss Baker."

"That's what I like in a man," she quipped, checking her clipboard. "Any chance there's more of you who aren't taken?"

Clay sent her an amused glance. "If you're willing to relocate, I think I might be able to find a couple of cousins or a reasonable facsimile at least."

"Sorry. I'm an East Coast girl and I plan to stay that way. Now, let's get you situated, shall we. Billy," she called to her assistant who was checking with the florist.

"See that the Buchanan men are where they're supposed to be and I'll check with the caterers that we're on schedule, then I'll see to the bride and her party."

As they walked outside to where the assorted guests were sitting, they were still chuckling over the very efficient young woman. "I could use a few more of her at the office," Clay said with a laugh.

"Or at the ranch," Burke added. "She'd be a great foreman."

Meanwhile, upstairs at Kate's house, Kate was surrounded by Buchanan women of all ages, not to mention her own mother and sister, plus her former sister-in-law. Champagne flowed freely there, too, except that she, Emma and Linda declined to have any, choosing instead sparkling water with a twist.

Linda had a special gift to pass along to the bride. "This was given to me as a borrowed item and now it should be yours." She extended her hand and gave Kate the handkerchief.

"It's lovely."

Emma, her arm around Jessie's shoulders, said, "You can return the favor someday and give it to Jessie. It'll be her turn next."

The teenager rolled her eyes. "Not hardly, Mom."

"Someday you'll change your mind," Emma insisted. "Wait and see."

"You'll meet someone who'll change your life."

"Suppose that I don't want it changed?" Jessie demanded.

"Spoken like a true Buchanan," Santina retorted.

"It can happen when you least expect it, whether you want it to or not," Linda insisted. "Trust me on that."

Everyone there nodded their heads in unison.

It certainly had for her, Linda thought as she admired

the striking picture Kate made in her wedding gown. One meeting with Clay had altered Linda's life forever. Love at first sight had transformed her, awakened her to life's possibilities. Shown her that in loving another as she loved Clay, she could see the face of the divine.

Her gamble on love had paid off.

She exchanged glances with Emma and Kate. They'd done the same and come out winners, as well.

Music drifted up to the second-floor window. A vocalist was singing an extremely popular love song from a long-running hit musical.

Rising from her chair, Kate smiled. "I'm ready."

Admiring her soon-to-be sister-in-law's choice of wedding dress, a figure-molding medieval-style gown in sapphire blue velvet with a matching cloak, Linda left the room with Santina and Jessie to join the other friends and family outside where the ceremony would take place.

Autumn had worked its magic on this area. Colors were splashed everywhere, outdoing themselves for glory.

Her own life was awash with color, Linda thought as she caught her husband's eye and joined the rest of the Buchanan family. She whispered the words "I love you," to him and was rewarded when he did the same.

Her left hand slipped over her stomach, fingers spreading out, lips curving in a deep smile of contentment.

Some dreams did come true and were worth any price.

* * * * *

COMING NEXT MONTH

COWBOY'S LOVE Victoria Pade

A Ranching Family

Fifteen years ago, Savannah Heller had to flee from her first love, Clint Culhane. But now she is back; will he forgive her the secret she's kept from him or will she be forced to leave him a second time?

WITH THIS WEDDING RING Trisha Alexander

When the custody of her unborn child is threatened, young widow Emily Pierce finds herself saying 'I do' a second time. Her boss Matt Thompson jumps at the chance to play devoted husband and father...but will the marriage be in name only?

SPUR-OF-THE-MOMENT MARRIAGE
Cathy Gillen Thacker

Hasty Weddings

When Max McKendrick fixes up Cisco Kidd with the beautiful but mysterious Gillian Taylor, he is sure that theirs is a match made in heaven. But none of them realise that dark secrets from the past will come to haunt them all...

BABY IN HIS CRADLE Diana Whitney

When Samuel Evans shelters a very pregnant stranger from a fierce snowstorm, he gets more than he bargained for. Not only does he save Ellie Malone's life, but he delivers her baby! How can Ellie help but fall in love with her knight in shining armour?

HONEYMOON RANCH Celeste Hamilton

His bride-to-be, sexy and sophisticated Paige McMullen *seems* like a woman of the world to handsome rancher True Whitman. But he is shocked to discover that she is still a virgin... Can he live up to the ideal husband that Paige has always dreamed of?

LUCKY IN LOVE Tracy Sinclair

Michelle Lacey is far from pleased with her mother's choice of friend, just who is this mysterious 'millionaire'? And how dare his sexy nephew, Jonathan Richfield, accuse *her* of being a fortune hunter? It's not Jonathan's *money* that she finds attractive...

COMING NEXT MONTH FROM

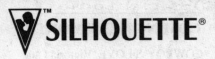

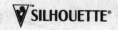

THE MacGREGOR BRIDES

NORA ROBERTS

The illustrious MacGregor clan's irrepressible patriarch—and relentless matchmaker—is determined to have his three gorgeous granddaughters engaged by Christmas. And he's hand-picked three unsuspecting hunks as their prospective mates!

"Nora Roberts is simply the best there is—she's superb in everything she does."

—Romantic Times

Available at most branches of WH Smith, John Menzies, Martins, Tesco, Asda, Volume One and good paperback stockists.

There must be something in the water in the little town of New Hope, there are certainly a lot of babies on the way! In this exciting new series, meet five delighted Mums-to-be. And the handsome hunks who get some surprising news...

Starting next month with:

THE BABY NOTION
Dixie Browning
DESIRE October 1998

Followed by:

BABY IN A BASKET
Helen R. Myers
DESIRE November 1998

MARRIED...WITH TWINS!
Jennifer Mikels
SPECIAL EDITION December 1998

HOW TO HOOK A HUSBAND (AND A BABY)
Carolyn Zane
DESIRE January 1999

DISCOVERED: DADDY
Marilyn Pappano
SENSATION February 1999

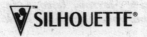

4 FREE
books and a surprise gift!

We would like to take this opportunity to thank you for reading this Silhouette® book by offering you the chance to take FOUR more specially selected titles from the Special Edition™ series absolutely FREE! We're also making this offer to introduce you to the benefits of the Reader Service™—

- ★ FREE home delivery
- ★ FREE gifts and competitions
- ★ FREE monthly newsletter
- ★ Books available before they're in the shops
- ★ Exclusive Reader Service discounts

Accepting these FREE books and gift places you under no obligation to buy; you may cancel at any time, even after receiving your free shipment. Simply complete your details and return the entire page to the address below. *You don't even need a stamp!*

YES! Please send me 4 free Special Edition books and a surprise gift. I understand that unless you hear from me, I will receive 6 superb new titles every month for just £2.50 each, postage and packing free. I am under no obligation to purchase any books and may cancel my subscription at any time. The free books and gift will be mine to keep in any case.

E8YE

Ms/Mrs/Miss/Mr ....Initials ....
BLOCK CAPITALS PLEASE

Surname ....

Address ....

....

....Postcode...........................

Send this whole page to:
THE READER SERVICE, FREEPOST CN81, CROYDON, CR9 3WZ
(Eire readers please send coupon to: P.O. BOX 4546, DUBLIN 24.)

Offer not valid to current Reader Service subscribers to this series. We reserve the right to refuse an application and applicants must be aged 18 years or over. Only one application per household. Terms and prices subject to change without notice. Offer expires 30th April 1999. You may be mailed with offers from other reputable companies as a result of this application. If you would prefer not to share in this opportunity please write to The Data Manager, P.O. Box 236, Croydon, Surrey CR9 3RU.

Silhouette Special Edition is a registered trademark used under license.

SHANNON OCORK

SECRETS OF THE
TITANIC

**The voyage of the century
—where secrets, love and destiny collide.**

They were the richest of the rich, Rhode Island's
elite, their glittering jewels and polished manners
hiding tarnished secrets on a voyage that would
change their lives forever.

They had it all and everything to lose.

"Miss OCork is a natural writer and storyteller."
—New York Times Book Review

1-55166-401-1
MIRA® Available from October 1998 in paperback